ADRIAN

"Adrian has a gift for drawing her readers deeper and deeper into the amazing world she creates."

—Fresh Fiction

"With an Adrian novel, readers are assured of plenty of dangerous thrills and passionate chills."

—RT Book Reviews

"Nothing beats good writing and that is what ultimately makes Lara Adrian stand out amongst her peers . . . Adrian doesn't hold back with the intensity or the passion."

—Under the Covers

"Adrian has a style of writing that creates these worlds that are so realistic and believable . . . the characters are so rich and layered . . . the love stories are captivating and often gut-wrenching . . . edge of your seat stuff!"

—Scandalicious Book Reviews

"Adrian compels readers to get hooked on her storylines."

—Romance Reviews Today

Praise for Lara Adrian's books

"Adrian's strikingly original Midnight Breed series delivers an abundance of nail-biting suspenseful chills, red-hot sexy thrills, an intricately built world, and realistically complicated and conflicted protagonists, whose happily-ever-after ending proves to be all the sweeter after what they endure to get there."

—Booklist (starred review)

"(The Midnight Breed is) a well-written, action-packed series that is just getting better with age."

—Fiction Vixen

Praise for
THE 100 SERIES

"I wish I could give this more than 5 stars! Lara Adrian not only dips her toe into this genre with flare, she will take it over . . . I have found my new addiction, this series."

—The Sub Club Books

"There are twists that I want to say that I expect from a Lara Adrian book, and I say that because with any Adrian book you read, you know there's going to be a complex storyline. Adrian simply does billionaires better."

—Under the Covers

"This book had me completely addicted from page one!! There were several twists and turns throughout this super steamy read and I was surprised by how much mystery/suspense was woven in. Loved that! If you're looking for the perfect summer read, look no further than this book!"

—Steph and Chris Book Blog

"I have been searching and searching for the next book boyfriend to leave a lasting impression. You know the ones: where you own the paperbacks, eBooks and the audible versions...This is that book. For those of you who are looking for your next Fifty Fix, look no further. I know, I know—you have heard the phrase before! Except this time, it's the truth and I will bet the penthouse on it."

—Mile High Kink Book Club

"For 100 Days is a sexy, sizzling, emotion-filled delight. It completely blew me away!"

—J. Kenner, New York Times bestselling author

"For 100 Nights is an erotic delight that will have you on the edge of your seat! An instant addiction and a complete escape, with an intriguing storyline and an ending that will leave you gasping for air. This series has quickly become one of my favorites!"

—Shayna Renee's Spicy Reads

"There is only one word that can adequately describe For 100 Nights: PHENOMENAL. For 100 Days was one of my favourite books of last year and this book has topped that. . . . Move over because there is a new queen of erotica on the charts and you don't want to miss her."

—The Sub Club Books

"If you're looking for a hot new contemporary romance along the lines of Sylvia Day's Crossfire series then you're not going to want to miss this series!"

—Feeling Fictional

"Lara Adrian has once again wowed me with her writing. She has created a complex erotic romance that has layers upon layers for both of her characters. Their passion for one another is romantic, sizzling, and a little bit naughty. Lara has added intrigue and suspense that keeps the reader completely involved. Each small revelation is leading to an explosive conclusion. I cannot wait for the third and final book, For 100 Reasons, to release."

—Smut Book Junkie Reviews

THE 100 SERIES

For 100 Days
For 100 Nights
For 100 Reasons
The Complete 100 Series (ebook)

100 SERIES STANDALONES

Run To You
Play My Game

Other books by Lara Adrian

Midnight Breed series

. . . and more to come!

Paranormal Romance

Hunter Legacy Series
Born of Darkness
Hour of Darkness
Edge of Darkness

Historical Romances

Dragon Chalice Series
Heart of the Hunter
Heart of the Flame
Heart of the Dove

Warrior Trilogy
White Lion's Lady
Black Lion's Bride
Lady of Valor

Lord of Vengeance

PLAY MY GAME

A 100 Series Standalone Novel

NEW YORK TIMES BESTSELLING AUTHOR
LARA ADRIAN

ISBN: 978-1-939193-32-2

PLAY MY GAME

www.LaraAdrian.com

Available in ebook and trade paperback. Unabridged audiobook edition forthcoming.

Play My Game

1

JARED

She stands out like a flame in the dark.

Surrounded by beautiful people, hundreds of bodies dancing and gyrating to the music throbbing inside my new club, Muse. But she is the one my gaze locks on and won't let go.

Hair the color of a fiery sunset, cascading down her back in gleaming waves. Long legs and a superb ass wrapped in white denim. Her small breasts float buoyantly under a silky, pale blue blouse as she dances with one of the female friends she arrived with a short while ago.

I track her with singular focus from where I stand overlooking the dance floor two stories below.

She's damn hard to miss in the roiling sea of black-garbed clubbers that swarm like a hive of drones around their queen. She doesn't even seem to notice how naturally she draws the energy and attention of the room.

She is out of place here. A bright splash of color in an abyss of darkness.

An innocent in a den of sin.

And I, Jared Rush, am a master of corruption.

I don't apologize for that fact. I make no excuses, either.

Like my paintings--dark, carnal images that have crowned me the king of the avant-garde art world while also making me a very rich man--I don't flinch away from my baser instincts. I exploit them.

I fucking revel in them.

Right now, every one of those instincts is gnashing at the bit, hungry for a taste of the fresh-faced, auburn-haired beauty who made the mistake of wandering into my lair tonight.

I don't know her name, but that's inconsequential.

I know who she belongs to.

Over the years I've accumulated my share of enemies, but few worth counting.

Fewer still worth the effort to wound.

To vanquish.

To ruin.

She has nothing to do with the bad blood that's been left festering inside me for decades. Yet as I watch her dance and laugh with her friends, it isn't just the idea of a simple sexual conquest that has my cock going hard, no matter how powerfully I want her. If that were the case, I'm confident I could have her beneath me before the night is over.

No, I'm thinking about slaking something more than mere pedestrian lust.

Something sharper, colder.

I'm thinking about an old, unsettled score. One that,

until recently, I thought I'd buried deep.
Now, I'm thinking about payback.
And I already have a price in mind.
One that begins with her.

2

Two weeks later . . .

MELANIE

The chain of pale blue gemstones circling my wrist twinkles under the glow of the dining room's soft lighting. I can't stop admiring the unexpected gift, or beaming at the man who gave it to me moments ago over dinner at GC, one of Manhattan's finest restaurants.

"It looks stunning on you," Daniel says as the waiter clears our dessert dishes. "I saw it while I was in Vegas last week and knew I had to get it for you. The tourmalines match your eyes."

I glance down, my smile faltering a little now. My eye color is changeable, more often gray than blue. It's silly that I should feel even a small disappointment that he doesn't know that.

Daniel Hathaway and I have only been dating for three months. I can't expect him to have memorized every minute detail about me in that brief time. After all, he's a busy, talented man with a demanding career. His architectural work claims much of his time and attention.

I knew that when we began seeing each other. In fact, Daniel's professional drive was one of the qualities I admired most in him when we first met. That and his kindness.

He's a good man in a world that's shown me so few of them in my twenty-five years.

Sometimes I wonder if he's only a dream I've conjured, a wish I never dared to speak aloud.

I reach across the intimate table to slip my fingers into his. "The bracelet is perfect. This whole night has been perfect."

"I want it to be. We're celebrating," he reminds me. He brushes a lock of my unbound auburn hair behind my ear, his grin lighting up his handsome face. "Business at the firm has never been better. The way things are going lately, I could make partner before the year is out. You must be my lucky charm, Mel."

He lets go of my fingers to pay for our expensive dinner and the three-hundred-dollar bottle of wine he ordered even after I reminded him I don't drink. I've never been much of a drinker. Given my family history, I suppose that counts as something close to a miracle.

Since I started back at college part-time to finish my MBA last year, the strongest thing I consume now is coffee. But not tonight. I'm in the middle of summer classes and I have an exam in the morning. The last thing I need is to lie awake half the night wired on caffeine.

"Ready to go, beautiful?" When I nod, Daniel rises from his chair to help me up from mine.

His hand at the small of my back steers me through

the busy dining room. On our way out, Gavin Castille, the handsome Australian chef and owner of the popular restaurant, stops us to chat for a few minutes with Daniel and make sure we enjoyed our meal. Daniel's easy charm and gregarious openness win him friends wherever we go. It certainly worked on me when we met over a lunch order mix-up at my favorite deli near the university.

The valet brings Daniel's Jaguar around and soon we are merging into the crush of Tuesday night summer traffic. When he heads in the opposite direction of the bridge that would take me home toward my place in Queens, I assume he has ideas of capping off our celebration by making love together at his Midtown apartment for an hour or two before I have to think about getting home.

But he's not driving that way, either.

I swivel a confused look at him. "What's going on?"

He smiles. "You look gorgeous tonight and I want to show you off. Actually, things have been going so great at the firm the past couple weeks, I'm feeling like I could take on the world right now. Especially with you on my arm."

"Daniel, what are you talking about?"

He pulls a black envelope from the interior pocket of his suit jacket and hands it to me. The seal has been broken, but I can still make out the stamped monogram of the stylized initials *J* and *R* in the pressed glob of antique-gold wax.

A crisp white invitation is inside. At least, I assume it's an invitation.

All that's printed on it is today's date and a Lenox Hill address on the Upper East Side.

A very expensive address.

"I don't understand."

Daniel's eyes gleam in the glow of the dashboard. His grin is practically giddy. "That's a ticket into one of the highest stakes poker games in the city. Extremely exclusive. Invitation-only."

"You're taking me to a poker game? Now?" A current of unease passes through me. I set the invitation down in my lap and glance at him. "I didn't even realize you play."

"I guess it never came up." He reaches out to touch the side of my face. "Does it bother you?"

I shrug, trying to decide if it does, or why it should. I'm sure there are many things about Daniel that I have yet to discover. But something about this feels like a secret, and for the first time in our relationship, the ground beneath me seems a little less solid than it did just a moment ago.

I meet his concerned stare. "I'm just . . . surprised, that's all."

"Relax," he says gently. "It'll be fun."

I wish I could be as enthusiastic as he is. Suddenly, I just want to go home. "Maybe you should go without me. You know I don't like staying out late--"

"If you're stressing about your exam tomorrow, don't. You're brilliant, Melanie. One late night isn't going to derail your perfect GPA."

"It's not only that."

My studies are important, but I'm also thinking about the other obligations waiting for me at home. My mother and six-year-old niece have been living with me since my older sister died four years ago.

Even though Mom says she doesn't wait up or worry about me when I'm out, I know better than to believe that. And I try hard not to let her down.

Daniel's only been to my place a few times, but he knows what my family means to me.

He gives me an understanding smile. "We don't have to stay long, I promise."

Reaching over he retrieves the invitation and envelope from my lap, tucking them back into his jacket. "And it's not just a poker game tonight, Mel. It's a chance to rub elbows with anyone who means anything in this city. With any luck, maybe I'll clean out some of their deep pockets while I'm there. Besides, it's not as if I could refuse when the host is none other than the firm's biggest new fish, Jared Rush."

Even though I've never met the man, my heart stutters at the mention of his name.

Famously talented and renowned for his dark, edgy portraits that seem to expose even his most beautiful and vaunted subjects down to the barest cores of their broken souls, Jared Rush has been a legend in the art world for a decade.

Although it's been a while since he's produced anything new, his paintings always command millions. Even if his art disturbs, few would deny its raw, seductive beauty.

Much like the roguishly handsome, rebel artist himself.

"The Gramercy Park project you told me about tonight. The bid for the boutique hotel and gallery your firm recently landed? Jared Rush is the client?"

Daniel slants me an amused glance. "Don't sound so shocked. He doesn't seem that bad, actually."

I know I look skeptical. It's impossible to live in New York City for any length of time without having at least heard of the arrogant artist and his work.

Or about his rumored carnality.

It is that reputation I can't seem to ignore now, no matter how hard I try.

All the words I've ever heard used to describe Jared Rush fly at me in the dark of the vehicle as Daniel drives us deeper into the posh area of the city near Central Park.

Depraved.

Debauched.

Deviant.

Dangerous.

In the seat beside me, Daniel continues talking, oblivious to my growing unease. "You know, I'd heard Rush was a real asshole beneath a facade of good ol' boy charm, but landing his account has been one of the smoothest deals we've negotiated at the firm. He practically handed the project to me when I met with him in person for the first time last month. Apparently, he's investing some of his sizable fortune into entertainment ventures these past couple of years. Dance clubs, hotels, that sort of thing. Sounds like he knows what he's doing, too. He just opened a new club in the Meatpacking District a few weeks ago and it's been turning big profits from day one."

"Muse."

Daniel grunts. "What's that?"

"The new club is called Muse. I went there with Eve and Paige one night while you were in Las Vegas."

"Did you?" He seems taken aback by the news. His dark brows furrow slightly. "This is the first you've mentioned that."

I offer him a smile, but it feels tight on my face as I

toss his words back at him. "I guess it never came up."

And as we turn onto East 63rd Street and continue toward the 19th century, five-floor brick-and-brownstone mansion at the address on the invitation, my sense of foreboding deepens.

I can't shake the feeling that I'm approaching the edge of a deep abyss. We haven't even stepped foot inside the door and I'm already desperate to leave.

Because something tells me if I'm foolish enough to enter this place tonight, I may not find my way out.

3

MELANIE

"Didn't I tell you we'd have a good time?"

Daniel's voice is a low, confident whisper beside my ear as he and the other players take a short break after the second round has ended.

And he's right. I am having a good time.

If I had imagined myself walking into a cavernous, multi-million dollar BDSM dungeon filled with half-naked women and coarse, leering men hunkered over a poker table in a gloomy, smoke-filled room, I couldn't have been more wrong.

After being welcomed into a warmly lit, opulent foyer by a polite doorman in a black tuxedo while a similarly dressed valet took the Jag and whisked it away from the curb, Daniel and I were brought into an elegant second-floor salon. Inside nine other men and a handful of their beautiful companions--male and female--had gathered for cocktails and fancy hors d'oeuvres before the start of the game.

I'd nearly choked when the urbane, silver-haired man in charge of the private gathering presented Daniel with twenty-five thousand dollars in chips, instructing him that he may settle the credit whenever he wished to leave the game.

Twenty-five grand.

Even now the idea makes my stomach clench. It's more than I make in a year working part-time at my office job in between classes and waiting tables at my neighborhood diner.

The staggering sum hadn't seemed to faze Daniel in the least. "It's all right. Only a drop in the bucket compared to the commission I'll pocket from Rush's project. Besides, I'm going to win at the table tonight, I can feel it."

And so he is winning.

Running the table, in fact.

In the hour and a half since we arrived, he's more than doubled his original stake. I have to admit I'm impressed. Daniel plays like a seasoned professional. Bold moves and clever bluffs. Steep bids that have me holding my breath in my seat behind him.

After the brief pause between rounds, we head back to the table with the others. I'm relaxed even without the cocktails everyone else is drinking, and as I exhale some of my earlier apprehension, I take a moment to soak in the sumptuousness of our surroundings.

Strains of classical music drift quietly through the mansion. High above our heads a massive chandelier sparkles like diamonds. The air is rich with the mingled fragrances of the oiled and polished mahogany millwork and the large arrangement of freshly cut flowers that graces the center of a gleaming Louis XVI table complementing the rest of the luxurious furnishings in the spacious salon.

Everywhere I look I see refined, Old World style and class.

What I haven't seen so far tonight is the host of this exclusive evening.

I've only seen a photo or two of Jared Rush on society websites and gossip pages. Still, I find myself scanning the small group of men, searching for the features I recall with surprising clarity now. Shoulder-length waves of thick, sandy-brown hair. Broad shoulders on a tall, muscular frame. Suntanned skin, sharp brown eyes, and a cocky smirk that always seems a little too amused, a little too insolent, despite his handsome looks.

But he's not in the room.

I'm not even certain he's in the building.

I don't know why I should feel so relieved.

The riffle of shuffling cards draws my attention back to the table as the first new hand is dealt. I settle in and watch the game pick up where it left off during the break. The men who'd been chatting over drinks and small bites a few minutes ago are silent now, faces schooled into unreadable masks as the cards fly and the stacks of chips rise and fall on the table.

Daniel's lost none of his confidence, but his luck is off to a shaky start.

I wince as he loses a quarter of his holdings in a couple of hands. The next one returns some of his money, but I can tell from the tension in his spine that his cards are not coming the way he would like.

Instead of dialing back on his wagers, he grows

bolder. Reckless.

I watch in shock as the game quickly devours all but a couple thousand dollars' worth of Daniel's chips.

"Ah, well. Easy come, easy go," he jokes after the final card is turned.

His quip earns a few chuckles and some shared commiseration from his fellow players. But Daniel's humor is a front. I know him well enough to understand that.

After downing the shot of bourbon he's been nursing in the crystal glass in front of him, he glances back at me with an unconvincing wink. Then he signals to the floor manager who introduced himself to us simply as Gibson when we arrived.

"How may I assist, Mr. Hathaway?" the older gentleman asks in a discreet tone.

I hope Daniel's going to say he'd like to exit the game and take me home before he ends up losing even the last two grand of the twenty-five thousand dollars he put up at the start of the night.

But that's not what he does.

"Would it be possible to extend my credit a bit tonight?"

The older man inclines his silver head. "I'm sure it won't be a problem, sir. How much would you require?"

Daniel considers for less than a second. "Fifty."

Holy shit. It's all I can do not to gape.

"Of course, sir." Gibson's expression doesn't even flicker in reaction. "I'll go see to it at once."

As soon as the man has left us, I pull Daniel away from the table. Panic is drumming inside me, rising into a growing sense of dread. "Let's go now. Please."

"Go?" He looks at me as if I'm the crazy one.

"Sweetheart, I'm in the middle of a game."

I shake my head. "You've already played. You've already lost a lot of money. Now you're talking about risking even more. Seventy-five thousand dollars, Daniel?"

"I can win it back. I just need the means to try." Where my hushed voice sounds strangled, his low tones are measured and resolute. He cups my face, drops a reassuring kiss on the tense line of my mouth. "Everything's under control. Trust me."

Trust him. He doesn't know how much he's asking of me. How hard it is for me to surrender my trust to anyone, particularly a man.

But I do trust Daniel. In three months, he has never given me the slightest reason to doubt him. He's never let me down, not even once.

Gibson returns with a tray containing five rows of chips. With a nod at Daniel, he sets the additional stacks down on the table for him.

"Come on, now. Give me another kiss for good luck."

I comply half-heartedly, tilting my face up to meet his lips. "Good luck."

He resumes his place at the table and the new game begins. I don't have the stomach to watch anymore. My chest feels as if it's got a swarm of bees buzzing inside it. My skin feels flushed and tight, crawling with prickles of anxiety.

I have to get out of this room.

What I really want to do is call an Uber and go straight home, but I can't abandon Daniel. I never would, but especially not when the stakes are suddenly so high.

But if I don't move my legs and get a little air, I just might pass out.

With the game underway, I approach Gibson where he stands near the bar. "Is there a restroom somewhere I could use?"

"Of course." He walks me out of the salon and gestures down the hallway. "Third door on the left, miss."

"Thank you."

The door is locked when I get there. I decide to wait the several minutes it takes before the ornately carved panel swings open and a pair of model-thin, beautiful women about my age stumble out together. I recognize them from the salon, the much-younger companions of a couple of the middle-aged men playing cards with Daniel.

They giggle as they step past me in their body-hugging sheaths and designer shoes. I don't miss the dismissive flick of their gazes as they take in my simple black A-line dress and kitten heels. I'd felt pretty when Daniel picked me up for dinner tonight. Now, I may as well be wearing jeans and a T-shirt.

"Excuse us," one of the women says after a moment.

Her friend just giggles, brushing her fingertips under her nose and wiping away the traces of cocaine that dusted her nostrils when they emerged from the bathroom.

I step inside the powder room and lock the door behind me. Even this room is luxurious. Whorled-wood millwork and gleaming brass fixtures. Warm golden light softens the tension I see in my reflection in the large mirror.

I don't know how long I linger there, letting the cold

water run into the marble sink as I stare sightlessly into the glass and wonder what the hell I'm doing.

Not only tonight, but with my life.

I don't belong here.

Not in this place. Not among any of these people.

And neither does Daniel.

I want to go home. Right now. If he doesn't want to leave with me, then he'll have to understand that I'll be leaving without him.

I head back into the salon and find Daniel speaking privately with Gibson. His face is ashen, his posture hunched . . . defeated.

"Is everything all right?" I ask as I approach, even though it's clear that nothing is even close to all right.

Beyond Daniel's slumped shoulders, the poker game continues--minus him and a couple of other players who seem to have left the gathering.

My heart sinks. I don't have to ask him if he won back the twenty-five thousand. Or the extra fifty he borrowed on credit to keep playing.

"Oh, my God. Daniel."

He doesn't look at me. His voice is pitched low, his words rapid, his eyes pleading with Gibson. "One more extension, that's all I'm asking for. Another twenty, just to give me another shot. Hell, I'll take ten and not complain."

His desperation is shocking. Embarrassing. "Daniel, please."

It's as if I am invisible to him. That's how tight a grip his panic has on him. "Come on, Gibson. You gotta help me out here, man."

The older man's face is sober, his calm unwavering. But then he releases a slow breath. "I will see what I can

17

do."

Retrieving his phone from his pocket, Gibson calmly exits the salon.

"Are you insane?" I hiss at Daniel when we're out of earshot from anyone else in the room. "You can't possibly be crazy enough to keep borrowing money and gambling it away. What's wrong with you?"

"I don't have it." His reply is toneless, wooden. "I can't pay back seventy-five grand tonight. I need to recoup my losses and then some, or I'm fucked."

I step back, mutely shaking my head. "You said you had it under control. You said the money you were getting from the new project was enough to cover the risk."

"It is. It *will be* . . . but not until the work is under way. If I can't make good on what I owe Jared Rush from this game tonight, there might not be a project anymore."

Oh, God.

I can't believe what I'm hearing. I can't believe this is happening.

Gibson returns, his schooled expression telling us nothing. He puts his phone back into his pocket, then formally extends his arm toward the salon's exit. "If you would follow me, please, Mr. Hathaway."

I'm not sure if I'm supposed to accompany them or not. I have no idea where they're going, but the last thing I want to be is left alone to wait for Daniel in the salon or anywhere else in this strange place.

Besides, I've never seen him so unnerved and anxious before.

As upset with him as I am for his stupidity tonight, I'm scared for him, too.

I'm scared for both of us.

I slip my hand in his and walk with him to whatever awaits us at the other end of the long hallway.

4

MELANIE

We are taken to a private elevator, then up to the top floor of the five-story mansion.

Daniel fills the short ascent with nervous chatter about the unlucky cards he was dealt during the last game and second-guesses about how he could have turned the odds in his favor if he'd been able to play a few more rounds.

He doesn't seem to notice the other man's silence. He's still talking as if he's going to get another chance to sit at the table again and try to recoup his losses with more of Jared Rush's money.

I have no such delusions.

Gibson leads us out of the lift and down an opulent corridor. This floor seems more personal, more intimate than the one we just left. I might be tempted to gape in awe at the fortune in framed art on the walls and the beautiful museum-quality furnishings everywhere I look, but I can hardly focus on a thing. My heart is pounding.

Every fiber in my body is taut with apprehension.

Gibson pauses with us outside a pair of towering, closed double doors at the far end of the hallway and I feel as if we're being brought to the gallows.

His sober announcement only confirms my dread.

"Mr. Rush thought it would be best to discuss the matter with you in private," he says to Daniel.

"Oh. I didn't realize he was here." Daniel swallows, his palm going a little sweaty against mine.

Gibson inclines his head without comment. "He's expecting you inside, sir."

Daniel clears his throat and offers a stiff nod. "Sure. Okay, thanks."

As Gibson turns the antique brass handles and the doors start to swing inward, Daniel swivels a blanched look over his shoulder at me.

"Maybe you should wait out here, Mel. This business is between Rush and me."

Honestly, there's nothing I'd like more than to avoid whatever awaits inside this room. But I've never been afraid of confrontation before, and as much as I appreciate Daniel's attempt to shield me from his problems, that's not how I'm wired.

If we're a couple, that means his problems are mine as well.

I shake my head and lace my fingers more solidly through his. "It's okay. We came here together, so I'm going in with you."

Gibson remains in the hallway as we enter the room. He closes us inside the masculine study with a soft clack of the latch at our backs. It echoes in my ears like a gunshot.

Facing us is a massive walnut desk that looks like it

belongs in an English manor. The piece dominates the dimly lit chamber, but the big chair behind it is empty.

Not that my gaze lingers there for long. Like the rest of my senses, my vision is pulled toward another point in the enormous room.

The place where Jared Rush is seated on an oxblood tufted-leather sofa.

He's even more arresting than any photo can convey.

Dressed in a dark suit and snowy white dress shirt unfastened below his tan throat, he is leaned back against the glossy leather, one ankle resting on his opposite knee. In his long-fingered grasp a lit cigar smolders, tendrils of fragrant, cedar-and-spice smoke curling up from the glowing tip.

Although he's staring straight at us, he hardly acknowledges our arrival.

No greeting. No pretense of friendliness.

"Hey, Jared. Thanks for seeing me," Daniel says a bit too cheerily. He steps farther inside, pulling me along by our clasped hands. "Hell of a game going on down there. It's damn hard to walk away when there's a million-plus in chips on the table just waiting to be won."

His chuckle is met with a prolonged silence.

"I understand you ran into some bad luck tonight."

The flat statement of fact is voiced in a deep baritone, carrying the smooth traces of a Southern accent. His hair is long, a tawny mane that extends below his broad shoulders, lending a savage edge to the refined cut of his jacket. An end-of-the-evening beard shadows the squared angles of his face and jaw.

In photos there is always an untamed quality about Jared Rush, as if he were a man more suited to rambling mountain ranges and wide-open spaces than to the bristling skyscrapers and concrete jungle of Manhattan. In person he *is* the mountain. The power of his presence alone seems to diminish everything else in the room.

Including Daniel, whose entire demeanor seems to deflate by the second. "Unfortunately, my luck did take a bad turn. But I was having a great night at first. Isn't that right, Mel?"

I jolt at the mention of my name. "Um, yes."

Until that moment, I think I had myself convinced I was invisible in the room. At least, invisible to Jared Rush.

Now I feel the weight of his stare as if his dark eyes are boring right through me. He appraises me from across the room, his gaze seeming to take an hour as it moves over every inch of me. I feel it like a stroke of a hand, an illicit caress of his eyes that speeds the breath in my lungs and makes me wish I had stayed outside.

Maybe Daniel noticed the shift in the other man's focus, too. His grasp on my fingers tightens possessively, and he moves his body partially in front of mine.

"Come in and sit," Rush offers now, less invitation than command. "There's no reason for you and your pretty date to stand there all night."

"I'm not Daniel's date, I'm his girlfriend."

The words leap off my tongue before I can hold them back.

Why on earth do I feel compelled to clarify anything to him?

Who I am is no business of Jared Rush's. Neither is my relationship with Daniel. But some instinctual reflex makes me feel it's important to draw that line, even if I get the sense this man is accustomed to not only blurring established lines but obliterating them.

"This is Melanie Laurent," Daniel says as we approach the sofa and take our seats on the two chairs opposite it.

Now that we're directly across from him, Rush seems in no hurry to release me from the grasp of his stare. "Ms. Laurent, a pleasure."

I only nod, eager for this conversation, and the rest of the night, to be finished.

Daniel clears his throat. "Look, Jared. This is not how I expected things to go. I don't know if Gibson explained the situation to you, but--"

"He did. I invited you to come to my home tonight and play a private game among my friends. You had some bad hands, you ran through your credit, which was sizable, and now you've come to ask me for more. Correct me if I'm missing something."

Daniel shifts on the chair. "I realize this is a rather awkward situation."

"Not for me." Rush's deep drawl is indifferent, impossible to read. "It's awkward for you, maybe. Awkward for your girlfriend, I have no doubt."

"All I'm asking for is a chance to win some of my money back."

"Using more of my money to do so."

Rush leans forward to snuff his cigar in the heavy crystal ashtray on the cocktail table in front of him, fragrant smoke curling up from the bowl. A glass of whisky sits next to an opened bottle of expensive Scottish single-malt. He picks up the glass and drains it in one shot.

He has elegant fingers. An artist's fingers on large, strong hands that look too powerful for wielding

24

paintbrushes. He catches me watching his movements as he sets the glass down and for an unnerving second, our gazes meet and hold.

I glance away first, my face awash in an uncomfortable heat.

"I'm not in the habit of trusting anyone," he says. "Least of all when it comes to my money. That's why you won't ever see me at the table. I enjoy hosting private games--and other diversions--for friends. But we're not friends, Mr. Hathaway. Until several weeks ago, you were only a name on a business card."

"We're colleagues now," Daniel adds. "I'm not going to do anything to jeopardize our relationship or the project."

"That's reassuring. Some men's honor is worth a lot less than seventy-five thousand dollars." Rush reaches for the phone lying next to the bottle of Macallan. "I'll call Gibson in to join us. After you and he authorize a bank transfer for tomorrow morning to cover the current debt, I'll extend you another twenty-five to get back into the game."

"Um." Daniel clears his throat again, and I can practically feel his mounting panic beside me. "A bank transfer's going to be a bit of a problem."

"A problem? You either have it or you don't."

I brave another look at Rush as his low voice vibrates into my bones. I was wrong to think he didn't seem at place in the cutthroat environs of Manhattan. Right now, while his handsome face is held with utter calm, there is no mistaking the danger in the man.

"I'll, ah, I'll need to rearrange some finances, that's all," Daniel hedges. "I can have everything cleared for you in a couple of days."

"A couple of days." It's not a question, and a person would have to be deaf not to hear the threat in that calm reply. "Are you saying you came to play tonight knowing you couldn't cover your losses?"

"I have some of it now." Daniel clasps his hands between his spread knees as if in prayer. I hope to hell he's praying, because I have no idea how he intends to get out of this. "I swear to you, I'm good for it."

"The same way you're good for the ninety-grand marker you skipped out on in Vegas last week?"

"What?" It's not Daniel who balks in reply. It's me. Shocked, I swing a stunned look at him. "What's he talking about? Is it true?"

But I don't have to ask. The truth is written all over his face.

The fact that he doesn't even try to deny it makes nausea swirl in my stomach. Earlier tonight I didn't even know he knew how to play poker. Now, I'm hearing he's got gambling debts in excess of a hundred and sixty thousand dollars.

"As I said," Jared continues. "The men downstairs are friends. I have an understanding of their worth, as well as their ability and reputation for paying their debts. You, on the other hand, were an unknown. I don't invite anyone to play without first examining my exposure for risk."

As upset as I am with Daniel, I level a glare at Jared Rush. "So, you knew he had a gambling problem and you still invited him tonight?"

"He's a big boy, Ms. Laurent. It's not my job to coddle him. Or anyone else for that matter."

"Well, congratulations. You rolled the dice tonight, too. Now, you're out seventy-five thousand dollars."

"Melanie, please." Daniel grabs my hand, visibly horrified. "For fuck's sake, I don't need you fighting my battles."

"She's loyal," Rush remarks, drawing my attention back to him again. "Loyal and a fighter. I'll bet you can't turn either of those qualities off, no matter how thinly someone deserves them."

I stare at him, stunned by how accurately he's assessed me. I've been in the room with him for hardly a few minutes and already I feel him nipping at the fabric of who I am, trying to expose me.

Is this how he unravels the subjects he paints on his canvases?

I drag my gaze away from the intensity of his dark eyes.

"Daniel, I think we should go now."

I stand up, but he remains seated.

"He knows he can't go, Ms. Laurent. Not without throwing away the biggest project his firm has landed in more than a year. And then where will he be? No job. No way to repay what he owes to me and the loan shark that must already be breathing down his neck. If Daniel walks out of this room now, he knows he'll have nothing left. Maybe not even you."

I swallow my indignation because in my heart, I know Jared Rush is right. Daniel made a grave mistake coming here tonight. A mistake compounded by the one he left behind him in Las Vegas.

But the even bigger mistake would be in thinking he could outrun those problems.

"What do you want me to tell my friends downstairs?" Rush presses. "I don't think those men from some of the biggest banks and corporations in the city are going to agree to your IOU. Your associates in Vegas won't wait much longer, either."

A curse slips past Daniel's lips. "No, they won't. I know that."

"I have the means to cover both of those debts for you, but my generosity isn't free. It's going to come at a price."

Daniel's head snaps up, hope blazing in his eyes. "Name it. I'll do anything. Forgo my commission on the project. Sign away my condo, my car, anything you want."

Jared Rush leans back as he listens to him plead, but his expression is impossible to read. His dark gaze is shadowed by the low light in the room, but I can feel the irritation crackling off the man in the stillness of his big body.

"I'm not interested in any of those things." His deep voice cuts the silence like an animal growl. "I don't see that you've got anything of value I could possibly want, Mr. Hathaway."

He shifts forward now, bringing his face back into the light. His eyes lock on me and I feel the power of his regard the same way I would feel an illicit stroke of his hands on my skin. Every nerve ending in my body explodes with warning.

"Then again," Jared Rush drawls, "perhaps that's not entirely true."

5

MELANIE

"What do you have in mind?" Daniel's voice lifts with hope beside me. I feel the change in his stance, the instant flicker of his relief--and his desperation--to learn what he'll be required to do to get out of this trouble tonight.

I wish I could say I feel some sense of hope or relief, too.

All I feel is the heat of Jared Rush's smoldering gaze still fixed on me.

He stares unflinchingly, unapologetically, while Daniel hurries to reach for the bait now dangling in front of him.

"Tell me what you want, Jared. I know we can work this out."

"I hope we can." Those hot, molasses-brown eyes don't leave my face for a second. "Ultimately, that's going to depend on Ms. Laurent."

"Melanie?" Daniel's head swivels toward me. "What's she got to do with this?"

"I want to paint her."

My breath seizes in my lungs. I wasn't sure what I expected him to say, but this is the furthest thing from my mind.

I want to bolt. I want Daniel to grab my hand and race with me out of the room, out of this mansion--away from Jared Rush--as fast as we possibly can.

That's what I want, but my feet stay frozen beneath me.

As for Daniel, he doesn't move, either. "What do you mean, you want to paint her?"

"Was I unclear? I want Ms. Laurent to pose for me. In my studio."

Jared Rush wants to paint me?

Images of his notorious artwork bombard my memory. I'm nothing close to an expert when it comes to the art world, but I've spent enough time near Manhattan to have seen at least a few of his provocative nudes, whether hanging in galleries or museums, or making headlines at exclusive auctions.

I'm also aware that it's been some time since he's produced anything new. Easily a couple of years. The fact that he's looking at me as his next subject would be laughable if his expression wasn't so joltingly serious.

"I'm not a model," I blurt. "And definitely not the kind you're known for painting."

His head cocks slightly, making some of the thick chestnut waves at his shoulders break against the crisp white silk of his shirt. A ghost of a smirk plays at the corner of his mouth. "You're familiar with my work?"

"I know enough." My reply sounds brittle,

disapproving. Maybe it is, but it's the sudden hammering of my heart that puts an edge to my words.

He doesn't seem fazed either way. "Few of the women I've painted were models. I'm not interested in professionals."

That still doesn't explain why he would be interested in me. But he is. The current of heat arcing toward me from his hooded stare leaves little room for doubt.

I wonder if it's obvious enough that even Daniel senses it now. He clears his throat. "I don't think I like where this conversation is heading. Melanie's not part of this, Jared."

"One hundred and sixty-five thousand dollars," Rush replies evenly. "She can make it all go away. I'll clear both your debts personally, the one you incurred tonight and the one closing in on you from Las Vegas. In exchange, all I'm asking for is a few hours of Ms. Laurent's time in front of my canvas."

"Naked," I point out, and just saying the word aloud in front of him makes me feel as if I'm already unclothed. A shiver dances down my spine, not chilled, but warm. Much too warm. Heat spirals through me, flushing me from my face to my toes. I fold my arms in front of me, the only shield I have against the unwanted heat this man is igniting in me.

Daniel makes a sound of discomfort in the back of his throat. "I'm familiar with some of your work, Jared. What kind of painting are we talking about where Melanie's concerned?"

"The only kind I'm interested in creating." Those dark eyes still hold on to me as he speaks. "I paint what's real. Things I find beautiful, provocative. Raw. Anything less is a waste of my time, and, frankly, my talent."

God, the arrogance. Not that he hasn't earned the right to some of it. His ability and critical acclaim as an artist has made him an extremely wealthy man. His power and fame in this city isn't in question, but neither is his reputation as a debauched manwhore. I'm not sure which of those traits bothers me the most.

Jared Rush wears his confidence as comfortably as he fills out his expensive suit and unbuttoned shirt. I'm sure he's used to women fighting over his attention wherever he goes, which makes me wonder all over again why he would want to paint me.

I'm not sure I want to know. I sure as hell have no intention of finding out.

I glance at Daniel, expecting him to shut this whole ridiculous conversation down. Instead, he stands there in silence, a tendon twitching anxiously in the side of his cheek.

My pulse kicks. He can't possibly think any of this sounds reasonable, can he? The fact that his tongue is apparently glued to the roof of his mouth doesn't give me much reassurance.

As for Jared Rush, he remains unmoving on the large Chesterfield sofa, a force of nature even at rest. Of course, he is not at rest, not even close. He is a tiger about to pounce. He is the wild animal I sensed the moment I stepped inside the room with him.

The knowing look on his face tells me he's aware of my reaction to him, then and now. Since I tend to wear my emotions on my face, he must also be aware of my outrage at his ballsy proposal.

My chin hikes up. "You've got a very high opinion of your own work, Mr. Rush. If you ask me, what you have is a sadistic eye, not to mention a disturbing concept of beauty."

"Mel, don't." Daniel's voice is a tight, strangled whisper next to me.

He's terrified of Jared Rush. After tonight, he's got good reason to be.

Seventy-five thousand reasons. Never mind about the rest he owes someone in Las Vegas.

Reminded of those enormous sums, my heart sinks. I grew up poor and struggling, the oldest of two girls with a hard-working single mom since the time I was thirteen. I don't know what it's like to gamble away that kind of money. Until tonight, I wouldn't have guessed Daniel could be so reckless and stupid. I know how hard he works, the hours he devotes to his career. What the hell was he thinking, racking up gambling debts nearly the sum of my entire student loans?

I've never been so furious with him in the entire time we've known each other. Yet as upset as I am, I'm also scared for him because I care.

I don't turn my back on people I care about, and as much as I may wish I could right now, I'm not going to start tonight.

While I don't want to make things worse for Daniel, I can't stand here and pretend I'm not taken aback by what Rush is suggesting. And I'll be damned if I'm going to cower in front of the arrogant man.

No more than I'm going to stoop to posing for him.

"Tell me what else you think about my art, Ms. Laurent." He leans forward, those elegant, powerful fingers lacing together between the wide sprawl of his knees. "I'm interested to hear your full, unvarnished assessment. It's obvious you'd like nothing more than to let me have it."

Daniel's sharp inhalation beside me should be enough to keep my tongue in check. It probably would be, if not for the challenge sparking in the depths of Jared Rush's stare.

I force myself not to blink. "Your paintings are masterpieces, no one can argue that. But they're also cruel. I don't see any beauty in them at all."

"Is that right?"

"Yes. You peel your subjects to their bones with your paintbrush. You might as well use a scalpel. I can only imagine what it takes for someone to sit for you knowing you'll expose every flaw and imperfection you can find--not only on their bodies, but in their souls."

Have I shocked him? His brows quirk in response, but there is no humor in his schooled expression. "I paint the truth, Ms. Laurent. It can be difficult to look at, and painful to reveal."

A charged silence crackles between us. When it lengthens, Daniel awkwardly clears his throat. "I think what Melanie's trying to say is that she's uncomfortable with some types of art, Jared."

"I heard what she said. I don't need you to translate."

Daniel chuckles, a nervous sound that scrapes up the back of my neck. "I'm just saying, you'd understand if you knew Mel. I mean, we're talking about a twenty-five-year-old woman who refuses to sleep unless there's a nightlight glowing in every room."

I nearly gasp at the intimacy of what he just shared. I flinch internally, not out of embarrassment, but from anger. I don't want Jared Rush picturing me outside of this room, in my bed or anyone else's.

I don't want him already clued in to a weakness only the people closest to me are aware of. Dammit, after three months together, Daniel ought to realize that much about me.

I tear my gaze away from Rush's probing stare. "I want to leave now, Daniel."

Pivoting, I begin to take a step in the direction of the study's exit. Daniel reaches for me. His fingers catch mine, his unmoving feet an anchor holding me back. There is a pleading desperation in his eyes. "Melanie, wait. Shouldn't we at least . . . consider Jared's offer?"

"We?" I nearly choke on the word. "You're not the one he wants to eviscerate on his canvas, I am."

"I know that." His handsome face collapses with regret. "Don't you think I know what I'd be asking of you if you do this for me? Jesus, Mel. I'm the man who loves you more than anything. I messed up tonight. I never intended to drag you into my problems. You've got every right to walk away right now and forget I even exist."

"It's good advice, Ms. Laurent. I reckon you oughta take it."

I glance over and see that Rush has poured himself another glass of whisky as he intrudes on what should be a private conversation. The longer we're in his company--and the more alcohol he consumes--the more pronounced his accent has become.

"Are you saying you've changed your mind about painting her?" Daniel asks.

"Not at all. I want to have Ms. Laurent in my studio very much. But only if she's willing." He brings the crystal to his lips, watching me over the rim as he drinks. "Some people may consider me sadistic and disturbing, but I'm not a monster. In fact, I can be downright reasonable."

I scoff under my breath.

"You don't believe that?" He arches a brow, his mouth tilting with the beginnings of a smirk.

"I believe you're a man who will do--and say--anything he needs to in order to get what he wants."

"One hundred and sixty-five thousand dollars. That was my offer." He leans forward and sets down his now-empty glass. "To show you how reasonable I can be, I'll better it."

"You're only proving my point."

"A hundred-and-sixty-five grand," he restates. "Each."

I can't hold back my incredulous laugh. "You're unbelievable."

Although, I'll admit, the figure staggers me. It's a hell of a lot of money and he's throwing it around like it's nothing. To him, I'm sure that's all it is. I have to believe that's all Daniel or I represent to him, too. Nothing.

Except his intense, searingly grim stare seems to say otherwise.

"Three-hundred and thirty-thousand dollars," he says. "Half to erase Mr. Hathaway's debts, and the rest for you, Ms. Laurent."

Daniel's grasp on my fingers tightens a bit. "Jared, thank you. That's extremely generous of you."

Frowning, I pull my hand away. "I don't want his money. I don't need it."

"Everyone needs money, Ms. Laurent."

He's right about that. I can hardly pretend that kind of windfall wouldn't be life-changing for me. It would wipe out all of my student loans and leave plenty to spare.

It would mean only having to work one job instead

of two, giving me more time to devote to my studies, not to mention time to spend with my Mom and my niece, Katie. Precious time, considering the fragility of my mother's health this past year.

But not like this.

I know Daniel needs my help, too. His well-being also hinges on my decision. I didn't create his problems, but my answer now will either leave him to drown in them or throw him a needed life-line.

And as much as my own financial situation could stand a little rescuing as well, I can't do it by selling a piece of myself to a man like Jared Rush.

God, can I?

He stares at me, giving me no room to hide as I consider all the reasons I need to refuse.

"Some things aren't worth trading for any price."

"Such as?"

"My privacy, for one thing. I live and work in this city. If I pose for one of your paintings, I'll never have any kind of anonymity again."

"There are ways to protect your privacy. I'm willing to guarantee never to release your name publicly."

"People I know will recognize me."

"Only if I decide to put the finished painting up for sale or on exhibit."

"What else would you do with it?"

He tilts his head, those molasses-dark eyes drinking me in for longer than I can bear. "I'll decide that once I've painted you, Ms. Laurent. Tell me the rest of your terms."

"We are not negotiating, Mr. Rush."

"Aren't we?"

Shit. Is that really what's happening here? I brave a

glance at Daniel, checking for his reaction. He looks uncomfortable, and God knows he should be. His girlfriend of the past three months is in the process of bartering her body and part of her soul in order to save him.

But it's not my body that's up for sale. It's only a painting of it. As for my soul, I'll be the one to decide how much of it I surrender to Jared Rush and his ruthless talent. If I am crazy enough to go through with this, I'm not going to give up anything except the hours he demands in front of his canvas.

Daniel takes my hand in his again. "I'm not going to let you do this alone, Mel. I'll come with you to Jared's studio--"

"Out of the question."

We both glance at him, into the flinty hardness of his expression. Rush slowly shakes his head.

"No one is allowed inside my studio while I'm working. Ms. Laurent will come alone, and she will agree to be cooperative and open to my instruction while we're in the session."

He's speaking to Daniel, but looking at me, waiting for my acknowledgment. I want to refuse him, but the words don't come. "How long will it take? The sessions, I mean. How long will I need to be there?"

"Some days I'll have what I need in a couple of hours. Other days, we could go longer, possibly into the evening if I feel it's required."

"No." I shake my head. "Daytime only. Preferably mornings, and no more than four or five hours at a time. No Saturdays or Sundays, either."

I don't volunteer about my commitments at home or the fact that I'm attending classes part-time between the two alternating temp jobs I juggle during the week. Every Wednesday I do accounting work at a dentist's office in Brooklyn. On the weekends, I wait tables at a diner near my house in Queens. I'm relieved that Daniel doesn't volunteer those personal details, either. I intend to keep my real life separated from anything having to do with Jared Rush and his unexpected proposal.

A proposal I am on the verge of accepting, I realize with no small amount of reservation.

"I'm not in the habit of being held to working on the clock," he says, pinning me with narrowed, studying eyes. "But I'll make an exception . . . for now. If I feel I need more of your time, we can negotiate those terms as they arise. Either way, I expect I'll have what I need from you in roughly a couple of weeks' time. Is that acceptable to you, Ms. Laurent?"

I shrug. "I guess so."

"Good. Then, we're settled on the terms?"

I nod. Daniel lets go of a heavy sigh before turning to me and pulling me into a tight embrace. "Thank you, sweetheart," he murmurs against my ear. "Christ, I don't know what I've done to deserve you, Melanie."

"I wouldn't make her wonder about that, if I were you."

I didn't realize he could hear Daniel. I didn't realize he'd moved off the sofa, either, but now he's standing tall on the other side of the cocktail table, watching as I extricate myself from Daniel's arms.

Rush extends his hand and Daniel wastes no time reaching for it. "Thank you very much for your understanding tonight, Jared. I hope we can put all of this behind us."

"Ms. Laurent," Jared Rush says, turning to me

without indicating whether he feels tonight's arrangement has satisfied him where Daniel is concerned. He holds his hand out toward me. "I'll have my lawyer draw up a contract for our signatures before you leave. Until then, I trust a handshake will suffice."

I place my fingers in his palm and they are immediately swallowed up in the warmth and strength of his grasp. Electricity travels through each digit and up my arm as I stare into the shrewd, unreadable depths of Jared Rush's deep brown eyes.

He doesn't smile, but there's no mistaking the glimmer of triumph in his gaze.

A shiver of unease chases the current of awareness that's still vibrating through me as he holds both my hand and my gaze captive.

Whatever Jared Rush set out to accomplish with us tonight, that look tells me he believes he's already won.

6

MELANIE

J ared Rush's lawyer slides the contract across the desk for my signature.

His name is Nathan Whitmore, and it turns out he was one of the players at the poker table downstairs. Tall, with espresso-dark hair and piercing gray eyes, I place him somewhere under forty. Definitely not the stodgy counselor I'd pictured when Jared announced his attorney would be drawing up our agreement and joining us in the study.

I glance down at the signature page of the contract we've all reviewed and agreed to, and are now signing in triplicate. The only name still missing is mine.

I pick up Whitmore's glossy black Montblanc pen and hurriedly scribble my name on the line below Daniel's neatly written signature on all three copies of the agreement.

To the left of ours, Jared Rush's scrawl is jagged and aggressive, as bold and imposing as the man himself.

"Thank you, Ms. Laurent." Whitmore's deep voice is all-business. We stand, and he presents one of the three executed copies to me, and another to Daniel. Slipping his pen into the interior pocket of his impeccably tailored suit jacket, he nods to his client. "Can I do anything else for you tonight, Jared?"

"No, I've got everything I need." Rush's gaze collides with mine across the cocktail table. "Unless Mr. Hathaway or Ms. Laurent have questions for you, Nate, you're free to go back to the game downstairs."

Daniel says nothing, while I shake my head. The contract terms were simple enough to understand. In exchange for three-hundred-and-thirty-thousand dollars, I belong to Jared Rush for up to four hours per day, three days a week, until his painting is completed.

Woodenly, I shake the lawyer's offered hand, trying to ignore the electricity that's been rolling off Jared Rush for the duration of our meeting. Every cell in my body is aware of him, aware of everything about him, no matter how much I want to deny it.

As Whitmore leaves the room, Daniel wraps his arm around my shoulders and brings me close. I lean into the familiar feel of him beside me, but it brings me little comfort now.

"If we're finished, Jared, I'm sure Mel would like to get home."

He nods. "Of course. I have your address on our agreement, Ms. Laurent. I'll send a car to pick you up tomorrow morning at eight o'clock and bring you here for our first session."

"Tomorrow?"

"So soon?" Daniel adds, his arm tensing around me. "Can't you at least give her a day to get used to the idea?"

"No," I blurt, shaking my head. "I can't do it."

They both look at me in question. Rush's brow furrows. "You just signed an agreement that says you will."

"I mean I can't start tomorrow. I have a personal commitment that I can't break."

"What could be more personal than the contract in your hand, Ms. Laurent?"

"I have an exam in the morning." It's not something I intended to explain to him, but he's not giving me much choice. "International Business. It's a requirement for my MBA."

He seems surprised. "You're a student?"

"Part-time."

Although his brow is furrowed, his beard-shadowed, square jaw rises in acknowledgment. "All right, then. We can begin on Thursday morning. I'll send my driver--"

"That won't be necessary. I'm fully capable of getting here on my own."

It's bad enough I had to provide my address for the contract. There's no way in hell I'll allow him to send one of his people out to fetch me.

Besides, what would my mother think?

I can't even go there. I'm not going to tell her about any of this. She doesn't need to worry about the choices I'm making--questionable as they may be right now. God knows she worried enough about Jen and her choices while my sister was alive.

I'm supposed to be the practical one. The level-headed one who's always walked a careful, if boring, path.

The one who's never let her, or anyone else, down.

"There's a subway station a few blocks up the street.

I'm used to taking the train into the city. I don't need a ride."

He acknowledges with a vague nod, but I can tell he's not happy with my pushback. "Thursday morning, eight A.M., Ms. Laurent." His deep voice makes it sound like a command.

"Fine," I reply, amazed that I can sound so cool and unaffected when every cell in my body is crackling with the need to get away from this man and the unholy arrangement I've just entered into with him.

An arrangement that's set to begin less than thirty-six hours from now.

Daniel thrusts out his hand and eagerly pumps Jared's. While he offers more thanks and relief for Rush's understanding tonight, I turn away and head for the door, folding the contract papers and stuffing them into my small evening bag.

I'm not sure I'm even breathing until I open one of the study's heavy doors and step out to the brighter light of the opulent corridor outside. With my face in my hands, I sag back against the millwork of the wall as all the breath in my lungs gusts out of me on a shaky exhalation.

I'm furious with Daniel, but I'm even more upset with myself. And with Jared Rush.

"Oh, God. What have I done?"

"Is everything all right, Miss Laurent?"

Gibson's quiet inquiry brings my head up with a jolt. I didn't even notice he was standing in the hallway. Now, my face heats with added humiliation.

I force a smile, which feels fake and tight. "Everything's fine. I'm fine."

He gives me a dubious, if polite, look. Before he's

made to offer some lame response, Daniel exits the study. Thankfully, alone.

"We should go," he says, glancing sheepishly at the silver-haired gentleman. "Goodnight, Gibson."

"Mr. Hathaway, allow me to see Ms. Laurent and you out." Gibson gestures for us to follow him back to the elevator we rode up on together. "I've already taken the liberty of having your car brought around. You'll find it waiting for you outside."

"Okay, thanks."

As soon as the elevator doors open, Daniel grabs my hand and practically pulls me through the grand foyer. The tuxedoed doorman lets us out to the cool night air and it's all I can do not to bolt for the idling car at the curb.

I slide into the passenger seat without meeting the valet's eyes, feeling paranoid that everyone in Jared Rush's employment knows I've just been bought by him.

I close my eyes, wishing I could blink and none of this would be real.

But it is real, all of it.

And for the duration of the drive to Queens, neither Daniel nor I seem capable of putting any of it into words.

He slows as we approach my modest house. Golden light and the flashing glare of the TV glows from behind the drawn curtains of the living room. Daniel pulls into the short driveway and puts the car in park.

When he turns off the engine, I glance at him in question. "What are you doing?"

"I'm a gentleman, Mel. I'm going to walk you to the door."

"No." My refusal comes out sharper than I mean it

to, and the look of guilt and torment on his face deepens. "I can manage on my own. Besides, it's late. Everyone is probably already asleep. I wouldn't want to wake them."

"Right. Of course, you're right." He reaches for my hand, clasping it between both of his. Shame edges his voice with a rawness I've never heard in him before. "Melanie . . . I'm sorry. Christ, I'm sorry about all of this."

I don't say anything. My confusion and anger with him is still ripe, even more so than my shock over what happened tonight in Jared Rush's study.

"I'll make this up to you, Mel. I swear, I will."

"It's late," I murmur for a second time. "I really need to get inside."

I pull my hand from his grasp and open the passenger door. As I climb out, he leans my way. "Melanie, I love you. You know that, right? What I said earlier tonight--that I love you more than anything else in my life--I meant it. I can't lose you. Please, tell me you can forgive me for all of this."

Can I? Right now, I'm not sure. But I give him a nod. It's the only response I'm capable of when the world around me seems to be spinning out of control. I quietly close the car door behind me, then walk to the house.

My legs feel boneless beneath me, despite that my little purse feels ten pounds heavier with Jared Rush's signed contract folded inside it.

I pause at the front door and wait to watch Daniel drive away. When he's gone, I unlock the deadbolt and step inside. Mom's dozing on the sofa with one of her European travel programs running on the TV. Six-year-old Katie's sleeping snuggled in front of her, still in her clothes when she should be in bed this late on a school night.

I'm not sure who's the bigger child, my niece or her grandmother, who spoils Katie the way she never could for Jen or me when we were growing up under my father's strict rule. Mom's gotten more indulgent about a lot of things since her heart attack last fall. Then again, so have I where she's concerned.

I shake my head and sigh, beyond the capacity for anything but gratitude and love when I look at what's left of my little family. We've been through hell and back together, thankfully the worst of it being over before Katie was old enough to understand or to grieve.

Moving silently, I shut the door and reset the locks. Placing my evening bag on the table near the door, I slip off my shoes before padding over to the sofa. Mom stirs with a soft, muffled snore as I carefully extricate Katie from her arms.

I carry my niece upstairs to her bedroom and get her into her pajamas. She's out before her pale blond head hits the pillow, and I pause inside the room for a moment simply to watch her sleep.

She is the reason I was able to agree to Jared Rush's very indecent proposal tonight.

As much as I care about Daniel, it wasn't him I was thinking of when I put my signature on that contract.

It was this little girl.

She and my mom, both.

For them, I can do this.

For them, I would do anything. Even take off my clothes for a man like Jared Rush, baring myself down to my soul if that's what it takes to help make a better life for us.

I step out of the room to let Katie sleep.

Mom's still snoring softly when I return downstairs to collect my purse and shoes after brewing a cup of tea to bring up to my bedroom while I study some more for my exam in the morning. As exhausted as I am, I know I'm not going to get much sleep.

And while I almost have myself convinced I can drown out everything that happened tonight with several hours of study on global supply chain management, it only takes a few minutes before I toss aside my books in frustration.

My thoughts are spinning, my head still vibrating with the deep baritone of Jared Rush's whisky-edged voice. My senses are still alive and thrumming with the unholy heat of his gaze.

God, what have I done?

Grabbing my evening bag off the edge of the bed, I pull out the contract and read it again, even though the terms are singed into my memory. His demands are clear, simple. Concise. As bold and aggressive as the jagged signature with which he sealed our agreement.

Jared Rush has secured my unclothed presence and cooperation in front of his canvas in exchange for the staggering sum of three-hundred and thirty thousand dollars.

He is a man who gets what he wants. I saw that firsthand tonight.

I felt it, and a part of me still stirs with that awareness, no matter how much I'd like to deny it.

And while it's only my time and body that belong to him for as long as our agreement stands, I can't help feeling that if I'm not careful, it will be nothing less than my heart and soul on the line.

7

JARED

After they're gone, I head downstairs to cover Hathaway's losses with my friends and other guests. As the host of this gathering, I have an obligation to make sure every player at the table belongs there. Allowing a financial risk like Hathaway--a rank amateur, compared to any of the men and women playing tonight--is a responsibility I fully accept.

Hell, I'd all but expected him to wager more than he could handle.

Call it a test. Call it a calculated move in a game he's not even aware we're playing.

Either way, tonight Daniel Hathaway gambled big-- and lost.

And I damn well mean to collect.

I mean to collect on everything I'm due.

The fact that I'll have the added pleasure of settling that debt in the company of a woman like Melanie Laurent only sweetens the prize. I knew she was gorgeous. I've been seeing her luminous eyes and silky auburn hair in the back of my mind for weeks now.

I've been wanting her ever since she walked into Muse. I hadn't been prepared for the intensity of that want tonight. She walked into my study and my cock took instant notice.

She's been gone for more than an hour and I'm still feeling the crackle of electricity that passed between us, no matter how hard she tried to pretend otherwise. I'm still craving her with a need that astonishes me.

A curt nod to the game room bartender as I approach sends him off to pour my usual. He returns a moment later with the aged Macallan. "Thanks, Adam."

"My pleasure, Mr. Rush."

I take a long swallow from the glass, but the whisky's smooth burn doesn't do a thing to take the edge off me. No more than the others that came before it had.

Melanie Laurent got under my skin tonight. Not only because she's a knockout, but even more so because of her fire.

I didn't expect the wholesome-looking beauty to agree to my proposal. I know she wanted to refuse. The way those glittering pale blue eyes of hers turned stormy gray and crackling with offense when I suggested she pose nude for me made it clear she would've liked nothing better than to smash one of her delicate fists into the center of my face.

She might yet, before all of this is over.

Fear for her boyfriend's wellbeing was probably the only thing that kept her fury in check tonight. Fear, and caring. It's obvious even to me that Daniel Hathaway is important to her. She's protective of him. Loyal. She stood up for him, fought for him.

But does she love him? I'm hardly one to guess.

Does Hathaway love her? He's already told me over half a dozen cocktails at one of our business lunches that they've only been together about three months. More than enough time for a man to get himself twisted into a knot over a woman like Melanie Laurent.

Any man but me, that is.

As for the state of their romance, I don't give a damn one way or the other, although there's a side of me that hopes he does love her. It will make seducing her away from him all the sweeter.

A ruthless smile pulls at the edge of my mouth as I bring the glass of single-malt to my lips.

"You look awfully happy for a man who just ate a seventy-five-grand overdraft for someone."

I glance over at my friend Nathan Whitmore as he joins me at the bar. Dressed in his bespoke dark suit and silk tie, few would guess that the polished, Ivy League-educated attorney spent the first fourteen years of his life scrapping around the city as a homeless runaway.

Our backgrounds couldn't have been more different, but eventually we both ended up in the same place. Both of us narrowly surviving dark nights filled with predators of every stripe. Both of us spared from that life by the grace of God, sheer tenacity, and the generous favors of a wealthy socialite with an unapologetic fondness for the companionship of younger men.

Nate and I weren't the only boys and young men Kathryn Tremont scooped out of oblivion or ruin and helped make into something better. There are others, including one of Manhattan's most celebrated titans of business, billionaire Dominic Baine. As some of Kathryn's "boys" we'll always share a bond, but over the years Nate and I have remained as tight as brothers.

I shrug at him, my grin lingering. "I'm not worried about the money. I'll get it back--and then some."

"I have no doubt." When Adam comes over to ask for his order, Nate waves the bartender away. "What the fuck happened in here tonight?"

His expression is concerned, sober. Too much of both when I'm feeling my whisky and still coasting on a sense of cold satisfaction that the night went even better than I'd hoped.

"What do you mean, what happened?" Chuckling, I clap the solid muscle of his bicep. "It shouldn't be a mystery to you, Nate. You drew up the contract."

"Yes, I did. I also drew up the contract with Crowne and Merritt, the firm we hired to do the Gramercy Park hotel and gallery project. Daniel Hathaway is the lead architect on that deal."

I nod and take another drink. "So he is."

Nate stares at me for a second, then exhales a low curse. "As your lawyer, I feel it my duty to point out there's about a hundred reasons why it's a bad idea to gamble with current business colleagues."

"I never gamble."

It's a fact, and he knows it. He's one of the few people who also knows why. But not even Nate knows everything.

He frowns at me. "Until tonight, I wouldn't have questioned you on that. But what do you call it when you invite someone like Hathaway to a seat at your poker table without first making damn sure he's liquid enough to be there?"

I did look into Hathaway, months ago. I've been watching him for a lot longer than that, but Nate isn't aware of how far my interest in Daniel Hathaway goes. If he were, he'd only try to talk me out of it. I've known Nate long enough to have seen his unmatched prosecutorial skills and his uncanny ability to apply logic and reason to untangle or defuse any situation.

I don't want to be talked out of anything.

I'm not an impulsive man, but in this, I have no use for logic or reason. My mind is made up. It has been for years.

It's too late now, anyway.

What was done before cannot be undone, and tonight the wheels have been set in motion on a long-overdue reckoning.

Nate's shrewd gaze narrows on me like a laserbeam. "I can't believe you didn't run background on him, Jared. That Las Vegas debt should've disqualified Hathaway from playing, right out of the gate. Hell, it ought to disqualify him from the hotel project, too. If you want him off the deal, say so, and I'll make it happen."

I shake my head, contemplating the last few drops of liquor in my glass. "I'm not concerned about the project. I'll deal with that when the time is right. As for tonight's game, Hathaway's a big boy. He knew what he was doing. He shouldn't have accepted my invitation if he wasn't willing--or able--to pay for his potential losses."

"We agree on that much," Nate says. "But what about the woman?"

"What about her?"

"Unusual collateral, don't you think? Not that I completely object. She's stunning, although with her girl-next-door face and figure, she seems better suited for teaching Sunday school than posing for one of your paintings."

I can't say he's wrong. Despite her fire, there is an innocence about Melanie, an obvious goodness, something I haven't seen in a long time. Certainly not in my chosen circles. And never once in my studio.

I grunt. "Maybe that's why I want her."

Part of the reason, anyway.

I would have made my offer regardless of what she looked like, however, carrying through with the rest of my plan to thoroughly corrupt and seduce her wouldn't be nearly as enjoyable. Now that I've met her, I can hardly wait to get started.

I'm reminded of the way she laid out her terms, pushing back on things--including the delay in our start date--as if she were the one in control of our negotiations. I didn't see any harm in letting her believe that, at least for the time being.

Two more days and she's mine.

Then I'm going to take great pleasure in peeling away all of her resistance. She's right; I do want to expose her on my canvas, body and soul. I want her to surrender everything to me, to my painting.

Before I consider this debt with Hathaway settled, I want to leave no doubt in his mind, Melanie's, or anyone else's that she belongs fully and completely to me.

I will be satisfied with nothing less.

Knowing the resulting piece of art will make headlines in Manhattan and the rest world is just icing on a cake I've been waiting years to taste.

"I guess I shouldn't argue with inspiration," Nate says after a moment, shaking his head. "Whatever gets you behind your canvas again can't be a bad thing. No offense, my friend, but you're a real prick when you're not painting."

"None taken."

I know damn well what I'm like when I'm unable to create. Boredom isn't a good look for me. Then again, neither is festering contempt.

Ever since I learned who Daniel Hathaway is, I've been consumed with little else.

In two more days, I will begin showing him who I am.

In the end, I want him to know I've taken everything that matters to him.

I want him to feel the justified totality of my revenge.

And I want him to understand with cold certainty that every debt--no matter how old or how deeply buried--eventually demands payback.

8

MELANIE

I report to Jared Rush's Lenox Hill mansion on Thursday at precisely eight A.M.

I've actually been in the city for about an hour already, trying to kill time, but I'll be damned if I want him to think I'm anxious. I am anxious, though. I'm nervous as hell.

My palms are damp, my heart racing, as I wait alone in the luxurious sitting room just off the foyer while one of Jared Rush's house staff alerts him that I've arrived.

For the past thirty-six hours, I've been trying to get accustomed to the idea that I've agreed to take my clothes off for a man I know nothing about.

The internet helped fill in some of the blanks. Not that I feel any better about my arrangement with Rush after reading dozens of photo articles about his most acclaimed and controversial paintings, or scouring countless online rags for paparazzi photos of him. And I found plenty of those. Image after image of him at events all over the world--complete with an accumulation of enough gorgeous female companions to circle the globe.

The knowledge of his staggering net worth came as a shock, too.

While his art incites multi-million-dollar bidding wars at the most prestigious auction houses, Jared Rush's savvy investments in real estate and entertainment ventures in recent years are estimated to have earned him close to half a billion dollars.

I'd assumed he was rich, but holy shit.

"Ms. Laurent?"

I lift my head at the familiar sound of Gibson's voice. "Good morning," I say, greeting the polite older gentleman as if I'm here on a social call.

His answering smile is kind, perhaps even a little sympathetic. He must know the reason I've come has nothing to do with a casual visit.

Right. Of course, he knows. He was there in the corridor when I practically broke down outside Rush's study the other night.

I'm sure by now the entire household staff knows about Daniel's humiliating loss in the game room and my contractual obligation to help him fix it.

Gibson gently clears his throat. "If you're ready, Ms. Laurent, Mr. Rush has asked me to show you upstairs now."

Am I ready? I'm not sure I ever will be.

I get up from the silk-upholstered settee, my long hair swishing against my back as I smooth my hands over the skirt of my sleeveless, pale blue cotton wrap dress. I haven't worn the summery frock since last year at Katie's kindergarten class graduation party at the school.

This morning as I was digging through my closet, searching for something appropriate to wear, the unfussy dress seemed the best of my limited options. Especially considering I was only going to be required to take it off, anyway.

God, I still can't believe I've agreed to this.

I should turn on the soles of my ballerina flats and run all the way back to Queens before it's too late.

I should tear up my agreement with Jared Rush, apologize to Daniel for abandoning him to the consequences of his own recklessness, then go back to living my life. Back to working my two extra jobs to keep a roof over Mom and Katie's heads while I'm barely nibbling at the edges of my mounting student loans.

That's what I *should* do.

Instead, I dutifully follow Gibson through the foyer to whatever awaits me upstairs.

He leads me into the same elevator Daniel and I rode in with him two nights ago. Instead of stopping on the second floor as we did then, today we ride all the way to the top of the five-story residence.

There is no long, broad corridor on this floor as we step out of the elevator car. This floor is even more private; a vast, beautifully appointed living space. Gleaming white marble floors. Soaring walls embellished with carved millwork and crown moldings. Floor-to-ceiling windows overlooking some of the most costly, historic real estate in Manhattan.

Gibson leads me through the heart of the stunning residence, pausing outside a pair of French doors that are opened into a spacious living room and solar. Turning to me, he gives me a nod of permission to enter.

I glance inside, hesitant. I don't see Rush, but I can *feel* him. That dark, electrical charge that traveled through me when I stood before him in his study two nights ago is back now, waking every nerve ending in my body. Sumptuous furnishings in butter-soft brown leather and creamy fabrics accented in masculine earthtones are arranged in a conversation-friendly cluster in front of an entire wall of bookcases lined with what I guess to be hundreds upon hundreds of hard-bound volumes. A large, elegant fireplace completes the inviting interior, unused at the moment, but flanked by a tidy basket of logs and gleaming tools.

From somewhere deeper inside the enormous room and out of my line of sight, I hear the quiet clink of silverware and china dishes, accompanied by the aromas of bread and bacon and freshly brewed coffee.

"Ms. Laurent," Gibson says, whether to prompt me into motion or to announce my presence to his employer, I'm not certain.

I step inside the room. Behind me, Gibson discreetly closes the French doors and departs the hallway in silence.

"Come in," Jared Rush tells me, his deep voice calm and relaxed as it rumbles from somewhere off to my right.

I follow the vibration and the heavenly smells of his breakfast. He is seated at a dining table in front of another set of French doors, this pair looking out onto a private terrace green space and patio off the back of the mansion.

Last time I saw him, he looked like a decadent lord of the manor, smoking his cigar and drinking whisky in his expensive, dark suit and partially unbuttoned, crisp white shirt. His thick tawny hair had been loose around his shoulders that night, the wild mane of a beast on a man surrounded by luxury and fine things.

This morning he is dressed casually in an ecru-colored linen button-down with the sleeves rolled up over his tanned forearms. Beneath the pressed white tablecloth, his long legs are encased in relaxed, faded denim. His large feet are bare inside soft leather loafers, and spread wide on the beautiful Persian rug that runs from one end of the expansive room to the other. It must have cost a fortune. Everything in this room, in this mansion, must have come with a staggering price tag.

Including me, I realize with no small amount of chagrin.

He's taking a sip of coffee as I approach. Today, his long hair is swept back into a loosely fastened queue at his nape. The hint of brown whiskers shadowing his lean cheeks and squared jaw the other night have been scraped away, but even clean-shaven there is still an untamed quality to his handsomeness. A wild, savage edge that no woman with warm blood in her veins could possibly ignore.

I wish I could say I was the exception, but even as I take the last few steps toward him at the table, my senses prickle with uninvited awareness.

He watches me over the rim of the china cup that looks like a doll's toy in his big, elegant hands. "Eight o'clock sharp. You're prompt."

"Isn't that what you told me to be?"

Amusement plays at the edge of his sculpted lips as he sets the delicate cup back onto its saucer. "Prompt, and you follow instructions. We're already off to a promising start, Ms. Laurent."

That brief smirk and the refined hint of the South in his rumbling voice almost disguises the danger in him.

Almost, but not quite.

He may be trying to project an air of casual disregard, but he hasn't taken his eyes off me since I arrived.

"Join me."

Another command, this time disguised with a smile and a dip of his beard-shadowed chin to indicate the breakfast feast of eggs, meats, breads, and fruit laid out before him on the elegant round table that's been set for two. My mouth waters at the mingled aromas, but even if I were starving, I'll be damned if I'll accept so much as a crumb from Jared Rush's table.

"I've already eaten," I murmur, trying to ignore the way the stale plain bagel and bitter cup of coffee from the shop down the street is currently rolling in my stomach.

He shrugs. "I hope you don't mind if I finish my breakfast in front of you, then."

"Feel free." Anything to delay the purpose of my being here today.

I can't help but notice there is no easel or art apparatus of any kind in this room. He doesn't paint in here. A degree of relief washes over me at that realization.

When my gaze comes back to Rush, I find him studying me. "If you're wondering where my studio is, it's not in the city. It's in Sagaponack. I have a house on the beach there where I work."

"The Hamptons," I acknowledge. Sagaponack being one of the most expensive enclaves in that playground for the rich, which is roughly two hours away from

Manhattan. Thank God.

"I thought it would be best if we start here today," he says. "Take some time to get comfortable with each other first."

"Nothing about this--or you--makes me comfortable." I practically wince as the words leap off my tongue. Why would I admit that to him? Why give a man like him any inkling he's got the upper hand over me?

But it's too late to take it back.

I've allowed the slightest crack in my armor and I can't expect this man to let it go unchallenged.

He leans forward, placing his elbows on the edge of the table. "I'd be disappointed if you were comfortable with our arrangement, Ms. Laurent. Or with me."

Is he saying that because he understands how out of my depth I am in his world, or because he wants me to be on edge? Maybe this is how he begins deconstructing everyone he exposes on his canvases. Or is he taking some kind of personal, extra enjoyment out of seeing me squirm?

I don't have the nerve to ask, especially not when his dark stare makes me feel as though he can already see through my cool replies and through the breezy cotton of my dress. All the way down to everything I'm desperate to keep hidden from him for as long as our arrangement lasts.

He indicates the lone chair across the table from him. "Please, have a seat."

"No, thank you. I prefer to stand."

"The whole time?" He leans back in his chair, one of his tawny brown brows arching. "I should warn you, I haven't even gotten started."

I want to assume he's talking about his breakfast, but I'd have to be either blind or stupid to believe that. As much as I want to indulge my stubborn side and stand for the duration of his meal and anything else he has in store for me this morning, all I've done is make myself the focus of his full attention.

And I realize now that he is stubborn, too. He doesn't touch any of the silverware at his place setting, nor glance at any of the mouth-watering food in front of him. With another nod toward the empty chair, he waits until I finally lower myself into it.

Evidently satisfied, he reaches for a braided silver basket containing half a dozen fresh, flaky croissants nestled on a bright white linen cloth. I can smell the butter and airy dough from across the table, and it's all I can do to control the small growl of my stomach as he offers the fresh-baked goodness to me.

I shake my head.

"You're sure? My chef trained in Paris. I've got friends who'd kill just for one of her croissants, never mind the rest of this feast."

When I decline to take one, he shrugs and puts one on his plate next to the fluffy omelet that's bursting with cheese, spinach and other vegetables, and chunks of smoky ham. I'm not sure if I interrupted his breakfast, or if he was waiting for me to arrive before he began.

I glance down at the formal place setting in front of me and can't help wondering what kind of game he thinks he's playing now. Did he actually expect me to sit across from him and share a meal with him as if any of this is normal?

Maybe it is normal for him.

Maybe he plays the part of the polite, albeit arrogant,

Southern gentleman for all of his models before eviscerating them on his canvas. I watch him reach for the sharp knife next to his plate, then slice into his omelet with a surgeon's precision. Those elegant, strong hands mesmerize me. The way they move with nuanced, utter control, no matter how mundane the task.

I don't want to think about all the wicked things he does with those hands. I don't want to think about all of the wicked things I've heard about his other appetites, but I can't stop the flood of rumors that fill my mind.

As I sit in silence while he devours his breakfast with gusto and a total masculine lack of self-consciousness, I'm thinking of the rumors about wild sex parties and BDSM clubs. Rumors about his insatiable hunger for beautiful women and the seemingly revolving door that leads to his bedroom. I've seen some of the supporting evidence for that last rumor in the pictures I found online.

As for the other rumors, they wouldn't surprise me, having gone to his new nightclub, Muse, two weeks ago with my friends Evelyn Beckham and Paige Johansson. Although Muse is billed as a dance club, part of its allure-
-and its phenomenal success--is the flashing, strobe-quick glimpses of people having sex behind one-way glass in the private VIP rooms that circle the multi-story dance floor. That night with my friends, I'd dismissed what I saw as an illusion, a gimmick designed to play on the club's name, but now I have to wonder.

Now, I have to wonder about a lot when it comes to Jared Rush.

His plate emptied, he wipes his mouth on the starched white napkin, then pours another cup of strong black coffee from the French press on the table.

"How do you think you did on your exam yesterday?"

For a moment, I'm startled by the question--by the idea that he not only remembers about my test, but bothers to ask. It feels too personal, too intimate, that he should know anything about what I do with my private time. I swallow to recalibrate my nerves, but it's not easy to project calm under the intensity of his gaze.

"I'm sure I did fine. I take my studies very seriously."

He chuckles. "I wouldn't doubt that for a minute."

"What's that supposed to mean?" Anger nettles me. I scowl at him across the table. "Are you mocking me because I'm trying to get a better education and improve myself?"

"No." He sets down his cup without drinking. "I'm telling you what I see when I look at you, Ms. Laurent. I see a good girl, too good. The kind who protects the people she cares about, even if they don't deserve it. Even to her own peril. The kind who gets perfect grades in all her classes and wears her Sunday best to an appointment with a man who's only waiting for the chance to get her out of it."

Heat surges into my face. I don't know what upsets me more, the accuracy of what he sees in me, or his audacity to say it.

His words send another kind of heat through me, too, a darker one that blooms deep inside me no matter how hard I want to deny it. I discreetly cross my legs, but squeezing my thighs together only makes the heat twist tighter.

"First of all, Mr. Rush, I'm not a girl. I'm a twenty-five-year-old woman."

He grunts. "I've got more than ten years on you,

darlin'. A hell of a lot more than that, if we're talking about anything other than age."

"I wouldn't doubt *that* for a minute," I say, tossing his words back at him. "As for protecting the people I care about, yes, you're right. That is important to me, regardless of what it might cost me in the end."

"He doesn't deserve you," Rush utters tersely. "Deep down, I think you already know that."

I can't believe his gall. What can he possibly know about Daniel, or me, for that matter? "Daniel cares for me. And I care for him, too."

"That doesn't answer my question."

"I didn't hear you ask one."

My flippant reply irks him. Well, good. He needs to be irked.

He needs to be put in his place--especially before he starts thinking he's going to deconstruct me the way he does everyone else. I'm not letting him in, no matter how hard he pushes. If this chat over his breakfast table is supposed to get us familiar with each other before our arrangement officially begins, then I want him to understand I'm drawing a hard line between us, here and now.

"All right, Ms. Laurent. Then I'll ask the question plainly." His stare penetrates deeper as he leans forward on his elbows--as if he's two seconds away from leaping at me from across the table. Maybe he is. "If you and Mr. Hathaway have such a strong, loving bond, why didn't you know he has a gambling problem?"

"Just because he made a couple of mistakes doesn't mean he's got a problem--"

"One hundred and sixty-five thousand mistakes," Rush interjects grimly. "And you had no idea. In fact, you were blindsided by it."

I can't deny anything he's saying. If I try to, Rush will only see through me, anyway.

He slowly shakes his head, studying me. "He's keeping secrets from you. Think about that next time you hear him say he loves you. Think about that the next time you let him fuck you."

I draw in a sharp breath, not that I'm actually shocked by his crudeness. He's needling me now, trying to find my soft underbelly.

Right now, what I want to show him are my claws.

"I didn't come here to discuss Daniel or my relationship with him. I didn't come here to discuss anything with you at all." My voice climbs along with the rapid beating of my heart. "My private life is just that--private. Now, we have an agreement, Mr. Rush, and I intend to honor it. I'll sit for you in your studio and let you paint me, but I will not let you dissect me. Not on your canvas, and for damn sure not here, over your French-pressed coffee and croissants, you arrogant asshole."

His gaze stays rooted on mine through the entirety of my angry outburst. His face is unreadable, schooled into a mask of indifference. Maddeningly, he reaches for his coffee and takes a slow drink before replacing the cup on its saucer without making the slightest sound.

Those artist's hands of his move deliberately, in measured, total control.

"You're right," he says after a long moment. "I've overstepped the bounds of our agreement. I apologize."

His contrition takes me aback. I was expecting fury. Hell, I was half-expecting him to void our contract and have me thrown out of his mansion.

Hoping, maybe.

As uncertain as I was about being alone with Jared Rush before, this encounter has only fortified my apprehension. Because that spark that ignited between us in his study two nights ago is still alive now. Stronger, as if that were possible.

It's explosive, dangerous.

He's dangerous.

All the more so when he's showing me a glimmer of humanity beneath the exterior of the untamed beast seated across the table from me.

"I'm glad you understand," I murmur, dropping my gaze momentarily if only to avoid his searching, penetrating stare that refuses to let me go.

Abruptly, he pushes back from the table and stands. My eyes flick up, following him as he stalks over to a sturdy mahogany sideboard on the other side of the room.

I don't know where to look first, at the glorious way his broad shoulders and muscled back move beneath the creamy linen of his loose shirt, or at the way the loose denim of his jeans call attention to his long stride and tight, round ass as he walks.

He opens the cupboard door at the front of the sideboard and reaches inside, withdrawing a bottle of Macallan and a short, cut-crystal glass. He pours more than two fingers' worth into it, then pivots around to face me, leaning casually against the bar.

"Take off your clothes, Ms. Laurent."

"Excuse me?"

He lifts the whisky to his mouth and tosses all of it back in one swallow. When his molasses-brown eyes meet my gaze again, his stare carves right into the center of my being.

"Remove it all," he says. "I want to see what I have to work with."

9

MELANIE

He can't be serious.

Yet, of course, he is. His hard expression leaves no room for doubt. His dark gaze is demanding in the heavy silence that stretches between us. With his broad mouth held in an unsmiling line against the edge of his emptied glass, he continues to stare at me. Waiting for me to obey.

Even though I know what I've agreed to with this man, I bristle at the way he seems to think he can command me as if he's got any right. As if he owns me the way he does any other object in his orbit.

I stand up, refusing to sit in subservience while he attempts to lord over me from across the room. My spine feels rigid and unnaturally straight as I face off against him with my hands fisted at my sides. "I came here this morning to begin my obligation in your studio, as your model. Since you have no intention of painting me today, I don't see why you should expect me to take off my clothes for you."

His eyes narrow on me. "Did I say I wasn't going to begin painting you today?"

I blink. "You said your studio is in the Hamptons."

"That's irrelevant to this conversation, Ms. Laurent." He sets his glass down on the edge of the sideboard. "And whether we're in my studio or somewhere else, when we're together, you're mine to observe and to instruct."

You're mine.

That's not exactly what he said, but that's what I hear. That's what his possessive stare is telling me as he casually folds his muscled arms over his chest.

All my life--since I first learned enough to mistrust men--I've recoiled from arrogant, domineering cavemen who think women were put on Earth for their personal use and entertainment. In fact, I've run long and far from that type. That's how I ended up with Daniel, my safe, steady port from all those earlier storms. My faith in him was shaken a bit the other night. I'm still furious with him today, but everyone makes mistakes sometimes. Even terrible, expensive ones.

Daniel's not perfect, but God knows neither am I.

And he needs me. He needs me to be here for him now, no matter how difficult Jared Rush might intend to make that for me.

I shake my head. "That's not fair. You led me to believe our agreement extended only as far as your canvas and your studio. Making me undress in front of you here, now, doesn't have anything to do with the terms of our contract and you know it."

"I disagree," he replies evenly. "Do you think I only create when I'm holding a paintbrush? I've been visualizing how your body will look on my canvas from the moment I decided I wanted to paint you. I've already imagined every supple curve and tender hollow. In my mind, I've already stroked my brush over every naked inch of your form. Having you remove your clothing so I can confirm what I already know is just a formality-- one our contract grants me permission to demand."

As he speaks, it's as if his words are painting a picture in my mind, too. I can see myself alone in a barren, cold studio in front of him, my skin bared for him. I can feel the power of his gaze as he commits all of my features to memory, along with my flaws.

I can hear the wet lick of his brush bringing all the hidden, most vulnerable, parts of me to life on his canvas through his skill and mastery. I can hear his low voice commanding me, coaxing me, seducing me into surrendering everything I've promised him and more.

My throat goes suddenly dry, in direct opposition to the liquid, molten ache that's unfurling within me. Beneath the meager covering of my dress and bra, my nipples have gone tight and hard. I don't want to acknowledge the traitorous response of my body.

I can't acknowledge it. What would it say about my loyalty to Daniel? What would it say about me?

Instead, I cling to my righteous outrage. "Obviously, you have about as much shame as you have morals, Mr. Rush."

His answering chuckle only demonstrates he's also impervious to insult. I can hardly pretend to be surprised.

"You're stalling, Ms. Laurent."

"And you're trying to bend the rules of our agreement."

"Would you like to be released from it?"

It's not a question I expect from him, especially not in the solemn tone in which he asks it.

He means it.

He studies me in prolonged silence, his head cocked slightly toward the bulk of his shoulder. As triumphant as he seemed the other night after Daniel and I had signed his contract, I can tell he's seriously willing to let me go now.

Is it because I've pissed him off? Because I'm not falling at his feet the way he seems accustomed to with other women?

Somehow, I don't think it's either of those things motivating him to let me break our contract. No, this is something else. I can see the truth of it in his consuming, dark eyes.

It's a small act of mercy--a shocking one, coming from a man like him.

Or maybe he's just having second thoughts now that he's seeing me in the sober light of day.

I shouldn't care why he's offering this. There is a cowardly part of me that wants to scramble out of this room and never look back. But if I break the contract, where will that leave Daniel?

His debt to Rush will be due immediately. I'm sure it will also mean the swift cancellation of his big project with him, which will probably cost Daniel not only the partnership he's hoping for at the firm, but his entire career.

I don't even want to consider what his problems in Las Vegas could mean.

And then, there are my own personal reasons for seeing this through.

Without the money Jared Rush has guaranteed me at the end of our arrangement, where will that leave me? How long will it take before I can even dream of paying off all my college loans? At the rate I'm going, Katie will be in high school by then, and my mom . . . ?

"You're taking an awfully long time to answer, Ms. Laurent. It's a simple question. But I'm only going to ask it this one time. Do you want me to let you go?"

There is so much meaning in that question, despite his claim of its simplicity. Do I want him to let me go? I don't belong to him, no matter what our agreement states. Yet it's impossible to deny that what's taking hold between us reaches far beyond the written terms of any contract.

And no matter how afraid I am of what that means, I can't seem to convince myself to break away from it. I can't seem to break away from him.

I swallow, and my answer falls off my tongue. "No."

His chin lifts fractionally, a look of mild surprise flickering in his eyes. I hear the quiet release of his breath, followed by his toneless, deep-voiced reply. "All right, then. Your clothing, please."

My movements feel slow, as if my limbs belong to someone else. I toe off my ballet flats, barely resisting the urge to sigh as the luxuriously thick Persian rug crushes beneath my bare soles. My fists unclench slowly, then rise to where the fabric belt of the wrap dress is tied at my waist. As much as I want to look away from Rush as I work the knot loose, I refuse to release him from my stare.

I know my eyes are defiant, filled with challenge, as the belt goes slack in my fingers and the front of the dress slips open to reveal my simple white cotton bra and a good deal of my bare abdomen.

He doesn't blink or react in any way. I'm not even sure he's breathing as I draw the dress off one shoulder, then the next. The light blue cotton floats down the length of me, as soft and airy as a whisper.

A tendon jerks in his jaw when I reach around for the clasp of my bra. The hook-and-eye closure pops apart in my fingers, but I hold the two ends together, not yet prepared to give in to this new reality. I'm not someone who jumps from one man's bed to another. It took nearly two months of dating before I felt comfortable enough with Daniel to take my clothes off in front of him the first time we slept together.

I've spent barely two hours total in Jared Rush's company and yet here I am, about to drop my bra and panties merely because he's ordered me to.

No, not because he's demanded it. Because he's paying me to do it.

I'm not sure why that makes me feel better, but somehow it does. Because this is a job. That's all it is; all I can permit it to be.

Judging from the bland, indifferent way he's waiting for me to finish, his muscled arms still folded against his chest, I have to believe that Jared Rush considers this nothing more than a job as well. That doesn't mean he won't continue attempting to rattle me. I can't let myself forget for a second that he is at his coldest, most brilliant best as an artist when his subjects are uncomfortable.

So, he's not going to get that from me. I won't give him that satisfaction, no matter how much he's paying for it.

I release the ends of the bra and shrug out of it. Cool air hits my bare breasts, making my already tight nipples contract into firmer peaks. The modest undergarment drops to the floor without hesitation or fanfare. I'm not performing a striptease, after all. I'm unwrapping purchased goods for inspection.

At least, that's the mantra I repeat over and over again in my head as I reach for the waistband of my panties, then strip out of them as casually as I would on my way into the shower.

Fully naked, I hold my arms out slightly, hiding nothing from Rush's inscrutable gaze. "Satisfied?"

He doesn't say anything. His eyes slowly travel the length and breadth of my body before returning to mine. "Walk over to the light."

His voice is as rough as gravel, hardly more than a growl. I feel as awkward as a bug under a magnifying glass, but I'll be damned if I let him know that. With my head held high and my hands moving casually at my sides, I pad toward the nimbus of sunlight streaming into the room from the terrace's French doors.

The new location puts me on the other side of the small dining table with him now, only a few feet of angled distance between the place where I stand in the heat of the morning light and his unchanged position in front of the sideboard. Those handful of feet feel as insignificant as a couple of inches as I wait for him to speak again.

"Gather your hair away from your face and neck."

No "please" or semblance of a request, just a tightly spoken command as if I'm standing on a stage or the auction block. Teeth gritted behind my closed lips, I reach up and lift my tangle of auburn waves into a loose ponytail in my grasp.

I can do this. I can weather his assessing gaze and

maddening arrogance the same way I handle any other obstacle thrown in my path. God knows, I've had enough training in twenty-five years of living that I can get through these next weeks, too.

"You have a scar under your left arm."

"Yes." His abrupt remark jars me, not that I expected the significant flaw to pass without his notice. As bad as it was, I don't try to think about that old wound. It's easier not to think about it in the daylight. In the dark, it's harder to keep the memories away.

Now that he's pointed it out, my thoughts flash back to that spring night when I was thirteen, when the trauma of my home life came to an explosive, final end. I can still hear my father shouting and swearing, railing at the world from behind the wheel of our speeding Buick. I can hear Mom screaming for him to slow down, that he was going to get us all killed.

Most of all, it's Jen's wooden silence, her resignation in those horrific moments, that haunts me to this day. Her terror never ended, not even after he was gone.

"How'd it happen?"

I shrug. "Just an accident that happened when I was a kid. No big deal."

He doesn't believe me. His gaze locks on mine as if he can sense I'm holding something back. I wait for him to dig deeper. If he is anything like his ruthless art, he won't be content with my vague answer.

I hurry to formulate viable explanations in my head, mundane scenarios to bore him and deflect his curiosity. But he doesn't seem interested in talking.

Unfolding his arms, he pivots around to the sideboard to serve himself another generous serving of the Macallan.

"I've seen enough," he utters tersely, his back to me. "Get dressed. I'll wait for you outside."

He sounds so disinterested, I have to wonder if I'm not at all what he was expecting. Is it my scar that he finds so offensive, or the fact that I haven't told him where it came from? His sudden lack of interest is curious, coming from a man who's made a fortune from exposing human frailty and pain.

I let my hair go, watching the rigid lines of his shoulders and spine as he pours his drink.

"That's got to be at least four shots of whisky since I arrived. Isn't that a lot for eight o'clock in the morning?"

He grunts, eyeing me over his shoulder. "I wasn't aware you were keeping track."

"Maybe someone should."

My reply brings him around to face me, his sensual mouth drawn up in a faint sneer. Then, as if in defiance of what I've said, he downs the whisky in one swallow while holding me in that scorching gaze of his. He sets the glass down with a hard thump.

"You drink too much," I inform him, as if he doesn't already know. "Is that why it's been nearly two years since you've produced anything new?"

The question leaps off my tongue before I can hold it back. His stare bores into me as he steps toward me. His legs are long and powerful. Two strides carry him within arm's length, close enough that I can smell the smoky whisky on his breath and see the hauntedness in his dark eyes. I can also see the barely restrained anger in his handsome face.

"Your clothes, Ms. Laurent. Put them back on." The smooth Southern edge of his low voice is far from soft now. "As soon as I leave this room, one of my staff will be in to clear away these dishes. I suggest you dress quickly and preserve your dignity, unless that good-girl attitude of yours is only a facade."

God, he's an arrogant bastard. I should let him go. I should not say another word. I should simply be thankful this awkward exercise is finished, and pray the remainder of my time with him will be over just as quickly.

But maybe there's something ruthless inside me, too, because I can tell I've hit a nerve and it only makes me want to probe deeper. He's trying to shut me out, and for some reckless reason, I don't want to make things that easy for him.

"Why start painting again now?" I press. "And why start with me, aside from the fact that you want to recoup the seventy-five thousand that Daniel owes you?"

He scowls. "Isn't that reason enough?"

"Obviously, you don't need the money."

"Are you suggesting I should forgive your boyfriend's stealing just because I don't need what he took from me?"

"Daniel didn't steal anything from you."

"Didn't he?" He steps closer to me, closing the meager distance. A dangerous fire smolders in his consuming brown eyes. "Only a cheat gambles with money he doesn't have. A thief, Ms. Laurent."

He sounds so indignant, I can't help myself; I scoff. "Then why not offer to have Daniel pose naked for you instead of me?"

"Because I wanted you. And you said yes."

His voice skims over my bare flesh like a stroke of

his hand. Dark, heated, and utterly in control. I swallow, my mouth as dry as the core of me is drenched. He hasn't touched me, yet my skin tingles as if his hands have stroked every bare inch of me. Arousal coils deep within me, uninvited, yet undeniable.

Just from the power of Jared Rush's gaze and the smoky rumble of his voice.

A cold, knowing smile pulls at the hard edge of his mouth. He leans in a little closer, his deep voice going even lower, a vibration I feel all the way to my marrow.

"And just for the record, Ms. Laurent, if you were mine, I would've put a fucking bullet in my head before I'd ever give you up to a man like me. Not for any reason. Not for any price."

I stare at him, unable to speak. My lungs don't seem to function, except to soak in the dark, enticing scent of him.

He takes a step back, and his eyes make one final sweep of my nudity. "We'll be leaving for my studio in ten minutes."

10

JARED

I feel her stare on me as I stalk away from her. It carves into me even though I can't see her changeable blue-gray eyes. Intelligent, inquisitive eyes. Brave, beautiful eyes that see more than they should, more than I intend to allow.

She's fearless, too, marching into my house wrapped in a sweet summer dress and haughty defiance, like a virgin sent in to face a dragon and determined to not go down without a fight.

I hadn't expected to begin seducing her over my breakfast plate, but damn if the idea hadn't taken on immense appeal the instant her gaze clashed with mine.

I'd told myself to show her some gentleness today, exercise some patience. I'm generally in short supply where those two things are concerned, but with her, at least for today, I wanted to try.

Fuck. So much for that.

Making her strip in front of me was a cheap shot,

one beneath even a bastard like me.

I'd like to tell myself it was contempt for Daniel Hathaway behind my demand. After all, he's the reason she's here with me in the first place. He's the reason I'm going to have Melanie Laurent on my canvas and in my bed before these next weeks are over.

But when I told her to undress for me, I wasn't thinking about Daniel Hathaway or debts to be settled-- new or old. I wasn't even thinking about my painting. I wasn't thinking about anything except the proud, smart, incredibly attractive woman seated alone with me in the room.

A woman who seems determined to challenge and push back at me with every turn.

She made it clear she wants to draw a hard line between her real life and our arrangement. I get that. Hell, I respect her for it and wholeheartedly agree. I'm not going to let her get inside my head or my personal life any more than she wants me in hers.

None of that changes the fact that when she's with me, she's at my mercy.

I thought taking her clothes off would unravel some of the fight in her. Instead, I'm the one who's nearly undone. I've seen hundreds of beautiful, naked women, both professionally in my studio and laid out before me for my pleasure. But none of them ever affected me as powerfully as her.

My heart hasn't stopped banging in my chest since the moment she reached for the knot on her innocent-looking wrap dress. Like a teenage boy who'd just discovered his father's porno stash, my body's reaction to Melanie undressing was swift and uncontrollable. Blood that surged to my cock in a hot torrent has left me with a massive hard-on that has yet to subside.

As I step out of the room now, the image of her confidently complying to my heavy-handed command runs on repeat in my head.

Her high, firm breasts studded with tight pink nipples. Long, lean legs crowned with a modestly trimmed thatch of light curls covering her sex. Miles of milky skin I'm certain will feel as soft as velvet under my hands, my lips, my tongue.

And a scar hinting at something more than just a badly healed physical wound.

I'd been struck mute and stupid with lust as she took off her dress and underwear. I told her I'd been picturing her unclothed since that first night. That much was true, but I'd been wrong to think I was prepared to see her in the flesh.

She is exquisite. Sexy as fucking hell.

She's broken in places, too. That scar is only trace evidence of bigger things she doesn't want me to see. I'd be lying to myself if I said it didn't intrigue me as much as her outward beauty and sharp intellect.

She should have snapped up my offer to end this game before it begins. The fact that she stood firm didn't surprise me. She's too loyal, too strong. She may even be a little desperate, though whether it's for the money to spare Daniel or herself, I'm not sure. Regardless, she wouldn't have come here in the first place if she wasn't fully prepared to adhere to the terms of our contract.

Evidently, retreating is no more in her nature than it is in mine.

God help her for that, because now that I've seen her it's too late for either one of us to turn back. She only thinks she can't stand me now; when this is over,

I'm certain she's going to hate me. And rightfully so.

A low curse grinds past my clenched teeth as I close the French doors behind me.

One of my household staff notices me and approaches from another area of the penthouse. "Is everything all right with your breakfast, Mr. Rush?"

Her cheerful smile dims when she sees my thunderous expression. I don't have the patience to smooth my scowl, particularly not when I'm still sporting an erection along with my surly attitude.

"No one goes in this room without first getting my permission, Carolina."

"Of course, sir. I'll convey your instructions to the rest of the staff at once."

I nod curtly, dismissing her to carry out my order. Threatening to allow any of my employees to barge in on Melanie while she was undressed had been another cheap shot. It was also a bluff. I would never do that to her, but I need her to understand she's in my world now.

I need her to understand that I'm the one in control, no matter how thin that control is already proving to be.

Retrieving my phone from the pocket of my jeans, I start tapping out a text to my personal assistant to arrange for my driver and a private charter service to East Hampton airport. I've barely typed the first couple of words when a call from Nate interrupts.

He's here at the house today, working on contracts in my office downstairs. For all he knows I'm still in a closed-door breakfast session with Melanie, so this can't be good news. I abandon the text and answer my lawyer's call.

"What's going on, Nate?"

He clears his throat. "Sorry for the call, but we have

a situation."

"What kind of situation?"

"Alyssa. She seems pretty upset."

Shit. Just what I don't need to deal with right now. Unfortunately, I don't have much choice. "What's going on?"

"I don't know. She's asking to see you, Jared. She's down here in the office."

"You mean she's at the house right now?"

Behind me, the French doors open and Melanie steps out. Fuck. Talk about even more bad timing.

Every article of her clothing is fixed in place as primly and perfectly as it was when she arrived, her clear gaze leveled on me with the same disapproval and mistrust.

The bright flush of color in her cheeks is new, though, and I'm not sure if that heat is directed at me in outrage or something else. After the way I just treated her inside that room, I wouldn't be surprised to feel the heat of her palm striking my face in another second.

I wrench my focus back to the other problem at hand.

"Did Alyssa say what she needs?"

"You know her. She only wants to talk to you. She looks like shit, Jared."

I curse under my breath. When I glance at Melanie I am met with a scathing look of rebuke--and not a little amusement.

"I'm sorry," Nate says. "I should've told her you were tied up for the day. I'll take care of it--"

"No." My answer is clipped, but firm. "Tell her to stay put. I'll be right down."

"Female trouble?" Melanie asks as soon as I end the

call, challenge gleaming in her stare.

I'm tempted to explain, but that would mean blurring the line that's been drawn between us in the sand today. Besides, Alyssa is my personal business. I'm not going to air her problems in public any more than I would my own. Where mine are concerned, Melanie Laurent has already seen more than I'd like.

I slip my phone back into my pocket. "As much as I was looking forward to getting started with you, Ms. Laurent, unfortunately, it will have to wait until tomorrow."

I can hardly say she looks disappointed.

"Eight o'clock," I tell her. "I don't expect you'll be a second late."

"Why would I be? The sooner you start your painting, the sooner we can be done with each other."

I grunt, stifling a smile. "Come, I'll walk you out."

She refuses my gesture to accompany her. "Don't bother, I know the way. It sounds like you have your hands full enough as it is."

Without waiting for my permission or my reply, she turns away from me and leaves for the elevator on her own.

11

MELANIE

With a large serving tray balanced on my hand, I carry five orders of Thursday's turkey-and-gravy lunch special out to the group of silver-haired women chattering over iced teas at the back of my section at the diner.

"Here you go, ladies." I set the heaping plates down in front of them, tucking the emptied tray under my arm while I ask if I can bring them anything else.

I wasn't supposed to work until Saturday, but with an entire day to kill after my abrupt dismissal from Jared Rush's mansion this morning, I decided I'd rather pick up an extra shift than spend the rest of the day at home steaming over the infuriating audacity of the man.

I'd also like to forget that I took my clothes off in front of him, but that's never going to happen. Even though I had almost convinced myself it was simply a requirement of the job I've entered into on my own free will, it didn't feel like a job.

Standing naked in front of him while his inscrutable, assessing gaze drank me in from head to toe felt more intimate than I want to admit. It felt like being caught in a storm, all of my senses heightened, my skin too tight and too hot, alive with a million tiny electrical charges.

Now, several hours later, all I feel is anger and awkwardness.

Based on his unreadable, almost harsh expression while he stared at me I have to wonder if he'd suddenly regretted offering to paint me.

Maybe my scar put him off.

Maybe he didn't appreciate the fact that I hadn't swooned on top of his breakfast table the way I'm sure he's accustomed to with any other woman he meets.

Or maybe he'd prefer to paint Alyssa, whoever she is. Though he didn't exactly seem happy to be dealing with her this morning, either. Not that Jared Rush's women or his no doubt well-deserved problems with them are any concern of mine.

"Melanie, dear?" One of the ladies breaks into my thoughts with a pleasant, sing-song voice. "I hate to be a bother, but didn't I ask for the vegetables in place of mashed potatoes?"

Shit. I blink and shake my head. "Oh, yes you did. I'm sorry, Mrs. Augustino. I'll be right back with that for you."

It's not like me to be so distracted, but my mind has been in a scramble all day. Not only because of my unsettling reaction to Jared Rush, but also because of the things he said to me.

Things about Daniel.

They may be colleagues on the hotel project, but Rush's mistrust of Daniel is clear. Anyone would have a right to be upset over a sizable debt like the one he racked up the other night, yet Jared Rush seems to disapprove of Daniel on a deeper level, as a person.

Why hire him for the project if he didn't like him? For God's sake, why invite him to a private, high-stakes poker game at his mansion--especially when he was aware of Daniel's situation in Las Vegas?

I didn't even know about that myself. Jared Rush is right, I was blindsided to learn about Daniel's gambling. I felt foolish; I still do. Why had he kept it from me? How long would he have tried to keep it a secret?

As I return to the kitchen for the side plate of veggies, other questions gnaw at the edges of my thoughts, too.

Not only about the man I fell in love with over these past three months, but about the one I don't know at all, yet who seems able to reach all the way into my soul with a single burning glance and a few shockingly intimate words.

If you were mine, I would've put a fucking bullet in my head before I'd ever give you up to a man like me. Not for any reason. Not for any price.

I can still hear the dark vibration of his deep voice so close to my ear. I can still feel his heated breath against my bare skin. I feel it so intensely, I shiver with it even now.

God, what is wrong with me? I need to forget about Jared Rush. I need to forget about all of the confusing things he makes me feel every time I'm near him. He is a means to an end, an opportunity for a new start for both Daniel and me. Once he has his painting and pays for it as promised, Daniel and I can try to get past this whole troubling situation and move on with our lives.

Although, I can't deny my trust in him may never be fully repaired.

As for the way Rush behaved with me this morning and his unsettling remarks, for all I know it's just preparation for him getting me in front of his canvas. I should expect him to probe for weak spots, to look for cracks in who I am.

He won't find them. I can't let him.

Blowing out a sigh, I push through the swinging door into the kitchen, which is operating at full tilt for the busy lunch hour.

"Order up," the cook calls out, punctuating it with a ding of the bell beside him.

The plate of pasta marinara and garlic toast is for one of the other servers' customers, but I snag it after ladling a small bowl of steamed broccoli and carrots for my table.

"I'll take this out, Chuck."

He gives me a wink and a wave of acknowledgment while moving on to tend the burgers sizzling on the grill. When I step back out to the dining room to deliver the food, I practically crash into Daniel.

"Hi, Mel." He's wearing a suit as if he's come straight to Queens from his office in Midtown, which he apparently has. In his hand is a large bouquet of red roses.

He's never come to the diner before. It's so unexpected to see him now, I can only frown. "W-what are you doing here?"

He gives me one of his boyish smiles that never fail to charm me. Except for today. "Is that any way to greet a man holding a dozen long-stemmed roses?"

"I'm sorry. Just . . . give me a minute, okay?" I

gesture with the plates in my hands, then squeeze past him to bring the food to Mrs. Augustino and the other table.

Daniel is leaning against the lunch counter when I come back, his smile dimmed a little as our gazes meet. He's trying to be cheerful, but there's a note of worry in his expression. "I've been calling and texting you all morning. I got very concerned when you didn't reply."

"I've been working for the past few hours." It's not really an excuse for ignoring him, but I'd rather not lie, either. I feel my frown pinch even more. "How did you know I was working today?"

"I stopped by your house. Your mom told me you picked up a shift." He leans in close and lowers his voice to a whisper. "I thought you were meeting Rush this morning."

"I was. I did." I shake my head. "I really don't want to talk about it. Like I said, I'm working."

It's a brush-off and he knows it. I can see the note of rejection in his eyes. "Mel, are we okay?"

"Sure." I tilt my head at him. "Aren't we?"

"What's that supposed to mean?"

At that same moment, Shelly, the server whose order I delivered, swoops up from her break in a cigarette-scented flourish. "Ooh, roses for me? You shouldn't have!" She cackles, draping her arm over my shoulders. "Who's the good-lookin' suit, Mels?"

"This is Daniel," I murmur, an awkward tension pulsing unnoticed by my coworker.

"I'm Melanie's boyfriend." Without missing a beat, Daniel's gaze flicks to the plastic nametag pinned above her left breast. "Nice to meet you, Shelly."

She beams at him before glancing at me and

widening her eyes. "You better get those pretty roses into some water, girl. Go on, take your break. I'll watch your tables."

"Thanks, Shel." I'd have preferred to keep working, but avoiding Daniel isn't going to make things better. I take the bouquet from him and he follows me through the kitchen to the small break area near the back door of the diner. Although to call the battered card table and rickety metal chairs a "break area" is a stretch.

He takes a seat as if he intends to stay a while.

I can't resist inhaling the sweet perfume of the flowers, no matter how inconvenient it is to be given them while I'm in the middle of the lunch rush. "I'll go look for something to put these in."

I return with the roses placed in a water-filled iced tea pitcher. Daniel grins up at me while I choose to remain standing.

"Do you like them?"

"They're beautiful."

When I don't offer anything more, he puts his elbows on his spread knees, clasping his hands together as if in prayer. I've seen this pose before, when he and I stood in front of Jared Rush that first night. Now, I can't help but consider this Daniel's groveling stance.

"So, you did meet with Rush today, then?" he asks after a moment.

I barely nod.

"For how long?"

"Not long."

He swallows, his hands still fused together as he glances up at me. "Did it . . . go all right?"

"Not especially, no."

The breath he exhales carries a heavy edge. When he

speaks, his voice sounds contrite, almost pleading. "Aren't you going to tell me what happened?"

"No, Daniel, I'm not." I set the roses down on the table, then step back a pace. "The only way this is going to work between us is if I do this thing with Jared Rush and we never speak of it. Not now, and not after."

A tendon throbs hard in his jaw. "If he touches you, Melanie--"

"He hasn't."

"Goddamn him, if he hurts you in any way--I'll kill the son of a bitch."

"Maybe you should've thought about that before you asked me to agree to pose for him."

Daniel's anger stutters to a halt. "W-what?"

I didn't say it with any venom, but he sounds so horrified and wounded, I'm almost sorry I said it. *Almost.*

"Mel, what other option did we have? Rush wasn't going to let me leave that house without paying him what I owed. I don't have that kind of cash."

"Not to mention the money you owe in Las Vegas," I remind him.

His brow furrows. "That's right," he says, keeping his voice low enough to be drowned out by the rest of the kitchen activity. He reaches out and takes my hand between his. His palms are moist and cool, but his grip is firm. His eyes implore me. "Listen to me. I love you. I know I'm never going to be able to make this up to you, but I'm going to do my damnedest to try."

"Then you can start by telling me why you kept your gambling problems a secret from me."

He flinches, his head snapping back before he blows out a heavy sigh. On a low curse, he drops his gaze to our joined hands. "I didn't tell you because I didn't want to see you looking at me the way you are now. I didn't want to lose you. I *don't* want to lose you."

As I stare at the top of his lowered head, more of Jared Rush's words come back to me. All those little seeds of doubt that I wanted to deny have started putting down roots since I left his house this morning.

"Are you keeping any other secrets from me?"

"What? No." His head comes up, his gaze stark. "I'm not, I swear to you, Mel."

I want to believe him. God, I'm desperate to believe him. After several months together, I need to be able to trust that this kind, loving man is who he's shown me to be. If the solemnity in his handsome face is any indication, he must be telling me the truth.

So why am I still hearing Jared Rush's deep voice warning me that Daniel is hiding something from me? That he doesn't deserve me?

Because I'm already allowing Rush to take me down a dark path, that's why. It has to be. Maybe he only said those things to manipulate me, to begin deconstructing me before his brush makes its first stroke on the canvas. Or maybe he just thinks I'm a fool for loving Daniel.

Anyway, it doesn't matter why Jared Rush said what he did.

It doesn't matter what he thinks.

If I have my doubts about Daniel, they're my own to either work through or leave behind. Right now, I'm not sure I'm ready to do either one. Especially not here, in the middle of the clamor and chaos of the diner.

"I should get back to my tables."

When I pull my hand away, Daniel comes off the chair to stand with me. His touch moves to my shoulders, resting lightly there, his thumbs stroking absently. "What time does your shift end? I have a client meeting in an hour that I can't miss, but I want to see you. I need to see you."

"Daniel, I can't." I step out of his touch, out of his reach.

"Can't, or don't want to?"

"I have a paper to write tonight." Which is true, but also a welcome excuse for some space to myself. It won't last nearly long enough, though. "In the morning, I have to go back to Rush's place," I say, feeling a strange mix of curiosity and trepidation over the idea. "We're going to his studio in the Hamptons tomorrow."

"The Hamptons." Daniel scoffs, his voice tight. A bleak acknowledgment settles over his face before he curses under his breath. "I hate everything about this damn arrangement. You belong to *me*, Melanie. I hate the idea of Rush being alone with you. I hate the idea of him looking at you, even if he says it's only to paint you."

I can tell he hates this, and for the first time, I wonder if that might have been the point. Knowing what little I do about Jared Rush, it wouldn't surprise me if he isn't taking some amount of satisfaction in the idea of causing Daniel distress.

"How long have you and Jared Rush known each other?"

He shrugs dismissively. "I guess about a month, a little more. We were introduced at the firm, when he approached us about his Gramercy Park hotel project. Why?"

"I'm just curious." But it's more than that. I am suspicious in a way that makes little sense to me. Suspicious of Daniel, of Jared Rush, of things I've never questioned before in my life.

Meeting Jared Rush has raised countless questions in my mind. He's stirring a paranoia in me, along with other, uninvited feelings I can't deny. Those feelings still linger inside me as powerfully as his dark, dangerous voice.

"Mel, what's wrong?" Daniel reaches for me and I flinch at his touch.

"I'm sorry," I murmur, distracted and edgy. "I should get back to work now."

"All right." He frowns, letting his hand fall slowly to his side.

He walks me out to the busy restaurant dining room. When we pause at the exit, he leans forward to kiss me and I move my head, giving him my cheek instead of my lips. I tell myself it's because we're in front of a diner full of nosy customers, but the small niggle of unease in my stomach is saying something different.

Daniel clears his throat. "Will you promise to call me tomorrow . . . after? I need to know you've gotten home safely. Can you at least give me that?"

"Okay." I nod, forcing a smile I don't really feel.

12

MELANIE

That next morning, I find myself seated between Jared Rush and the pilot of a sleek black helicopter chopping high above Long Island under beautiful, sunny skies. The private charter had been waiting for us at an exclusive heliport along the East River just a few minutes away from the mansion at Lenox Hill.

When Rush had accompanied me to his chauffeured Mercedes parked at the curb outside his home nearly an hour ago, I hadn't been expecting we'd be flying to Sagaponack. Least of all suspended in a small, speeding metal box with far too much window glass for my peace of mind.

"Nervous?"

His deep voice vibrates close to my ear. Every time I hear him speak, it unravels something inside me. Now is no different. The low rumble cleaves through my thoughts, and my anxiety, which is hardly insignificant.

My stomach climbed up behind my rib cage the moment we took flight and still hasn't come down. I want to chalk it up to the fact that I've never flown in a helicopter before, but part of the distracting flutter inside me has to do with the close proximity of Rush's body to mine.

I give him a half-shrug, half-shake of my head. "I'm fine."

He tilts his head, obviously unconvinced. "Is this your first time in a helicopter?"

"Yes." The bird dips a little at a hiccup in the air, and my hand shoots out in reflex to brace myself. Rush's denim-clad leg is the closest thing in my reach. I grab for him without even realizing it until I feel the heat of his hard thigh clamped under my fingertips.

Oh, God. I snatch my hand back on a wince. "Sorry."

"No worries." That easy Southern drawl sounds more pronounced with the low chuckle that accompanies it. Everything about him seems calm and unfazed the farther we get away from the city. All except the look in his dark gaze. It sears me with its intensity as he watches me. "I take it you don't like flying?"

"It's not flying that bothers me." The helicopter bobs again, and I suck in a breath. "I don't really like heights much."

"You don't like heights and you don't like the dark. I'm intrigued," he says, studying me with a look that seems more serious than his easy tone would indicate.

My stomach clenches for a different reason now. I hate that he remembers Daniel's careless blurt about my fear of the dark, but, of course, he would remember. I don't suppose Jared Rush is the kind of man who forgets anything. Just as he won't forget this added admission of weakness I've volunteered to him. I can only wonder how it might color the way he sees me, or the way he'll choose to depict me on his canvas.

"It's not a big deal." I lift my shoulder, trying to ignore the way his penetrating gaze moves over me. "Everyone's got their quirks."

He acknowledges with a slight nod. "True enough."

"Even you?" I ask.

As eager as I am to deflect his unnerving focus away from me, I can't deny I am curious about the man. I know he's arrogant and infuriating. I know he's dangerous in more ways than I want to admit, even to myself. Yet no matter how much I'd like to pretend differently, I want to know more about Jared Rush.

"Do I have quirks?" He grunts. "More than a few."

"Such as?"

He stares at me. "Ms. Laurent, are you asking me to share something personal with you?" A cool, sardonic humor glints in his dark eyes. "I thought we'd established fairly firm rules of engagement yesterday. As I recall, personal questions are off-limits."

The reminder of what happened at our breakfast meeting sends heat into my face, along with other places I'd prefer to ignore. He knows it, too. I can see the glimmer of awareness in his schooled expression.

He's used to being in control. Used to being the one who sets--or breaks--the rules. He demonstrated that clearly enough yesterday. I had marched into his house determined to let him know he wasn't going to rattle me. It took him only minutes to show me that he could not only rattle me, but leave me burning with a mixture of outrage and uninvited desire.

Jared Rush is not only used to calling the shots. He's

used to winning as well, and I can't dismiss the way he's just referred to our conversation in combat terms. Rules of engagement. The kind of rules made for entering into battle.

Is that what this is to him--some kind of war? If so, what does that make me?

Am I his enemy simply by association with Daniel? Or am I something even less? Something expendable, a pawn?

I suppose I'll have that answer soon enough. In approximately two weeks, Jared Rush will have his painting. Daniel's debts will be forgiven, my own financial concerns will be lessened, and this will all be over.

At least that's what I tell myself as the pilot radios our approach to the small tower up ahead. Over the vibration in the cockpit, he informs us we'll be on the ground in ten minutes.

With a nod, Rush leans back in his seat next to me and taps out a quick text to someone. No matter how hard I try to ignore him, my gaze follows the long, muscular lines of his body, the elegant strength of his hands and fingers.

The calm confidence that surrounds him, whether in motion or at rest, is starting to feel familiar to me now. His air of total control in any situation had felt abrasive when we met, but it also soothes me somehow, even though he's the last person I should look to for reassurance.

We land as softly as we took off, the helicopter parking on a small target not far from the gray cedar shakes-sided terminal building at East Hampton's airport. Rush guides me off the aircraft, the heat of his palm hovering at the small of my back until we clear the slowing rotors.

The salty summer breeze riffles my long ponytail and sends the hem of my loose dress dancing around my bare calves as we walk toward the terminal. He opens the door for me as we step inside, smoothly navigating us past the handful of attendants and locals who greet him like an old friend, not the rich and famous artist he is.

We head straight through to the entrance on the other side, where taxis and ride-shares jockey for positions at the curb. Rush leads me to one of the half-dozen idling vehicles.

"This one's us," he says, gesturing to a beige Toyota sedan with a decal in the window.

"You called an Uber?"

He glances back me, grinning. "Were you expecting a limo?"

It's the first time I've seen such a relaxed and purely natural expression on his face. With his thick, tawny-brown hair brushing his broad shoulders and his handsome face lit up with a boyish smirk, it's hard to reconcile this side of him with the ruthless, intimidating man who has bought and demanded my presence here today. The sight of him like this all but stops me in my tracks.

"Don't look so shocked," he says when I slow behind him. "My place is only ten minutes away. Let's get out of here."

His place, as it turns out, is a large cedar-shakes beach house and three-car attached garage situated on what appears to be a two-acre lot. The weathered gray shingles and creamy white trim are set off by pops of colorful hydrangea bushes, wild roses, and thick, green hedges.

Gravel and sand crunch under the vehicle's tires as we turn off the road onto the short driveway out front. The whole property is classic and laid-back, a far cry from the staid, Old-Money glamour of Rush's mansion in the city.

I slide out of the parked car's backseat while Rush speaks briefly with the driver. Fresh, salty air engulfs me, bringing with it the scent of blooming flowers and the low, rhythmic roar of the waves rolling against the beach on the other side of the property.

No wonder Rush's demeanor seemed to change the moment we landed at their airport. Even my own nerves smooth out as I drift toward the house and its inviting front porch and huge veranda.

Eyes closed, I pause and inhale deeply, allowing myself a moment to savor the calm. Having grown up poor in the city before being saddled with multiple jobs just to make ends meet, I can count on one hand the number of times I've been this close to fresh ocean air. And I've never breathed it from in front of a multi-million-dollar beach house in the Hamptons.

The car door shuts in the distance behind me, followed by the whine of the Toyota's engine as the driver leaves the property.

I sense Jared Rush's approach even before I feel the deep rumble of his voice at my back. "Welcome to my studio, Ms. Laurent. Ready to get started?"

He moves beside me and I glance at him, unsure how to answer. One part of me simply wants to be done with our arrangement, while another is desperate for it never to begin.

This man has already put an indelible stamp on my life. Whether I follow him inside or not, I know my life can never be the same. There will always be the time *before* I met Jared Rush, and the time *after*.

A challenge glints in Rush's smoky brown eyes as he waits for my response.

Does he think after the way he acted with me yesterday I won't have the nerve to see this contract through? I'd gotten the sense he'd been trying to test my limits, possibly scare me off. If anything, his behavior has only made me more resolved to prove to him that he can't intimidate me.

How far will he go to prove otherwise?

I'm not sure I'm ready to find out.

But then I think of my mom and Katie, of how this opportunity will make life better for both of them--for all three of us. I think of Daniel, too, despite how conflicted those thoughts have become these past few days.

I meet Rush's piercing gaze and hold it, my chin rising a notch. "Lead the way."

A smile tugs at the sculpted curve of his lips. "All right, then. Come on."

13

MELANIE

I follow him onto the covered porch as he unlocks the door and gestures for me to step inside ahead of him.

There is no doorman waiting to greet us, no household staff ready to tend his every need or whim. It's just the two of us beneath the soaring, dark wood rafters of a spacious great room painted in shades of white and ecru.

The simple, inviting furniture is similarly neutral, accented by a wall of filled bookcases and art of various styles and materials. The room in its entirety is like a blank canvas that's been arranged to make the most of the real star of the show, the tall windows looking out over a sandy, grass-covered dune and the sparkling expanse of dark blue water with its gently rolling waves that spread out as far as the eye can see.

"What do you think?"

"It's lovely." I glance over my shoulder and find him

looking at me. "This isn't the kind of place I imagined you working in."

"No?" He cocks his head slightly, a quiet grunt emanating from low in his throat. "How exactly have you been imagining me, Ms. Laurent?"

It's a loaded question, and I don't doubt for a second that he's aware of that fact. If I admit I've been thinking about him, picturing him at work, wondering about the unreadable man beneath the very public facade, I'll only feed into his already gargantuan ego. Not that my denial would hold any water with him, either. He's invaded my thoughts from the moment we met. He's dominated them, the way his presence dominates all of my senses now.

I avert my gaze back to the sun-dappled waves, because looking at Jared Rush only makes me intensely aware of the heat and size of him. Not to mention how insanely good he smells. Spicy and fresh, enticingly male. God help me, I'd be aware of all that even if he were standing in another room.

"Are you going to tell me what's in that pretty head of yours, or are you going to leave me to guess?"

His deep voice slices through my resistance the way nothing else can. If my curiosity wasn't so piqued I might ignore the bait he's daring me to take. His probing gaze is even harder to ignore. I can feel it boring into me, daring me to face him.

I draw in a breath as I look at him. "Do you want to know the truth?"

"Always. Especially from you." It's a crisp answer. A coldly serious one.

Something quick and dark flashes across his expression. A warning. Which is rich, coming from him.

I scoff quietly and it lifts one of his brows. "Is there something funny about expecting honesty from someone?"

"Not at all. I just think it's ironic that you'd demand it when you practically pulse with private agendas and secrecy."

"Is that so." I can't tell if he's amused or annoyed with me in the long moment that passes before he speaks again. "I thought my agenda couldn't be spelled out more clearly. You have a signed copy of it, in fact."

Until a few days ago, Jared Rush was nothing more than a distant name to me. An enigma in a city full of mysterious and sinister figures who existed far beyond my orbit. Now, here I am, alone with him in a remote, empty house for the next several hours with the full understanding that at any moment I will be obliged to take off my clothes for him.

Again.

The thought of being naked in front of him doesn't unnerve me as it did before. Jared Rush doesn't scare me, even though he probably should. He'd like me to be afraid, I'm sure. All the better to peel me apart, bit by bit, on his canvas the way he's done with everyone else who's come before me.

But I'm not going to play that game with him.

If I'm to be examined and dissected, exposed to the very core of my being, then so will he.

I pivot away from the glass to face him fully. He's unearthly handsome in the gilded morning light. Smooth, bronzed skin. Chiseled cheekbones and a stubborn, squared chin under the dark whiskers framing the generous line of his mouth. His absorbing, intense eyes are the only part of his face that seems immune to the warmth of the light. Filled with impenetrable shadows, they could pull me under with him if I'm not careful.

"I know what your contract states. What I haven't figured out yet is what you really want to get in the end."

"I want what I'm due, Ms. Laurent."

"You're not just talking about money. Are you?" In his cold silence, I scoff again, more sharply this time. "If that's all this was about, you wouldn't have offered double what Daniel owes."

"I offered double because that's what it took to get you here. I would've paid a great deal more."

A dark look smolders on his profanely handsome face. He holds me in that unnerving stare of his, the one that makes me feel like I'm already naked. It sends a shiver of heat through my veins, a look that should send me bolting for the door and the nearest escape out of here, away from him.

Instead, it does the opposite. It makes me determined to unlock whatever it is Jared Rush keeps walled up behind the cold indifference of his eyes. He's got secrets hidden behind the mask of his cool control, the kinds that carry deep pain and scars.

I want to uncover them all. Against every shred of logic and self-preservation I possess, I want to understand who Jared Rush really is on the inside.

"Come," he says. "My studio is on the other side of the house. I only have you for a few hours, so we should get started."

I swallow, then fall in beside him as he leads me away from the expansive living area and down an airy atrium hallway. Windows overhead frame blue sky and frothy clouds, inviting an abundance of natural light into every corner of the welcoming house. It's an artist's house, no question, each tastefully furnished room presenting an interesting and ever-changing backdrop of form and light and shadows.

Still, as polished and beautiful as it is on the surface, there's an emptiness to this place. A vacancy beneath the outward charm.

It's the same kind of aching hollowness I see when I look into its owner's eyes.

"Do you spend a lot of time here?"

"Not as much as I used to. And not lately."

"Why not?"

He shrugs. "I have other things in the city that keep me busy."

"Too busy to paint?"

"Busy enough."

"I thought artists lived for their work."

"Some do."

"But not you?" I walk alongside him for a moment, waiting for his answer. When it doesn't come, I can't help thinking about the question that's been plaguing me since that first night at his mansion. "You're one of the most talented, acclaimed painters of the last decade, but you act as though you could just throw it all away."

"Painting is everything to me," he replies with about as much emotion as he might announce the sun is shining outside. "It's the only reason I'm alive."

"Then why has it been so long since you produced anything new?"

He barks out a sharp laugh. "Have I been on a time table? Forgive me, I wasn't aware."

He doesn't pause. If anything, his long-legged stride takes on a stiffer pace as he leads me through the bright passageway to whatever awaits me at the end of it.

"Do you want to know what I think?"

He grunts. "Not especially."

"I thought you appreciated the truth, Mr. Rush. Just a minute ago, you said you expected it."

When he doesn't stop, I do. I watch him stalk away from me, impatience and coiled aggravation in every muscled line of his big body. I should let him go. I shouldn't care what he's running from or what's made one of the most singularly gifted artists of his time trade his talent for a bunch of flashy night spots, private clubs, and high-rise hotel projects.

It shouldn't matter how Daniel and I have gotten tangled up in Jared Rush's world. But I'm here now, and I'm getting more and more entangled every minute. I can't look away. I can't ignore the pain I see in this man, no matter how much every warning bell in my brain is trying to convince me otherwise.

"I think you're hurting, Jared. I think behind all your confidence and swagger, behind your scathing talent for stripping everyone else down to their soul with your paintbrush, all this time you've been the one who's bleeding."

He turns slowly, his face an unreadable mask. He walks toward me, the distance between us in the corridor closed with just a few measured strides.

He fills my vision, crowding out everything else that surrounds us.

"That's why you drink, isn't it? To dull whatever pain lives inside you."

"What's inside me, Ms. Laurent?" There is an airless quality to his deep voice now. The growl of sound holds both a threat and a darker challenge. "Trust me, that's one place you don't want to look."

"I think you're afraid I'll try. I think you're afraid to have someone expose you the way you enjoy doing to everyone else."

"You think you know a lot, don't you?"

"Am I wrong?"

I stare up at him for what feels like minutes, hours. I can almost see the shutters sealing closed behind his deep-brown eyes. I can feel how determined he is to bar me from getting inside. In the heat rolling off him as he looms over me in threatening silence, I can all but taste the electric current of his anger . . . and his arousal.

I take a step back in retreat. His answering chuckle is as cold as his smile.

"If you want to analyze me, Ms. Laurent, you'll have to work a hell of a lot harder than that. In case you've forgotten, you're not here for conversation. You're here to pose for me and do as I ask for the next few hours that I have you in my studio. Those were the terms of our agreement, were they not?"

"You mean our rules of engagement," I toss back at him. "Isn't that how you described them? Battle lines."

He scowls. "You and I aren't at war."

"Are you at war with Daniel?"

Those penetrating brown eyes narrow almost imperceptibly. "Is that what he told you?"

"No. When I asked him about you, he said the two of you hadn't even met until recently, when you hired his firm for your project. Is he lying?"

"The fact that you have to ask tells me he's already lost your trust." He studies me, contemplating for a long moment, perhaps waiting for me to defend Daniel. When I don't Rush lets go of a short breath. "He told you the truth, at least about this. Until recently, I didn't even know he existed."

I should be relieved, but all the confirmation does is bring more questions. "You only recently met, yet somehow in that short time he's managed to make you hate him?"

"Daniel Hathaway is nothing more to me than a red line to settle in a ledger." The words are so cold and toneless, I can't help but believe them. "Once his debt to me is paid to my satisfaction, I'll be finished with him."

"What about me, Jared?"

Oh, God. I don't mean to speak my thoughts out loud, but my blurted reply escapes before I can hold it back. Rush lets it linger between us for a long moment, so long it's all I can do not to squirm under his deliberate silence.

He tilts his head, his gaze searching mine. "What about you, Melanie?"

My pulse throbs at the sound of my name on his lips, the first time he's uttered it. Somehow, he's made those few syllables sound dark and sinful, full of demand even though his voice is as smooth as velvet. Awareness arcs in the small space separating us in the hallway. The current is heavy and pounding, like the coil of heat suddenly blooming in my core.

My heart hammers in my breast, in my temples . . . in all the places Jared Rush's nearness seems to awaken inside me. I draw in a breath and push the rest of my question out in a raspy whisper. "What am I in all of this?"

His mouth softens, but only at the edges. "That'll be up to you to decide."

His gaze travels over me, as palpable as a caress. But he doesn't touch me.

He doesn't press his mouth to mine, not even when his eyes drift to my lips and linger there.

On a low growl, he moves away from me, his dark brows furrowing. His hands are down at his sides, his fingers curled into tight fists.

"The studio is the last door at the end of this corridor. I'll give you a few minutes to get settled and undressed. Be ready to begin when I return."

14

A curse explodes off my tongue as soon as I've stalked away from her.

My hard stride carries me into the kitchen where the light from the morning sun is practically blinding in its brilliance. A few hundred yards out from the beach house, small blue waves capped in white froth ripple toward the shore. Normally, the sight of the ocean calms me the way nothing in the city ever could. Being here, away from all the noise and the claustrophobic press of skyscrapers and ceaseless noise, reminds me of wide pastures and simpler, easier times.

Normally, being here smooths out all the jagged edges in me. Edges that have only been getting sharper and deeper these past couple of years.

Right now, though, I feel anything but calm.

Not when the woman I crave more than any other in a damn long time is waiting for me at the other end of the house. I look at the endless miles of changeable blue-gray water and I see Melanie's eyes carving me up with each glance, searching for answers. Looking for truths I'm not ready to give her. Truths she can never know, not if I have anything to say about it.

I've lived my pain and the shame that followed it. I survived it. I buried all of my dead and moved on. So I'd thought.

Until a name I'd never heard before landed in my email, sent by someone I'd hired more than a decade ago to be my eyes and ears. It's true I hadn't met Daniel Hathaway before securing his firm for my newest hotel project. It's also true that the man means nothing to me, outside of what he owes me.

I might have been satisfied with ruining Daniel Hathaway, exposing him as the fraud I know him to be.

But then I saw her.

I saw her, and I knew I had to have her. On my canvas. In my bed. At my total mercy.

Except the more time I spend with Melanie Laurent, the less clear it becomes to me just who of us is the one with the most control.

"Fuck."

I walk over to an antique cabinet I keep fully stocked with every quality liquor known to man. It's damn early to be drinking, even by my own questionable standards. I don't consider it to be a problem for me, although I can't deny that the harmless glass of whisky here and there is becoming more of a habit than I'd like.

A fact Melanie picked up on after only a few hours in my presence.

She's the reason I reach for the bottle now. Frustrated desire courses quicksilver and hot through my body. My cock is heavy and aching in the confines of my pants, the bulge barely concealed by the loose drape of my untucked shirt. Jesus, I'm hard as stone and all I've done is look at her.

I should have kissed her like I wanted to. I should have shut up all of her questions and probing observations with a brutal mating of our mouths. I don't think she would have complained. Hell, the yearning in her eyes practically begged me to take whatever I wanted from her.

Instead, I retreated like a fucking coward.

My hands are clumsy as I retrieve the Macallan and a cut-crystal glass from the cabinet. Seeing the way my fingers tremble only adds fuel to my beastly mood.

It's getting worse over time.

The tremors that started out as a faint and fleeting lack of dexterity a few years ago are almost a daily annoyance now. I've been able to conceal it so far, but I know it can't last. It won't last. The whisky helps. At least, that's what I tell myself as I pour an oversized shot into my glass and throw it back in a single swallow.

The forty-year-old single malt cuts a warm, familiar path into my body. I gulp another large shot, then pour some more into the glass to take with me to the studio. By the time I make my way to the other end of the house, the whisky has worked enough of its magic that my hands feel loose and nimble again. The worst of the unsteadiness has passed.

My surly attitude is less persuaded by the alcohol, especially when I walk back to the studio and find Melanie standing there unclothed and waiting for me, just as I'd instructed her. At the sight of her nudity, my molars clamp down hard behind the flat line of my mouth. The erection I'd been sporting when I left her a few minutes ago comes raging back to life again, arousal twisting through me in molten coils.

Christ, she's beautiful.

Exquisite.

Having already seen her undressed once before, it's not like I'm unprepared for it now. But even if I'd seen her naked a thousand times, I doubt I'd ever be anything close to immune.

I stop just inside the studio and soak her in with a hungry glance. Long, graceful limbs. Lush curves. Creamy smooth skin that makes my mouth water with the urge to run my tongue along every lovely inch of her.

When our eyes clash, she lifts her chin a notch, defiance in her schooled expression. She doesn't try to hide herself from me, instead standing tall with her delicate shoulders squared and her arms loose at her sides.

The straightness of her spine only accentuates the thrust of her perfect breasts. The dusky nipples darken with each second my eyes linger on them, tightening into ripe little berries I'd like to take between my teeth. Below the hourglass curves of her abdomen, her sex draws my gaze like a magnetic force.

I have to give her credit. I know she's well out of her depth with a man like me, yet her poise is unshakable, even under the blaze of my lingering stare. At least until she notices the glass I'm holding. I see the flicker of disapproval move over her pretty face, and for some reason her reaction pricks a shame in me the way nothing else can.

Pushing the feeling aside, I give her an unrepentant smirk. "Pardon my lack of manners. Would you care for something to drink?"

"No, thank you." Her reply is clipped and cool.

"Suit yourself." Deliberately, I lift my hand and take a slow drink while I regard her over the rim of the glass.

Her gaze hardens on me. "Do you intend to be drunk every time we're together like this?"

"I'm nowhere close to drunk, darlin'." I walk over to my work area and take a seat on the stool near my empty easel. The table next to it holds assorted paints and containers of cleaned brushes, along with dozens of sketching tools.

It's been months since I've touched any of them. Months since I've even wanted to try. But she's changed all of that.

Not because of the contract we've signed. Not even because of Daniel Hathaway, either. I look at Melanie Laurent and I see a goodness I haven't known in a long time. I see a rare strength. Most of my paintings explore the fissures and frailties of human existence, the darkness, even depravity. With this woman, it's her light that draws me. It's what drew me to her that night at Muse, even more than the fact that she belonged to Daniel Hathaway.

I see a ferocity and a tenaciousness that makes me want to protect her. From struggle and pain, from Hathaway. From anything and anyone who might hurt her or do her harm.

If I were a better man, I'd want to keep her safe from me as well. Unfortunately for both of us, that's where my honor ends.

Because she refuses to look away from me as I get settled at my easel, I take another unhurried swallow of whisky, draining the glass before setting it down on the table next to me. There's only the slightest tremble in my fingers as I reach for one of the large sketch pads situated nearby. Thank fuck for that. I flip open the pad and prop the blank canvas on the easel, then pick up one of the charcoal pencils from the table.

I didn't expect to feel so eager to begin, but my hands move almost on their own, as if driven to capture every nuance of what my eyes are seeing. Christ, it's been so long since I've had this feeling, I've practically forgotten what it's like. And never has my impulse to create been as intense as it is when I'm looking at this woman.

I sense her uncertain gaze on me as I sweep the first few experimental lines across the paper.

"Um . . . what do you want me to do? Should I sit somewhere or is it better if I stand still?"

"Do whatever feels natural. I'm just warming up before we get started."

That's not entirely true. I'm only sketching rudimentary lines and arcs for now, trying to make sure the tremors are gone. As for warming up, I'm well beyond that. My hand moves with a speed and fluidity I can hardly control. Strokes of charcoal rasp swiftly against the paper, bringing pieces of her to life on the page. The shape of her body. The soft fall of her auburn hair around her shoulders. The elegance of her limbs. The enticing curve of her hip.

"Is it all right if I look around, then?"

I grunt a nonverbal reply, too absorbed to bother with words. I tear off the top sheet and let it fall to the floor as I begin a second sketch, my eyes flicking in rapid fire from the canvas to her and back again as she begins a casual tour of my studio.

I'm riveted to her movements, to the measured grace

she exudes in spite of the fact that I haven't exactly made this whole thing easy for her. If she is self-conscious about being nude in front of me, she seems determined not to show it. With her hands loosely clasped at the small of her back, she slowly investigates the art supplies and half-finished canvases that have collected in nearly every corner of the room.

She pauses in front of a crate of my paintings that I brought back last year from various gallery loans and exhibits in the city. Her hands are careful, respectful, as she combs through the half-dozen or so works. I hear her breath catch when she spots one of my more personal pieces, an unsigned portrait called *Beauty*.

It depicts a regal, yet weathered, brunette whose aging face and deflated nude body hints at the illness that almost destroyed her. But instead of sorrow or defeat in her intense stare, her expression while she brings herself to climax with one thin hand between her parted legs is one of pleasure. It is carnal. Uninhibited. Defiant.

Just like the woman who posed for me.

"I know this painting," Melanie says. "I saw it hanging in Dominion up in Midtown." With the faintest blush riding her cheeks, she casts a questioning look at me over her shoulder. "It's one of yours?"

I nod gruffly, my hands sketching feverishly as I try to capture the symmetry of her body and the way her hair seems to float like fiery, silken waves over her shoulder. From this angle, the way she's rotated slightly toward me, I can just see the hint of the brutal scar that runs along her side. I sketch that, too, because I've never allowed any lies on my canvas.

Except for the ones I tell myself.

"I've spent a fair amount of time in and out of that

gallery," I murmur, glancing up from my sketch if only to look at her for a longer moment. "I'm surprised we didn't run into each other there."

If we had, she would already be mine and everything about this conversation, this moment, would be different. Everything except my unfinished business with the man who's had the undeserved privilege of her trust and affection these past several months.

She shrugs, folding her arms in front of her and obscuring the pretty side view of her breast I'd been enjoying. "I've only been to Dominion once, about a year ago now. My best friend Evelyn's brother gave her tickets to a private reception. Some kind of fundraiser Baine International was hosting at the gallery."

I'm aware of her friendship with the African-American former runway model, having seen the women together that first night at my club. "Evelyn's brother is Andrew Beckham," I clarify. "He's Dominic Baine's personal attorney."

"That's right," she says, tilting her head. "Do you know Andrew?"

"I know both men. Beck's a decent guy and a damn fine lawyer. As for Nick Baine, he and I go way back. He's a good friend, one of the best anyone could ever want."

It hadn't always been a smooth road for the two of us, but what I didn't understand then was that the tormented artist-turned-billionaire-corporate-titan had been fighting demons that rivaled--possibly even surpassed--my own. Nick's amazing fiancée, Avery Ross, helped slay those demons with him. If anyone deserves a happy future, it's the both of them.

As for our fucked-up pasts, it's not an

understatement to say that Nick and I both owe our lives to the woman in the painting that's caught Melanie's attention.

She turns back to look at the portrait, studying it in silence while I start on a third sketch of her. She's just as gorgeous from behind, so fucking sexy it's all I can do not to snap my pencil in two as I follow the lean muscles of her legs and spine and the luscious curves of her ass. She leans forward for a closer look at the painting and my brain nearly explodes with the sudden urge to get up from my stool and bend her farther over so I can feast on her until she comes on my tongue.

"This one's so different compared to your other work," she says.

As if sensing the dark weight of my thoughts, she abruptly glances back at me. My animalistic-sounding grunt is pure caveman, but it must seem like disgruntled insult to her. I'm sure my scowl doesn't help.

She hurries to explain. "I mean, it's impossible to mistake your style for anyone else's. Dark, edgy, erotic. A little unsettling. Unflinchingly raw. But there's something about this portrait that seems . . . I don't know. It's tender," she says, her gaze soft and curious, piercing me like an arrow from across the room. "That's what I thought when I saw this painting in Dominion. I thought whoever painted this woman, this resilient 'Beauty,' must have cared for her very much. He must have loved her."

It's a question as much as a keen observation, one I'm under no inclination to answer. I've already warned Melanie that she can forget any ideas about peering under the hood of my personal life. That goes double for my past.

So, I'm not sure why the words gather in my throat as she levels that inquisitive look on me. My hand moves over the sketch paper, recreating the doe-eyed softness of her stare and the tempting sweetness of her slightly parted lips.

"Her name was Kathryn," I mutter as I focus on my canvas. "We were . . . friends."

"Friends." She glances at the profanely intimate painting, then back to me. "Were you in love with her?"

I shrug, considering. "For a while, I suppose, off and on. She'd been a part of my life longer than anyone else."

"How long is that?"

"Nineteen years, give or take. She took me in when I first came to New York." I say it as if the date is of no consequence, despite that it's seared into me as indelible as a brand. Nineteen years ago in April, the day after my mother's funeral, with both of my parents dead by then, I left the only home I'd ever known and boarded a bus bound for New York City.

"You couldn't have been more than a teenager then," Melanie says, a note of concern in her voice.

"I was sixteen."

"Just a boy."

I scoff under my breath. "Hardly that."

"And she was older?"

"Much," I say around a low chuckle that holds no malice whatsoever. "Kathryn Tremont was a friend, lover, savior, and mentor to a lot of young men over the years. She only took what was freely given, and her kindness knew no bounds. Neither did her generosity."

"Kathryn Tremont?" Melanie gapes. "The Manhattan socialite and philanthropist? That Kathryn Tremont? Her name is on the art building at the university I attend."

"One and the same," I confirm with a smirk. "Kathryn lived out loud, no question about that. She was still keeping a handful of new companions at her side when she died of cancer last year."

"I saw her obituary in the *Times*. They dedicated an entire page to her and her countless charitable works. I'm truly sorry for your loss, Jared."

"She was a good person," I admit, unable to diminish Kathryn's importance in my life, even if only to reject Melanie's compassion. "I made that painting of her after she beat cancer the first time. I gave it to her unsigned, thinking it was so revealing she'd want to keep it private. Not Kathryn. She hung it in the main salon of her Fifth Avenue mansion for several years before lending it out to her favorite galleries for the public to enjoy."

"She sounds like an amazing woman."

"Yeah. She was."

Melanie nods, then looks away from me. Continuing her exploration of my studio, she walks over to a paint-spattered table and plucks one of my old paintbrushes from a cup full of them. I watch her tap the soft, fan-edged bristles against her lips. My cock surges in response, going hard with hungered want.

"Where was home for you before you came to the city?"

"Kentucky." The word sounds strangled, little more than a growl. "I grew up on a horse farm in Lexington."

I shouldn't tell her even that much. It cuts too close to the beginning of everything for me. The beginning of the end. She doesn't know how much the words cost me, and right now, I'll be damned if I let her know.

She turns a curious glance on me as she places the

brush back in its container. "Now I understand why that smoky accent of yours makes me think of green, rolling hills and mist-covered mountain ranges." A small smile plays at the edge of her mouth. "Were you a little cowboy as a kid, Mr. Rush?"

I give a gruff shake of my head. "No. We raised thoroughbreds. The farm had been in my mother's family for five generations."

Christ, why am I still talking? I have no desire to crack open my past right now, least of all with her. Impatient to be done with this entire conversation and the arousal that's making my vision swim, I continue sketching at an even more feverish pace, hoping my lengthening silence will prove uncomfortable enough to close the subject.

Of course, it doesn't work on this woman.

She only peers more intently at me now. When she speaks again, there is a note of caution in her quiet voice. "You said it *had been* in your family for generations. Past tense. What happened to it?"

"We lost it." The words come out clipped and angry. "My father made a terrible mistake."

"What kind of mistake?"

"He trusted the wrong man with all his investments. Turns out it was a Ponzi scheme. The bastard sold him and several other investors phony stocks while he pocketed all his clients' money. When the scheme was exposed, there was nothing to be done. We lost everything, practically overnight."

"Oh, my God. That must have been awful for you," she says, her tone soft, compassionate. "I'm so sorry."

Her sympathy over this loss feels like a rake chewing up unhealed wounds. "Why should you be sorry? It's not like you had anything to do with it."

It's a dick thing to say, but too late to call it back. I'm not sure what to call the churning fire gnawing in my veins. Is it leftover fury at my father and his recklessness that carried such a steep price? Or does the heat raging within me have more to do with this innocent woman I've now dragged into the center of everything that's wrong and corrupted in my life?

On a snarl, I decide it's both.

I toss my charcoal onto the table and reach for the glass of whisky, forgetting I've already drained it. Anger spikes as I stare at the empty glass. But it's not the anger that drags a growl up the back of my throat. What truly sets me off are the faint tremors vibrating through my fingers, making the crystal tremble in my grasp.

Slamming the glass back down, I vault up from the stool. *"Goddamn it."*

Melanie flinches. No, it's something more than that. She *jolts* in response to my churlish outburst, most of the color draining from her cheeks in less than an instant. It's terror I see in her eyes, instinctive, visceral terror.

I've pushed and provoked her ruthlessly every time she's been in front of me, but this is the only time I've seen her composure slip. She shrinks back, staring at me like she's facing a wild animal.

Hell, maybe she is.

Her fearful gaze shreds me. I turn away from it, and three furious strides carry me out the door of the studio. I head back to the kitchen to retrieve the rest of the Macallan. Fuck the need for a glass.

I mean to kill the whole damn bottle.

15

JARED

I don't even hear Melanie following me until I wheel around with the whisky in one hand and find her standing right behind me.

She's dressed now, albeit hastily. She didn't bother with her lacy little white bra or the panties that she'd folded neatly on a chair in the studio. Her light cotton dress is wrapped around her like armor, her arms crossed in front of her like a shield.

She's wary of me, and with good cause. Even so, she holds my glare as she tilts her head up to look me in the eye. "What just happened back there? What's wrong with you?"

A cold laugh bursts out of me. Christ, I wouldn't even know where to begin.

Now that I'm squared off against her with only inches to separate us, the trace of palsy in my fingers seems the least of my concerns. I want her. Our agreement prohibits me from touching her, but I'm not thinking about contracts or legalities. I'm not thinking about Hathaway or how satisfying it would be to seduce his woman right out of his arms.

All I'm thinking about is her.

How breathtakingly beautiful she is. How bold and aggravatingly tenacious she is, even when she's afraid.

I'm thinking about how much I want to pull her into my arms.

And I'm thinking about what an asshole I am for putting those troubled shadows in her eyes.

Her brow creases as she searches my face. "I don't know what your problem is, other than that bottle in your hand. But for your own sake, I hope you get some help."

"Get some help?" Instead of laying out all the truths she won't want to hear, I settle on a sharp chuckle that sounds as brittle as it tastes. "Nothing's wrong with me that another drink won't take care of."

"No," she says, apparently unaware of how threadbare my control feels right now. "Another drink seems like the last thing you need right now."

"What I need? What the hell would you know about that?" I sneer down at her, my breath gusting through flared nostrils. My hand tightens around the neck of the whisky bottle, if only to keep from wrapping my fingers around the fiery tendrils of her long hair so I can pull her against me like I want to do.

She swallows, those luminous eyes of hers changing from uncertain, apprehensive blue to a tempest of dusky gray as her pupils darken and enlarge under my stare.

"What's the matter, Ms. Laurent? Afraid to take a guess? Or are you just afraid to say the words out loud?"

She doesn't have to speak for me to read what's

going on behind her silence and her disapproving stance. I can see her pulse beating in the pretty hollow at the base of her throat. I can feel the heat of her skin intensifying, practically burning me across the scant distance separating us. Her nipples are tight beneath the soft cotton sundress she's still clutching together in one small fist over her heart. Her lovely, all too tempting body vibrates with enough awareness to charge the air like the coming of a storm.

She knows damn well what I need, all right. She knows what I want.

She knows, because she wants the same thing.

A breath leaks out of her. "I should leave now."

Her quiet murmur is far from convincing. I should step away from her, but I can't convince myself to do that, either.

"Our session's not over yet."

"I can't be here if you're going to be like this. I won't." She gives a tight shake of her head. "I don't care that I signed your damn contract. I don't care about your money. I've been doing just fine without any help, and Daniel will have to clean up his own mess somehow. As for you, you'll have to find another outlet for your anger and abuse, because it's not going to be me."

Her words are raw, her vulnerability as she hurls them at me strike me harder than a physical blow. Vibrating with the force of her emotions, she starts to turn away. My free hand moves before I'm even aware of it.

"Hey." I halt her, wrapping my fingers around the delicate firmness of her arm. She freezes in my grasp, wary and untrusting, her gaze flying up to mine.

I scowl down at her, struggling with the self-directed

fury that's still running hot through my veins, and the remorse I feel for subjecting her to any part of it.

"I'm sorry," I mutter, my voice like gravel.

Sorry for being an asshole. Sorry for frightening her. Sorry for wanting her more than I have any right to.

Part of me knows I should let her go. I never should have brought her into any of this in the first place.

But it's too late for that.

Too late for either one of us. There's no undoing the connection that's been smoldering between us since our eyes locked for the first time. Now, those flames are on the verge of exploding into something neither of us can control.

If my desire for her was only about taking something of Hathaway's, I'd already be inside her. But this need is something different. It's something deeper. Something she's not ready for.

Maybe neither of us are ready to give in to what we both want from each other.

Maybe neither of us are ready to let someone look inside all those dark corners. God knows I've kept my demons locked up tight for years. That's where they need to stay.

That's why the right thing to do would be to let her go--from the contract, and from my grasp. Instead, my fingers flex a little tighter. A possessive urge floods me, overriding logic and what thin sense of decency I may want to pretend I still have.

"Why didn't you run when I gave you the chance, Melanie?"

She pulls in a breath through slightly parted lips, but it's nothing close to a denial. The slender bicep caught in my loose hold offers no resistance at all. She won't fight this any more than I can.

I'm still holding the whisky bottle in my left hand, but I move my right up the curve of her shoulder, then into the warm silk of her hair. Her breathing speeds in time with mine. Her eyes pull me in as I lower my head to hers. Our mouths meet and a rough groan rumbles out of me, half in curse for my own weakness, and half for hers.

Her lips are softer than I imagined, giving way beneath mine as I curve my palm around to the back of her head and pull her closer. I want to be careful with her. I've already scared her enough. I want to be gentle, even though this desire inside me burned right past that marker the instant she followed me out of the studio.

She moans against my lips, and her indrawn gasp is all the permission I need to sweep my tongue into the sweet inferno of her mouth. Her hands move up to my shoulders, and for the briefest second I wait to feel her push me away. She doesn't kiss like a woman who belongs to another man. She kisses like a woman created specifically to drive me mad.

Still, I can't ignore the fact that she's isn't mine. No matter how right she feels in my arms, against my questing mouth, she doesn't belong there.

I wait to feel her retreat, but it doesn't come.

Lifting up on her bare toes, she brings herself closer. Her palms create two points of heat that root me in place as I deepen our kiss. I try to rationalize it's the whisky burning away my control with this woman, but that's a lie.

It's her. It's the incandescent flame that is Melanie Laurent.

It's us, on fire together.

And I fucking can't get enough.

Arousal pounds in every pulse point in my body. I've been enduring the agony of that lust since the minute she arrived at my Lenox Hill address this morning in another prim summer dress, her naturally beautiful face pink and fresh, devoid of makeup or artifice, looking for all the world like a virgin on her way to be sacrificed.

And I am the Beast lurking in the dark, intent on devouring her.

A fitting growl unfurls in my throat at the very idea. The erection I've been trying to ignore all morning has surged to rampant life now. I can't get enough of the taste of her kiss, my tongue thrusting and demanding, my hips crushing against hers.

I drag her closer with my right hand still tangled in the soft hair at her nape.

I need her.

I think I've needed this woman even before she had the misfortune of walking into my club those weeks ago. Christ, I needed her even before I heard the name Daniel Hathaway and set out to claim some overdue payback. I just didn't know how much I'd need her, need this, until I met her.

I let go of her neck and bring my hand around to the front of her. She's free to move away, free to leave, and some desperate part of me hopes like hell she will. Instead, she moans against my questing mouth and I am lost.

Her sweet summer dress is already half-opened in front. Her breasts are bare beneath it, her nipples peaked and hard as pebbles under my palm as I run my trembling hand over one, then the other, caressing another moan out of her parted lips.

She's hot against me, her breath deep and rapid, her heart galloping at a pace to match my own. Her soft belly contracts as I skim my fingers downward. Her skin is impossibly soft, as warm and smooth as velvet under my rough fingertips.

Without breaking the contact of our mouths, I let my touch drift lower, down into the trimmed, silky curls of her sex. The fact that she's not shaved bare as a baby or waxed into the mere suggestion of a grown woman had made me hard as granite when I first watched her strip for me in my study back in the city. Now, with her body arching against me and the sweet, earthy scent of her arousal swamping my senses, I am beyond erect.

My cock throbs with hunger for her.

Everything male in me is gnashing with the need to taste her. To take her.

She gasps into my mouth as I cup her pussy in my palm and give the tender flesh a possessive caress. She's drenched and hot, searing my fingertips as I delve into the wet seam of her sex. I push inside, groaning at the snug fit of her around my finger.

She moves with me, not fighting the invasion as I explore her tightness. She melts into my palm, her juices searing my skin. I can't resist seeking out the swollen bud of her clit. With one finger inside her, my thumb caresses the taut pearl until her breath pants into my mouth as I kiss her and a climax shudders through her.

"Oh, God," she whispers brokenly around my fevered kisses.

My curse is guttural, a strangled noise. It's all I can manage when every cell in my body is ablaze with the need to get my aching cock inside her. "Christ, Melanie. I want to fuck you so bad."

If her breathless moan in response is meant to be a denial, my lust-fogged brain isn't getting the message.

One hand on her isn't enough. Not when the animal in me is gnashing with the impulse to throw her over my shoulder and drag her off to my lair.

The half-empty bottle of whisky feels like it's made of lead as I lift it toward the nearby countertop without interrupting our kiss. My hand shakes with the effort. I should recognize the odd sensation in my fingers by now. In some dim, desire-choked corner of my mind, I feel the tremor.

At the same time, my grip on the bottle falters.

Fuck.

I grab Melanie and swing her out of the way about a second before it hits the floor.

Glass shatters around her bare feet, glittering shards and spilled whisky flying everywhere. She lets out a small yelp, but it's barely audible next to my furious bellow.

"Don't move," I snap at her when she starts to step away from some of the mess I've made.

"It's okay," she says, her voice a soft rasp after I've plundered her mouth and body for the past five minutes. "Let me help you clean this up."

Another snarl rips out of me. "Damn it, I said don't move!"

She freezes, staring at me in confusion. That look of wariness is back again, along with something else, as she watches me hunker down and begin sweeping the largest of the shattered pieces away with my bare hands.

There's no hiding the shakiness of my fingers, even if my explosive rage might mask the tremors as something other than evidence of the neurological flaw I know them to be.

I bite off another hard curse under my breath and tear my gaze away from hers.

I hear her shallow inhalation as she continues to watch me. "Jared . . ."

"We're done here." My reply is short, dismissive.

It has to be. Another moment of her tender scrutiny--of her undeserved kindness and concern--and I'm going to put my fucking fist through a wall.

"Today's session is over," I tell her gruffly, keeping my fury aimed at the floor. "Once I clean this shit up, I'll arrange for your return to the city."

16

MELANIE

Twenty-seven hours have passed since Jared Rush brought me over the edge of a shocking climax with his kisses and his wicked touch. Twenty-seven hours since that bone-melting moment abruptly ended when he exploded like a grenade over a broken whisky bottle and practically shoved me out of his beach house studio.

One full day and I'm just as blindsided and confused as I was when it happened.

After furiously cleaning up the shattered glass, he'd called for an Uber to take me all the way back to my house in Queens. The pleasant middle-aged woman behind the wheel filled the silence of the two-hour drive from Sagaponack with chatter about her kids and grandchildren, a welcome distraction, but one I'd barely registered.

While I had nodded and smiled when expected, my thoughts had stayed fixated on Jared, my emotions running the gamut from outrage to concern and everything in between. Not the least of them being the banked, but still burning, desire that kept its grip on me for the duration of the ride home.

I'm still not sure what triggered the change in him from the man I was only starting to get to know as I explored his studio and the growling beast who stormed out a moment later for another drink. Where he'd seemed open to talking about other aspects of his past, it was clear I'd ventured too far when I asked him about growing up in Kentucky. The loss of his family's farm, and his father's evident role in it, obviously carved a deep wound in Jared that still wasn't fully healed.

Yet there was something more, something else that flipped the switch on his fury. When I caught up to him in the kitchen, his hands were visibly shaking with the force of his rage. And somehow, my noticing that seemed to set him off even more.

Why?

By the time the driver dropped me at my house I'd finally managed to convince myself that whatever Jared Rush's problems are, whatever trauma may lurk in his past, for my own sanity--for my own self-preservation--I need to keep my distance from him.

I'd like to say I'm long over the effects of his kiss and his strong hands on my body, but my reaction to the carnal side of him has proven the hardest one to shake. His total domination of my senses was like getting swept into a hurricane. Powerful. Dangerous. Electric.

I can't remember the last time I'd been kissed like that.

Never. That's why I can't remember it. Because the answer is never.

Jared kissed me as if he'd been wanting to do it forever and couldn't get enough. He claimed my mouth as if I belonged to him, and nothing else mattered. Foolishly, I tumbled right under his spell. I would have fallen much further if reality hadn't brought me crashing back to my wits.

I frown into my plate of grilled seafood, idly chasing a bite of mahi mahi around with my fork. When I glance up, I find my two best friends still gaping at me across our table for lunch at GC.

Evelyn's pale green eyes are lit with shock against the buttery mocha glow of her beautiful face. "Let me get this straight. You posed nude for Jared Rush and this is the first we're hearing about it?"

"Twice, technically," Paige Johansson adds in a mock disgruntled tone. "Our girl Mel's gotten nekkid for Hottie McDark-and-Deviant two times, Eve, and this is the first we're hearing about it."

A former model, like Evelyn, Paige is gorgeous, too. Now, she's perpetually auditioning for film roles and commercials, so it's no surprise to see her short black hair is growing out since I last saw her. The messy crown of choppy layers now falls around her impish face in inky waves as she reaches for a third slice of her flatbread pizza.

"You think he's deviant?" The question leaps off my tongue, despite that I'm sure I don't really want to know the answer. And if anyone would know these things, it's Paige.

She munches on a bite of pizza, giving me a look that says I'm an idiot just for asking. "I've heard he hosts private orgies at his mansion on the regular. And in case you didn't notice when the three of us went to his club,

Muse, a couple of weeks ago, there were people having actual sex behind all those walls of one-way smoked glass overlooking the dance floor."

Oh, God. I'd wondered if all those bodies moving in erotic positions behind the brief flashes of strobe lights and semi-opaque glass had only been an illusion, some titillating effect meant as a play on the fantasy-themed name of the club. Part of me knew it was real, but hearing Paige confirm it sends a note of shock into my veins.

Was Jared Rush one of those unclothed, undulating bodies that night? As for the rumored orgies at his house, it takes more effort than I care to admit to avoid picturing him being pawed at and pleasured by a den full of eager women. How many has he seduced with his dangerous, yet magnetic sensuality?

Dozens, I imagine. Hundreds? I wouldn't doubt it.

I stop myself from trying to guess, because it doesn't matter. All I know is I'm not going to be one of them. What happened at his beach house couldn't have driven that point home with any sharper clarity.

And that goes double for the fact that I refuse to be around another man with a drinking problem. Growing up with my father and his brutal binges was terror enough to last me a lifetime. I've got the scars to prove it, both inside and out.

Paige reaches for her glass of beer. "Tell us again how you ended up with Jared Rush's tongue down your throat and his hand up your skirt yesterday."

"Paige," Evelyn gasps. "You're kind of missing the point here, aren't you?"

"I don't know. Am I?" she asks, one brow arched as she eyes me over the rim of the glass.

Where Evelyn is measured and elegant, with a natural poise instilled in her from her modeling days, free-spirited Paige flouts conversational and societal guardrails wherever possible. Next to these two creative, successful women and their colorful lives, I'm the wallflower of our trio. I've long been the practical, quiet one who spends all her time either studying or working. That is when I'm not doffing my clothes for an arrogant and tormented, possibly alcoholic artist to bail out my closet-gambling boyfriend. Oh, yeah. Let's not forget, letting him thrust his tongue down my throat and his hand up my skirt.

My pulse throbs at the remembered heat of those incredible moments. It's been more than a full day and I can still feel the intensity of Jared's lips burning against mine. I can still feel his hand on my sex, his strong finger moving inside me until I came. I feel it so vividly it makes my thighs squeeze together under the table even now.

The truth is, I wanted him to kiss me. To touch me. I wanted *him*. Only the unexpected shatter of that liquor bottle and his unhinged reaction that followed was enough to jolt me back to my senses.

Thank God.

Any longer in his arms and I'm all but certain I would have let him do a lot more than he had, and then my stupid mistake would have become a disastrous one.

I set down my fork, my already weak appetite drying up altogether when I think about how recklessly close I was to the edge of something dangerous with Jared Rush.

"I'm not sure how I let any of this happen," I admit, miserable with all my questionable choices lately. "I just know it can't continue."

Paige tilts her head. "By 'it' are you talking about your contract to pose for Rush, or letting him melt your panties off you again?"

Eve smiles. "She wasn't wearing panties, remember?"

I groan, but I'm not sure if it's in reaction to my friends' teasing or to the way my core tightens at the thought of letting Jared's mouth anywhere near mine again. To say nothing of letting him near any other part of my body. The fact that I can be aroused by a man I'm certain can only be bad news and trouble for me is just more evidence for staying away from him.

"I'm talking about all of it," I say, pushing my half-eaten lunch away from me. "I never should've agreed to it in the first place."

"Daniel should have never pressured you to agree," Evelyn says gently. She reaches out and gives my hand a reassuring squeeze. "I know you're always the first one in line to help someone if you can, but this is different. I can't imagine any problem big enough for Gabe that he would be okay with me posing for one of Jared Rush's paintings in order to save himself, let alone encourage me to do it."

I can't imagine that, either. Gabriel Noble leads the security team for Dominic Baine's corporate offices, headquartered in a sleek glass tower on West 57th Street. He and Evelyn have been together only for a matter of weeks, but it's obvious to anyone who sees them that Gabe is head over heels in love with her and she with him. As a combat veteran who lost part of his leg in the war, he's been through the worst kind of hell on the battlefield. I know he'd walk through that much pain and more if it meant keeping the woman he loves safe.

"You deserve better than that, Mel," Evelyn says, her tone solemn. "Daniel shouldn't have let you agree to that contract for any price."

A small, ironic laugh dies in my throat. "That's what Jared said to me. The first morning I went to his house, he told me if he were Daniel, he'd rather put a bullet in his head than put me anywhere near a man like himself."

A strange look of surprise sweeps over Evelyn's face. "He said that?"

At my nod, Paige narrows her eyes. "If Rush really felt that way, then why the hell did he offer a hundred and sixty-five thousand dollars to paint you?"

"Because that's what it took for me to say yes."

It feels strange to hear his words coming out of my own mouth. I can't say them without reliving every electrically charged moment we've shared these past few days since Daniel's reckless loss at Jared's game table.

No more than I can help wondering how things might have been different if Jared and I had met under different circumstances. I must be crazy to even consider it, especially after yesterday, never mind all the troubling things Paige has confirmed about him today.

Not that my halo is without tarnish. After all, it's not as if he forced himself on me. I kissed him willingly, welcomed his touch without reservation. I took off my clothes to pose for him on my own volition, and I signed his contract despite every instinct warning me that my life would never look the same again afterward.

Whether I want to deny it or not, everything female in me has been buzzing with an intense kind of electricity from the instant I walked into Jared Rush's study the night of that poker game.

Even knowing he's likely the worst man I could ever

want doesn't make the craving any less strong.

I'm not sure what that says about my relationship with Daniel. What that says about me as a person, I'm pretty sure I don't want to know.

"Ladies, how are we doing today?" The Australian-accented, deep voice that interrupts my slide into self-inflicted misery belongs to Gavin Castille, the celebrity chef and owner of the eponymous GC restaurant. "I trust lunch was to everyone's satisfaction?"

"Superb," Paige purrs, leaning forward to give the handsome Aussie her full attention, along with that of her breasts, which are shown off to their best advantage in a pretty push-up bra worn beneath the gauzy material of a low-cut boho top.

Gavin's dimpled grin says he appreciates the effort, though his professionalism remains intact. "Excellent. Glad you enjoyed." He glances at Evelyn with a warm smile. "Nice to see you again. You know, I still appreciate you lending a hand with the catering station at the Baine charity event at the zoo last month."

"It was my pleasure, Gavin."

"Zoo catering?" Paige asks. "Have you picked up a new hobby we don't know about?"

Evelyn laughs. "Avery invited me to the event when we were reviewing my lingerie designs for her upcoming wedding to Nick. Since I was there anyway, I thought I might as well make myself useful and help out."

Gavin gives her a knowing look. "I have a feeling you had another reason to stick around that day. I ran into Gabe at the Baine Building last week. He told me you two are engaged."

"We are." She flashes the diamond solitaire on her left hand, beaming with unrestrained joy. "We haven't set a date or anything yet, but I hope it's soon."

"Congratulations," Gavin says. "He seems like a great guy."

She nods. "He's the best. I've never been happier."

"Glad to hear it. When the time comes for menu planning, let me know if you'd like help. I'm sure I could come up with something special for your big day."

"Are you serious?"

"It'd be my honor," he says, those dimples back for a return performance as he smiles at Evelyn, then nods at Paige and me. He pauses then, his brows furrowing as his gaze lights on me. "You were here a few nights ago at dinner."

"I was." God, that date with Daniel seems like it happened months ago.

"Well, it's nice to see you here again. I must be doing something right in the kitchen to bring you back so soon," Gavin says, pride making his bright green eyes gleam.

Paige lets go of a saucy laugh. "I'll bet you do everything right. In the kitchen and elsewhere."

I roll my eyes, even though he seems unfazed by my friend's blatant objectification. "Ignore her, please. Lunch was delicious."

"I aim to please." He taps the edge of our table. "Have a great day, ladies."

"Oh. My. God," Paige says once he's gone. "Talk about delicious. Which reminds me, I really need to get laid."

Evelyn nearly chokes on her white wine. "You're unbelievable. Are you going for a world record, or something? I think what you really need is to find a good man and settle down."

"That's easy for you to say, Eve. You found yours."

I thought I'd found mine in Daniel, too. Or maybe I wanted to believe that so much, I had myself convinced he was everything I could possibly want in a man.

Those illusions began to crack the night he brought me here for dinner, then on to Jared Rush's poker game. As hurtful as it was to learn about Daniel's gambling problems the way I did, it isn't fair for me to pretend any longer that things between us can ever be what they were before.

Meeting Jared Rush changed all of that, in more ways than I want to consider.

17

MELANIE

My thoughts are still churning after we've finished lunch and paid the bill. As we wait for the valet to bring Evelyn's Volvo around, a white SUV rolls up to the curb outside the restaurant. A group of three men dressed in suits on a Saturday afternoon climb out of the vehicle with another, more casually attired group wearing khakis and pastel-colored polo shirts. They're engaged in animated conversation, lots of grins and chuckling as they gather next to the SUV while a valet jogs over to assist them.

I might only give them a passing glance, but then I notice the *Crowne & Merritt Architects* logo on the passenger door of the SUV. One of the suited men is Daniel. I quickly turn my head away from him, an impulse I can neither control nor explain.

All I know is I don't want to see him right now. I'm not ready to deal with--

"Melanie?" His voice cuts through the traffic noise

and chatter of his companions, impossible to ignore.

"Well, isn't this some piss-poor timing," Paige mutters under her breath from beside me, echoing the reaction going on inside my own head. "Where the hell's our getaway car when we need it?"

"I can't ignore him."

Evelyn catches my troubled gaze. "You sure? Here comes my car. We can be gone in the next five seconds."

Part of me would like nothing better than to flee the scene and not look back, but running has never been the way I handle problems. Never mind that's what I fully intend to do where Jared Rush is concerned.

Daniel motions me over to him, a big, welcoming smile plastered across his face. "Melanie, sweetheart, come here for a minute."

I exhale a pent-up sigh. "I'll be right back."

The men all turn toward me as I approach their group. Daniel hurries forward to meet me with a quick kiss on my cheek before lacing his fingers through mine.

"Gentlemen," he says, leading me over to his colleagues. "I'd like you to meet my better half, Melanie."

They all chuckle politely at the tired adage and bob their heads at me in greeting. Daniel wraps his arm around my waist. He's trying to appear relaxed, but his hold on me and his grin are both too rigid to be sincere.

"We just came back from touring one of the firm's newest projects," he tells me. "Not only are we ahead of schedule, but it looks like we're also coming in well under budget."

"Congratulations."

The elder of the two other men in suits gives me a nod as he pats Daniel's shoulder. "Thanks to your fiancé, we've all got plenty of cause to celebrate today. You keep delivering the way you have been lately, son, and we'll have no choice but to promote you to partner."

"Thank you, Mr. Merritt." Daniel's tone is so deferential, I almost expect to see him bow.

"Young lady, would you care to join us for lunch and a cocktail?"

"Oh, I--"

"--She's already eaten," Daniel blurts over me. His anxious glance flicks to my face. "I mean, I assume you've already eaten with your friends."

"Yes, I have."

"But I'd love it if you joined us," he hedges.

"I can't."

"Well, then," Mr. Merritt says. "We're going to head inside now. Melanie, it was a pleasure to finally meet you. We'll have to have you both out to the house sometime. My wife is always eager to meet the significant others of the firm's shining stars."

Daniel inclines his head. "We'd enjoy that very much, sir."

I can't muster any kind of reply. All my words are clogged at the back of my throat, kept in place by the disbelief I'm trying desperately to bite back.

"My *fiancé*?" I gasp after the men disappear inside the restaurant. "You told your boss we're engaged?"

"It's no big deal," he says in a hushed tone. "It just slipped out one day when I was talking to him. You have to understand, Crowne and Merritt is a small family firm. They care about things like this. Stability and traditional values. Appearances matter, especially in their prospective partners."

"Do they care about the truth?"

He blows out a short breath. "I don't understand why you're upset over this. There's no harm in saying we're engaged."

"No harm, except it's not true and you've just dragged me into the lie."

I don't know why I'm arguing. I have no intention of spending any time with Daniel's colleagues or their wives. I'm not even sure why I'm still standing here talking to him at all.

Maybe it was only a careless fib, a small white lie blurted out because he was nervous or thought it would win his boss's approval. I don't care about the hows or the whys. It's the principle of what he did that bothers me most.

Because if he can lie about small things, how can I ever be sure he's not lying about the big things. Things like gambling problems and enormous debts owed to Las Vegas loan sharks.

Things I'm afraid I wouldn't discover until he has no choice but to admit them.

If not for what happened with Jared, I'd still be blindly believing I could trust anything Daniel Hathaway says.

But I can't now.

"I'm done, Daniel."

He frowns. "Done?" His face collapses momentarily, a look of distress, even panic, washing over him. "If I've upset you this much, let me fix it. I told Mr. Merritt we're engaged, so let's do it. Let's get engaged."

He says it as if the thought of marrying me is as life-changing to him as asking me out to a movie. As if the more important thing to him is propping up this lie with an even bigger one. He doesn't want to marry me. He only wants to smooth things over for himself.

God, I'm an idiot. For days I've been swamped with guilt over my uninvited attraction to Jared Rush. I've been mentally berating myself for kissing him when I'd left things with Daniel unresolved.

Now I feel nothing. I look at this man I thought I loved and I wonder how I ever could have thought he truly cared about me.

He reaches for my hand, but I pull it back. "Shit, Melanie. Please. I can't afford to lose you. Not right now. Not over something as stupid as this. Let me make it up to you. Marry me."

I laugh because I can't help it. As far as proposals go, this has got to be the lamest effort any man has ever uttered. Worse than that, I don't believe a single word of it.

Not that it matters. I wouldn't have said yes anyway. Not when my head has been full of doubts and misgivings about him ever since Jared exposed his first lie to me.

"My friends are waiting, Daniel. I have to go now. Goodbye."

I turn to walk away. He ducks into my path, his body an obstacle blocking my escape.

"Melanie, wait. You don't mean this." There is a wildness in his eyes, an authentic fear. "I agree, we can't have this conversation out here. I'll come by your house later today and--"

"No." I shake my head. "I don't want you to do that."

"All right. We'll talk tomorrow, then. You just tell me where and when, and I'll be there."

"I don't think you understand," I tell him, gently, because I want there to be no mistaking what I'm saying. "I don't want to see you anymore, Daniel. Not at my house. Not anywhere. You and I are over."

"Mel."

I step around him without answering. My feet carry me unhalting to the waiting Volvo where Evelyn and Paige wait for me.

"Let's get out of here," I murmur, sliding into the open backseat.

The weight of Daniel's stare follows me as my friends get into the car with me, then we merge into the river of traffic and drive away.

18

MELANIE

"Honey, are you sure you're feeling okay?" My mom eyes me with concern as I set our emptied picnic cooler down on the kitchen floor the next evening. "You haven't seemed like yourself all day."

"I'm fine." I give her a mild shrug and an equally vague wave of my hand. "I just needed some time with you and Katie, that's all. The park was nice today, wasn't it?"

"I loved it!" My niece grins at me from her perch on one of the four chairs surrounding our little dining table in the kitchen. "When can we do go again, Aunt Mellie?"

"Soon, I hope." I can't resist dropping a kiss on the top of her blond head as I hand her a juice box from the fridge.

The three of us spent the whole day on a blanket under a shade tree in our favorite neighborhood green space. Mom napped and read a book off and on, while Katie and I talked and fed a group of nearly tame chipmunks that sniffed out our lunch and came to beg for treats.

"It was a beautiful day." Mom eases herself onto another of the chairs. She blots her forehead with a wadded-up tissue that seems to materialize from somewhere on her person the way a magician would pull a rabbit out of his hat. "Whoo, it's a warm one, though."

I don't like the paleness of her face, or how easily she seemed to tire today. I asked her more than once if the sun was too much for her, but she insisted she was fine. In fact, she seemed more focused on how I was feeling, obviously homed in on my general state of distraction, even now.

"I'll get you some water, Mom."

I grab a glass from the cupboard and fill it from the filtered tap. She nods as she takes it from me, her hands a little shaky. The sight of her unsteady fingers brings my thoughts back to Jared and his jarring outburst just before he sent me away.

If I'm being honest with myself, it hasn't been more than a minute since the last time he took up space in my head today.

He'll be expecting me at Lenox Hill tomorrow morning to return to his studio for our next session. I'll be there, but only to tell him in person that I'm breaking our agreement.

Now that I've had time to process my feelings after our kiss--and the startling way it ended--I've decided the best thing for me is to keep my distance from Jared Rush. I can't deny I was moved to hear about his past. His hardship as a child, his drive to rise above it, struck a chord in me. I gained a new understanding of him, a compassion that makes it hard for me to turn my back on the fact that he's a troubled, tormented man.

But I've already watched one explosive drunk destroy himself and nearly everyone else around him. I didn't survive my father only to get entangled with a man who triggers every alarm bell in my system. No matter how much he intrigues me. No matter how intensely attracted I am to him.

Too bad I didn't have this same clarity when it came to dating Daniel.

My phone chimes inside my purse, which I hung on the back of the chair across from my mom. While she finishes her glass of water, I reach into my bag and silence the cheery ringtone I'd assigned to Daniel soon after we started seeing each other.

"Don't you want to answer that?" Mom asks. "Your phone's been ringing most of the day. It could be important."

"Not more important than spending time with you and Katie."

As for Daniel, he's left one message after another on my phone. The first few were filled with pleas for me to give him another chance to make things right again. Then he left another, awkwardly asking what our breakup might mean to the agreement we have with Jared and his half of the money I'm due to receive.

I haven't listened to any of his messages since. I don't want to think about Daniel or the agreement or anything else, except the pleasant day I've enjoyed with my family. The truth is, I needed the uninterrupted time together with my mom and my niece more than they could possibly know. I needed to remind myself what matters.

I glance at six-year-old Katie, who looks so much like

my sister Jen it breaks my heart sometimes. "You promised to start on your homework before dinner, remember?"

She rolls her eyes at me and slides off the chair with a dramatic sigh. "Okaaay."

Drink in hand, she shuffles out of the kitchen, then her footsteps lightly thump up the stairs toward her bedroom.

I slowly shake my head. "She may gripe about studying, but her teacher told me at our last conference that Katie's one of the top students in her entire grade."

"She's a smart one, like you." Mom smiles at me, letting go of a wistful sigh. "Jen'd be real proud of her, wouldn't she?"

"Yeah, she would." My sister was no slouch when it came to her studies, either, but as the situation at home spiraled downward with my father's drinking and violence, her schoolwork suffered. Eventually, everything began to suffer until one day she was gone. I gesture to the empty water glass in front of my mom. "Want some more?"

She nods, dabbing at her moist brow again. "Thank you, honey. You take such good care of me. Katie, too. You'll make a wonderful mother one day."

I scoff. "I don't know about that, Mom. You could be waiting a long time before you get any grandchildren out of me."

I balk at the idea, mainly because it's never seemed further out of reach. I thought Daniel might finally be someone I could see in my life for the long term, someone steady and reliable. Someone I could trust with my heart and my future.

Now, I'm not even sure I could trust him with my

car keys.

My mom stares at me with a tender look in her eyes when I return with her refilled glass. "I'm sorry I wasn't a better mother to you and your sister. I think about it so often, you know? All the things I could've done differently. All the times I should've been stronger--for you girls, if not for myself."

"No, Mom. Don't blame yourself for anything that happened. You did the best you could for us. I know that. I think Jen knew it, too."

She glances down, her brow furrowed. It takes her a long moment before she speaks. When she does, her voice is small. "You don't know how often I prayed for your father to finally kill himself. I should have packed up you girls and taken you as far away as I could instead of wishing for God to save us. I didn't have enough money for us to leave. No family to help us, or give us somewhere to stay. I couldn't bear the thought of raising you girls in a shelter somewhere, or worse, on the streets."

I reach out to her, gently laying my hand over her frail, trembling fingers. Her skin is cool, almost cold, beneath mine. "It's okay."

"No, it's not." She lifts her head, an almost palpable remorse written in every line of her face. "I should have protected you and Jennifer, whatever it took. Instead I just prayed for a miracle to save us. I prayed for him to die that night, Mellie."

She doesn't have to say anything more than that. I close my eyes, hearing the screams that filled the car. Feeling the sudden crash of impact, the horrible roar of twisting metal and breaking glass.

"I didn't realize he could be capable of that kind of

evil," she murmurs. "If I had, I would've killed him myself."

"No one could've known what he meant to do, Mom."

"I should have." She breaks down, letting go of a jagged sob. "I didn't realize the price of my prayers for him to die would nearly cost me both of you girls, too. Or that eventually, God would answer my failures as a mother a few years later by taking Jen away from me."

"Oh, Mom, no." I pull the chair next to her a bit closer so I can sit beside her. "Is that what you think? You didn't cause Jen's overdose. She did that to herself."

I clasp her hand with both of mine and hold it tight as a tear rolls down her cheek. I had no idea she's been harboring this kind of guilt, not only for my alcoholic father's abuse of us all and his heinous final act, but for my troubled sister's long slide into addiction and the accidental overdose that ended her life.

We tried to help her turn her life around. Jen's doctors and therapists tried to help her. Not even the birth of Katie was enough to give her the strength and willpower required to battle her addiction. Jen was gone by the time her daughter was barely two years old.

"None of it was your fault, Mom. Don't ever think that." I let go of her hand and gather her close, trying not to notice how fragile she feels in my arms. "Jen would never blame you. I think she'd be devastated to know you feel this way about what happened to her."

"I wish I could've saved her, Mellie." Her tears wet my shoulder. Her voice is quiet, choked with emotion. "I wish I could've been the kind of mother you both deserved. A strong woman. A brave one."

"You are." I ease back from her, if only so she can

see my face and know I mean what I'm saying. "You're all those things to me. To Katie, too. I can't imagine taking care of her without you, Mom."

She gives me a watery smile. "Oh, honey. You're my joy, you know that? That precious little girl upstairs is all my hopes for what Jennifer might have been, but you're my heart."

"Are you trying to make me cry now, too?"

She giggles around a wet sniffle, bringing her hand up to cradle the side of my face. "I love you, my sweet Mellie-Belle."

She hasn't called me that since I was Katie's age. Hearing it now is the balm I need after the way my world has seemed to tilt on its axis these past several days. "I love you, too, Mom."

She pats my cheek, then settles back against her chair on a sigh. Her eyes are still moist, her skin a bit too sallow for my peace of mind. "Do you suppose I have time for a quick nap before I help you with dinner, sweetheart?"

"Sure. If you like, I'll wake you when we're ready to eat."

"Oh, that'd be nice. Thank you, Melanie." She takes her time standing up, using the edge of the table for balance. When I move to assist, she shakes her head. "I'm fine, I'm fine. All that fresh air today's making me sleepy, that's all."

As if to reassure me, she straightens and carries her empty glass to the sink. I'd like to believe it's only a day spent outdoors that's got her looking so exhausted, but I can't shake the pang of concern in my breast as I watch her step out of the kitchen.

I turn back to finish cleaning the cooler so I can put

it away, and not a second later a loud crash sounds in the living room.

"Mom?" Dropping everything, I hurry out, my heart in my throat.

And for good reason.

She's lying on the floor where she fell, her book and glasses scattered beside her next to the end table she knocked over when she collapsed.

"Mom!"

I fly to her side. Above me upstairs, I hear Katie's footsteps pounding for the steps. She comes halfway down and sees the situation. Her frightened shriek sounds like the one I feel building in the center of my chest.

"Grandma!" she cries.

I have my ear down on my mother's breast, trying desperately to hear if her heart is still beating, if she's still breathing. I drag my head away only long enough to meet my niece's terrified stare.

"Katie, my phone is in my purse in the kitchen. Get it and call 9-1-1 for me right away, okay?"

She nods, snapping into action with a calm that's remarkable for her age. As she nears the spot where I'm stuffing a sofa pillow under my mother's head and reaching for more to place under her legs to elevate them, Katie pauses.

Her voice is as stark as her face. "Is Grandma going to--"

I don't let her finish the thought, mostly because I can't bear to consider it.

"Grandma needs a doctor right away, sweetie. Go make the call. We have to hurry."

19

She ghosted me.

I can't say I'm surprised. I can't even say I blame her. If she didn't think I was a first-rate jackass before, I'm sure she must now.

However, none of that does a thing to improve my dark mood over Melanie's absence for our Monday morning appointment to return to my studio.

"Shall I cancel the flight charter for today, sir?"

Gibson's polite inquiry interrupts the track I'm wearing into the rug in my study with my aggravated pacing. I grumble something unintelligible even to my own ears and give him a curt, affirmative wave. He nods politely, then closes me inside my cage to brood some more.

Because of her anxiety in the helicopter, I had arranged for a small private jet to fly us to Sagaponack today instead. Call it an olive branch, if not an overdue apology. It seemed the least I could do to make Melanie feel more comfortable with me, less afraid.

Not acting like a raving madman and a volatile, drunken prick might have gone a long way toward that effort, too.

Today I had intended to try on both counts.

As obvious as it is that she's not going to give me that chance, some pathetic part of me wants her to know I'm not a complete asshole. Why it feels important to me, I have no damn idea.

But that's not entirely true.

It's important because in the few times we've been together, I've glimpsed a goodness in her, something that shines past the pained shadows in her luminous gray-blue eyes. Her goodness shines through in spite of that pain she works so hard to hide.

The same goodness I set out to corrupt from the instant I first saw her.

If not for the clumsiness of my failing hands, that corruption would have started right there on the kitchen floor of my beach house. I groan at the memory, and at the fresh jolt of lust it chases through me.

A better man might regret the kiss I forced on her, along with everything else. I don't.

I can't.

Not when her mouth felt so perfect against mine, her body pliant and willing.

She burned so hot when I took her in my arms, I can still feel the singe of her warmth everywhere we touched.

Jesus Christ. The Macallan must have really soaked my brain, because even now, three days later, I still have myself nearly convinced she had wanted me every bit as much as I still want her.

My cock would like nothing better than to believe

that, too. Just the thought of kissing Melanie stirs a swift erection and sends fire licking through my veins.

Fuck.

On second thought, it's a damn good thing she didn't show up this morning. Not only for her, but for me.

I've never been this hungry for a woman before, this consumed with need. I don't like the feeling one fucking bit.

I've made it a point to always remain in control of every situation. It's how I've survived.

Detached. Opportunistic.

Numbed to everything but my own needs and pleasures.

Staying in control was the only way to navigate the brutal early days after I first arrived in New York. It's also how I've swum the equally shark-infested waters of the city I've since made my own through my art and the wealth it's earned me.

But all those years of hard lessons and discipline might as well have been built on sand because now, after one taste of Melanie Laurent's lips, all I've thought about since is how I can have another, deeper taste of her.

I have her phone number, though I've resisted calling it. I have her address, too, thanks to the hundred-dollar tip I gave the Hamptons Uber driver who took her home for me.

I could have Nate call and remind her that she's legally obligated to fulfill her contract with me. Or I could get in my car and drive out to her little house in Queens to tell her myself. That ought to solidify her contempt for me.

I've given her no reason not to despise me already,

so what difference would it make?

I pace another hard track in the rug, trying to talk myself out of caving to any of my worst urges where she's concerned. Instead, I decide to make the most of my day's suddenly cleared schedule and take care of a few business matters that require my attention.

First on the list is a face-to-face with my old friend, Dominic Baine.

Forgoing my driver, I head down to the mansion's underground garage where I have my pick of half a dozen luxury cars. I choose the fastest one, an aggressive black Aston Martin DBS Superleggera that crouches like a sleek predator among its staid, pricier German neighbors. The sports car starts up with a low, animal rumble before I send it screaming out onto the street.

A few minutes later, I roll up outside a private entrance for the soaring, dark glass tower of the Baine International building on West 57th. A uniformed valet takes my car while a similarly dressed doorman shows me into the modernly elegant lobby.

The place is bustling with suited corporate types and uptight-looking business executives coming and going from the gleaming elevators at the center of the spacious reception area.

I'm out of place in my jeans and boots and rolled up shirt sleeves, my hair loose around my shoulders. As I cleave through the center of the place, a few heads turn in my direction, though whether in disapproval of the rough beast prowling among them or in recognition of the artist with an equally crude reputation I can't be sure.

Nor do I care.

I'm used to being a disruption, a source of contempt as much as cautious curiosity. I've made my fortune off disturbing society's delicate mores and I do it unapologetically, both through my paintings and my various other business pursuits.

I nod at the pair of security personnel posted inside the lobby.

I haven't met the strawberry-blond female officer in the black suit and earpiece behind the desk, but I know the tall, chestnut-haired man standing on the other side of her. With his military posture and precise haircut, Gabriel Noble wears his dark suit like a uniform, unsurprising, considering the combat veteran's service time overseas.

"How's it going, Gabe?"

"Jared." He nods back at me as he accepts my outstretched hand in greeting, but there's an added coolness in his sharp hazel eyes. "Mr. Baine told me he was expecting you."

"Mr. Baine?" I grunt at the formality. Both Gabe and Nick, and Gabe's soon-to-be brother-in-law, Andrew Beckham, Nick's attorney, have been guests at my Lenox Hill house and my various clubs and private gatherings in the past. Where Dominic Baine is practically a brother to me, I've come to consider Gabriel Noble a friend, too. "Everything all right, Gabe?"

I can tell by the rigid set of his squared jaw that he wants to say something. Hell, based on the flat look in the former soldier's stare, he may even want to plant his fist in my face.

"Nick's waiting for you, Jared," he says, skirting my question. He glances at his female security associate. "O'Connor, will you call the executive offices and let them know Mr. Rush is here for Mr. Baine?"

Her nod is as crisp as a salute. "Yes, sir."

Gabe gives me another cool stare. "I trust you can find your way upstairs."

"Yeah, sure." Whatever's got his dick in a snarl will have to wait. I've got enough problems of my own to deal with, not the least of which being the reason for my in-person meeting with Dominic Baine.

I continue through the lobby to the bank of elevators and ride up to the executive floor. Nick's pretty assistant, Lily, meets me with a bright smile as I step out.

"Good morning, Jared. How nice to see you. It's been a while."

Her friendliness smooths some of my raised hackles. It doesn't hurt that the brunette knockout is as nice to look at as she is whip-smart and competent. She fills our short walk to Nick's office with easy small talk, a skill I imagine she's mastered over the past handful of years that she's shuttled visitors, colleagues, and adversaries between the gleaming elevators of the executive floor to the immense, windowed office overlooking some of Manhattan's most expensive skyline.

Nick is on the phone when we reach the open door, but he motions me inside while he wraps up the call.

"Thanks, Lily," I tell her as she discreetly departs to leave me alone with her boss.

A moment later, Dominic Baine walks around his large desk to shake my hand.

"I'm glad you called today," he says, his deep voice matching the sober look in his clear blue eyes. "I wish it was under better circumstances."

"Yeah, about that. Alyssa Gallo came to my house a few days ago. She told me what happened at the rec center."

Nick gives me a grim nod. "Have a seat."

I follow him to the conversation area of his office. He gestures for me to take the gray sofa beneath an impressive Jackson Pollock painting in black enamel, while he opts for a leather club chair situated just to the side of me.

"Before we get into anything else, Jared, I have to tell you that the art program's been a big success at Chelsea. I can't thank you enough for sponsoring it."

I wave off the praise, even though I know my old friend isn't the kind of man to give it lightly. "I'm glad to help. I really admire what you've done, Nick. Not only with the first community center in Chelsea, but at all the others you've built in the time since. You're making a real difference in a lot of kids' lives."

"So are you."

I shrug. "Hey, whatever. It's only money."

"No, it's not only money, Jared." Leaning back in the chair, he studies me over the tops of his steepled fingers. "If it was only money, I could've funded the program myself. It's your vision that made the art classes possible. Your connections in the art community have helped bring in top speakers and instructors from all over the world to teach and inspire kids who'd never have a chance at that kind of opportunity."

"Your fiancée's brought in her fair share of talent, too. And from what I hear, the classes she's taught have been some of the most popular ones."

He nods, and only a blind person would miss the pride that glows in Dominic Baine's eyes at the mention of the woman he adores. "I think Avery's having even more fun with the program than any of the students taking her classes. In fact, she's been doing her damnedest to persuade me to expand the program across all of our centers."

"No shit? That's a great idea."

"You think so?"

"Yeah, I do. I don't know how building all those centers for disadvantaged kids became a mission for you, but it's obvious to me that's what they are. A mission. An important one."

He nods, his expression sober, though not as shuttered and forbidding as I've so often seen it. He's changed somehow. Still the shrewd, unbreakable man he's always been, yet there is a deeper strength in him now, one that bores into me through the clarity of his cerulean eyes.

"I think you probably do know why, Jared. You and I aren't so different. Maybe we had different backgrounds, came to this city from different places, but deep down we're more alike than not. We both came through hell to get where we are now. We left behind pieces of ourselves we can never get back, but goddamn it, we're still standing. We're survivors."

I can't hold that unflinching stare. I let a curse slip past my lips as I drop my gaze and stare at the rug under my boots for what feels like an hour.

I wasn't prepared for Nick to bring up my past. He's one of the few people who knows where I've come from, what I had to do in order to make it from one day--and night--to the next.

I didn't come here to crack open that ugly part of my life, and I sure as hell don't want to see Dominic Baine's pity for what I'm struggling with now.

I clear my throat, but my voice still comes out as a sandpaper rasp. "I'm here because I want to talk to you about Alyssa."

It takes Nick a moment to respond. "All right," he says, unacknowledged permission to let me dodge other subjects I prefer to leave buried. The intensity hasn't left his gaze, but it's replaced now with the steely, inflexible look that must serve the corporate titan very well in his boardroom meetings. "I gather Alyssa told you we've barred her from the rec center."

"She did. She's pretty broken up over it, Nick. That center is her lifeline."

"She should've thought about that before she allowed her friends to vandalize and empty the place out last week."

I curse, giving a tight shake of my head. "She didn't allow anyone to do anything. And those kids aren't her friends."

"Kids?" Nick scoffs. "You want to see the security video from the break-in? They smashed their way in with sledgehammers and crowbars. They did thousands of dollars' worth of damage before they ran out with twice that much in computers from the STEM lab and other electronics."

"Alyssa had nothing to do with it, Nick."

"No? Her skinhead boyfriend was the asshole leading the pack. We've got enough of his face on camera for me to ID him. Now, we're just waiting for the police to track the bastard down and arrest him."

I nod, feeling no regard for the nineteen-year-old gang leader who's been manipulating and using Alyssa for the past year. As if turning tricks from the age of fourteen wasn't enough, she went and got mixed up with lowlifes who can only drag her further down.

"I hope they do get him," I mutter. "Chad Traynor's bad news. Best thing for Alyssa would be for him to go away for a long time. Best thing for her baby, too."

"Ah, fuck." Nick gives me a bleak look. "She's pregnant by that piece of shit?"

"Going on four months. She told me when she came to my house last week. Like I said, she was pretty upset after she found out she'd been banned from the rec center. She's got nowhere else to go, Nick. Her mother's been in and out of shelters with her since she was born, and that's no kind of home for a seventeen-year-old girl. Those art classes are the only place she can get away from Traynor and the rest of her fucked-up living situation. She's safe there. The center and the art classes she's taking there give her something positive to hold on to. It gives her hope. Kid like her? Having a little hope could mean the difference between life and death."

I know I don't have to remind my friend how true that statement is. He knows. He's lived it, same as me.

Although Nick hasn't said as much, I'd guess his determination to build his recreation centers throughout the city is an effort to give a few kids the kind of safe haven we both wish we'd had.

Especially the troubled ones, the ones whom life would otherwise swallow up and destroy.

Nick exhales a long, slow sigh. "You believe her that she didn't have any part in the break-in or the planning of it?"

"Damn right, I believe her. She loves the center as much as anyone, maybe more. It's all she's got."

He stares at me for a long minute, then shakes his head. "It's not all she's got. She's got you on her side, Jared. If you're vouching for her, then that's good enough for me."

"Thanks, Nick. I appreciate you giving her another

chance."

As we stand up and shake hands, he gives me a considering look. "Maybe Avery and I could convince you to teach one of the painting classes this year."

I chuckle. "Not a chance. Kids and me don't mix. That goes double for my art."

"I'm talking about teaching them basic technique, not giving them a master class on the Jared Rush method of erotic portraiture."

A grin tugs at my mouth. "Answer's still no."

Besides, the last thing anyone needs is to watch my hand shaking in front of the canvas. Worse, to see my rage over it explode like it did in front of Melanie.

I can't fix that mistake now. I'm damn sure not going to subject a classroom full of kids to a similar performance.

"When's the last time you were in the studio?" Nick asks. Since he doesn't wait for my answer, I assume it's because he's aware of how long it's been since I produced anything new. "You know, it might do you good to pick up a paintbrush and get back to work on something again."

"Actually, I am painting. Or, was. I was at the studio in Sagg a few days ago."

"Is that right?" He gives me a look of cautious surprise. "Who's the lucky muse this time?"

"You don't know her."

One of his dark brows wings up. "I'm even more intrigued now."

"Forget it. I don't like to talk about my work."

"Since when?" He balks, grinning. "The only thing bigger than your bank account is your ego, brother. No offense."

"None taken. It's the truth, after all." My laugh comes easily, and I realize this is the first time I've felt anything close to humor in longer than I can recall. Leave it to Nick to drag it out of me, especially on a day like today. "I'm gonna leave the rec center operations and hands-on work to you and Avery. Trust me, it's for the best."

"You're really not going to tell me what you're working on? Or, rather, who?"

I consider confiding in him about the whole fucked-up thing, starting with my discovery of Daniel Hathaway's presence in New York. Thankfully, the impulse only lasts for a second. "It's complicated."

He smirks. "In other words, situation normal for you."

He's got a point, but where my feelings about Melanie Laurent are concerned, complicated doesn't even begin to describe them. There's no point trying to explain now.

"I should go. Thanks for making time for me, Nick."

"Anytime," he replies, that sharp blue gaze of his too keen, too knowing. "I mean it, Jared. I know things haven't always been smooth between us, but I'm your friend. I always will be."

I nod. "Thanks. Likewise."

He walks me out of his office to the spacious reception area of the executive floor. "I'll inform the rec center that Alyssa's welcome to return--on the condition that going forward she's not seen with Traynor or any of his gang."

"Understood, Nick. Again, thank you for giving her another chance."

"Would you like to tell her, or would you prefer that

I do?"

"I'll handle it with her. For some reason, she trusts me more than most people."

Nick grunts. "She owes you her life, Jared. Don't think she doesn't realize that. If anyone else had found her that night instead of you, they would've turned her over to the police. They would've done worse than that, probably."

"I just want her to have a chance at a decent life," I murmur, reliving the night about a year ago when a scrawny, coked-out sixteen-year-old approached me outside a club and tried to sell herself to me for fifty dollars. The flashback brings another one fast on its heels, something even more personal, one I refuse to let materialize. "I just want Alyssa to be safe."

Nick puts his hand on my shoulder. "I'll help you do that, if I can."

As we talk, Andrew Beckham strolls out of his office nearby. Holding a manila file under his arm, the African American attorney approaches us. Smiling, he extends his hand to me. "Hey, Jared. How's it going? Didn't realize you were here."

"I'm just on my way out, actually."

"Jared came in to talk about what happened in Chelsea last week."

"Ah." Beck glances at Nick. "I spoke to the station commander down there this morning. He says they've got fresh a tip on Traynor's possible whereabouts. Sounds like they expect to make an arrest any day now."

"Good," Nick and I say at the same time. He gives me a nod. "I'll keep you posted on any new information we receive."

"Appreciate it."

The two men walk me toward the elevator. As we say our goodbyes, the chime dings with the arrival of the car on the executive floor. The doors slide open and Gabriel Noble stands there.

"Morning, Gabe," Nick says, moving aside to let his head of security step out. "What's going on? I haven't seen you look that grim since . . . well, in a long time."

"I need to take a couple hours off this morning, if that's okay."

"Sure, it's okay. Anything wrong?"

Gabe slants a brief glance my way before giving his boss his full attention. "Eve just called me. I need to swing by the hospital and pick her up."

Beck's face goes deadly serious next to Nick. "What's my sister doing at the hospital? Is she okay?"

"She's fine," Gabe assures him. "She's been there with a friend since I dropped her off before heading in to work."

"Anything serious?" Nick asks.

"It could've been worse." I don't miss the fact that Evelyn Beckham's fiancé now seems intent on pretending I'm not there at all. His clipped answers and deliberate avoidance of me puts an edge of suspicion in my veins. "Eve's friend's mother collapsed with a blocked artery at home yesterday afternoon. She almost didn't make it. They've got her under observation for the time being while they run some tests."

"Which friend?" My question sounds more like a demand. Curt and dark, my growled reply brings all three men's gazes swinging back to mine. "Who's Eve with at the hospital?"

I don't need to ask because the truth is written all over Gabe's grim face. "I shouldn't tell you. I heard what happened out at your studio."

Ah, fuck. I shouldn't be surprised that Melanie would confide in her best friend about the way I behaved.

Odds are good she told Evelyn about our arrangement, too. "No wonder you looked like you wanted to deck me downstairs."

"He still does," Beck points out.

Nick frowns. "What happened at your studio, Jared? Who are we talking about here?"

I shake off the question with a scowl. All my focus is locked on Gabriel Noble. "Where is she? What hospital? Tell me where Melanie is."

Beck's frowning at me now, too. "You mean Melanie Laurent? I know Eve's friend. What the hell was she doing out at your studio, man?"

I don't have time to answer questions or explain the twisted reasons behind my concern for a woman I have no right to feel so possessive of right now. But I *am* concerned.

The punch of visceral, possessive alarm hits me with the force of a tsunami.

"Damn it, Gabe. What fucking hospital?"

He grits out a low curse. "Presbyterian Queens."

My feet are in motion as soon as the words leave his mouth. As I step past him toward the open elevator car, the muscled soldier jabs a finger in my face, his hazel eyes full of lethal warning.

"I don't know what you think you're doing with Mel, but she's a good person. Too good for whatever's going on between you two. We may be friends, Jared, but if she gets hurt, you're going to answer to me."

I feel a tendon jerk in my jaw as we square off with each other.

"Point taken," I utter tersely, then step into the waiting elevator and punch the button for the lobby.

20

MELANIE

Standing in the hallway outside my mother's hospital room, I watch through the window as she sleeps. Her doctor has just left to continue his morning rounds after stopping to give me the latest update on her condition.

She's stabilized now, but they want to keep her under observation for another day to run further tests and to make sure there are no bleeding issues with the stents they inserted into two of her severely blocked arteries. The EMTs who reluctantly let Katie and me stay at Mom's side in the ambulance yesterday said if we'd been even a few minutes later getting her to the emergency room, we would have lost her.

Even now, the starkness of that reality hits me like a physical blow. I wipe at the sudden swell of tears that spills out the corners of my eyes.

I've saved my worry and tears for the few minutes here and there I've been able to steal away from Katie. I don't want her to know how scared I was yesterday. I don't want her to see how scared I still am that one day Mom's struggling heart is going to give out for good.

At six years old, she doesn't need to carry that fear along with me. I need to be strong for her. Strong for Mom, too. It's not a burden I resent even for a second. Still, sometimes it would be nice to have someone I could lean on once in a while. Fortunately, I've got a few good friends like Evelyn Beckham on my side.

Rallying myself to head back out to the family waiting area where I've left Katie with Eve, I make a quick stop in the restroom for tissues to dry my eyes. I make the mistake of glancing in the mirror over the sink and I groan at the horror staring back at me. The industrial-grade fluorescent light overhead gives my red-rimmed, dark-ringed eyes and ashen skin the full zombie effect. I'm sure my breath is no better for the countless cups of bad coffee I've had since Katie and I arrived at the hospital with Mom.

I manage to school my expression into one of calm confidence as I make the short walk from my mother's recovery room to the large, open space where I spot Katie reading a children's magazine seated next to my friend.

"Sorry that took longer than I'd planned. Mom's doctor was making his rounds and I wanted to catch him while he was on the floor."

"No problem," Eve says, her slender arm wrapped around Katie's shoulders. She doesn't voice her concern in front of my niece, but I can see it in her pale green eyes. "If you want me to stay a while longer, I can call my client and cancel her fitting."

"No, don't do that. You've been working on those

lingerie designs for months. Besides, Gabe will be waiting outside to pick you up before long, anyway."

Eve gives me a caring smile. "You're sure? I know my client will understand if you'd like me to stay."

"Yes, I'm sure. Katie and I will be fine here on our own. Right, kiddo?"

Katie lifts her head and nods. "Are we waiting to go home with Grandma, Aunt Melanie?"

I crouch down in front of her and brush some of her blond hair behind her ear. "Grandma's sleeping right now, sweetheart. The doctors want to take care of her for a bit longer here at the hospital. Hopefully, she can come home tomorrow."

When I stand up again, Eve rises with me. "You've both been here for more than twelve hours. Come with Gabe and me. He'll be happy to drop you off at home to freshen up and rest for a bit. You can't do anything more for her right now, Mel. She's in good hands."

"I know. And I'm fine. We won't stay too long, promise. We'll take the subway home before it gets dark."

She heaves a resigned sigh, then pulls me into a brief, tight hug. "I'll call you later to check in and make sure you're home."

"Okay. Good luck at the fitting."

"Thanks." She turns to Katie, holding her arms open to catch my niece as she pops off her chair to say goodbye to her favorite of my friends. "You take good care of your auntie for me, all right? She won't listen to me, but I know she'll listen to you."

Katie bobs her head. "I'll try. Grandma says Aunt Mellie's stubborn like a mule when she puts her mind to something."

Eve laughs while I gasp, feigning outrage. "What? When did she say that about me?"

Katie giggles. "All the time. 'Specially when you boss us about eating vegetables and not staying up late watching TV."

"Well, I'm about to get even bossier about those things. Grandma's doctor gave me a bunch of new rules for her to follow after she comes home."

Katie scrunches her nose. "She's not gonna like that."

"That's why I'm going to need your help making sure she behaves, okay?"

"Okay."

Eve smiles at us. "If I'm leaving, I should go."

"Go," I tell her, drawing my niece under my arm. "We're good."

"I'm calling you later."

I nod. "Thank you for being here. I love you, girl."

"Love you, too. And you," she tells Katie. With a wave, she turns away from us and glides out of sight as elegantly as if she's on a fashion runway.

When it's just the two of us, I glance down at my niece and the dog-eared kids' magazine clutched in her hand. "Are you reading something good?"

"Uh, huh. It's all about elephants in Africa. There are games and stuff in it, too."

"That does sound good." I smile at her sweet face that looks so much like my sister's. "Will you read some of it to me?"

"Sure."

We head back into the mostly empty waiting room. Traffic in the coronary unit has ebbed and flowed since we arrived yesterday afternoon. The brown vinyl recliner

I sat in while Katie slept in my arms last night is vacant, so we reclaim it. For several minutes I allow myself to unwind to the sound of my niece reciting facts about elephant social structures and efforts to conserve endangered species around the world.

I don't even realize I'm dozing until I startle awake and find my lap empty.

"Katie?" I vault out of the chair and step into the wide corridor outside the waiting room.

She's nowhere in sight. The halls are busy with nurses moving patients and people drifting out of one room or another along the passageway. But no sign of my niece. I start walking fast, panic rising in my breast.

"Katie?"

I round the corner toward another stretch of hallway practically at a skid. All my breath leaves my lungs in a relieved gust when I see her standing in front of a vending machine. Her small hand is splayed against the Plexiglas, her pale blond head tipped up as she looks longingly at all the beverages inside.

"Katie, what are you doing out here? I thought I told you not to wander off while we were at the hospital. I want you to stay where I can see you, remember?"

She glances at me, her sweet face contrite. "I know. But you were sleeping and I got thirsty."

"It takes money to use this machine, honey. Come on, I'll get you a drink from the water cooler near the nurse's station."

"But I want juice," she says, disappointment and fatigue in the puppy dog look she gives me.

She's tired and bored, which is understandable considering how long we've been keeping vigil outside my mom's unit. She's probably hungry again, too. We had breakfast in the cafeteria downstairs, but Katie barely picked at her toast and eggs.

I should see about getting her an early lunch.

What I really should have done was take Eve up on her offer to bring us home. Katie needs the rest and a proper meal. God knows I could use a little of both as well.

"All right," I relent, digging into my purse for a couple of dollars to feed the machine. "You can have juice. Which one do you want?"

"Apple." Then she shakes her head and points to another one. "No, grape. I want grape."

A deep voice sounds from behind me while I'm still foraging for my wallet. "How about one of each? My treat."

I swivel my head at the dark whiskey growl I'd now recognize anywhere. It doesn't lessen my surprise to hear Jared Rush's voice, or to see him standing in the hospital corridor with me.

"What are you doing here?" I'm sure my frown isn't any more welcoming than my tone, but I can't help it.

"Can I have both, Aunt Melanie?" Katie asks, oblivious to the change in the air that always seems to occur whenever Jared's nearby.

I wish I could be oblivious to it, too. Awareness of him arcs through me like an electrical current, hot and bright and intense. He looks good, dressed in jeans and boots, the sleeves of his white button-down shirt rolled up over his tanned, muscular forearms. His thick man of sandy-brown hair breaks in waves on his broad shoulders, wild and untamed, like the rugged handsomeness of the man himself. And he smells ridiculously good, spicy and warm, a comfort to my senses that I want to refuse but can't.

I break away from his smoldering stare to hand my money to Katie. "Choose one or the other, honey. I don't have enough for both." I glare back at Jared. "And we don't need anyone's charity."

"How about an apology?"

The only thing that could shock me more than his unexpected appearance here are those words falling off his tongue in a low tone that actually seems sincere. He seems a bit taken aback by them, too. Something flickers in his warm molasses eyes, something I'm tempted to call regret.

I lift my chin, refusing to give in to anything about this dangerous, volatile--obviously troubled--man. "I don't need your apology, either."

After Katie's bottle of grape juice clunks into the tray and she fetches it out, I steer her away from Jared, prepared to leave him standing right where he is.

"I heard about your mom, Melanie. How's she doing?"

I freeze, wheeling around to face him. "What do you mean you heard about her? How? Did Eve--"

He shakes his head. "Not Eve. I ran into Gabe this morning while I was at the Baine Building meeting with Nick. He was on his way to pick her up at the hospital."

"And he told you she was here with me?"

"He didn't want to tell me anything, so don't be upset with him. When I heard what happened to your mom, I pressed him to tell me where I could find you."

"Why?" The question blurts out of me like an accusation. "What do you care? Oh, wait. Let me guess. You're here because I didn't show up for our session today?"

Katie looks up at me as my temper swiftly moves toward a simmer. "Who is this man, Aunt Mellie?"

"Just someone I met recently. He's not important." I see Jared's jaw go a bit more rigid at my jab, but he says nothing. I paste a comforting smile on my face as I meet my niece's worried look. "Why don't you go back to the waiting room and read some more from your magazine?"

She frowns. "But you just said not to go where you can't see me."

"I know, and thank you for reminding me. I need just a minute with Jared, okay? I'll be right behind you."

"She's cute," Jared says as we both watch Katie skip back to the waiting room.

"She is," I admit softly. "She looks just like my sister."

"Your sister's not here with you?"

"Jen's dead. She died when Katie was two years old." I level a flat stare at him and find him watching me with a soberness in his gaze.

"I'm sorry."

I fold my arms over my chest. "Why are you here, Jared? If you've come to tell me I'm in breach of my contract with you, don't bother. If my mom wasn't in the hospital, I was going to tell you I want out of the agreement. I can't be around you, Jared. After what happened at the studio on Friday, I won't be around you anymore."

"That's more than understandable," he says, no inflection in his voice. "I'm here now only because I wanted to make sure you were all right."

"You didn't have to do that. You shouldn't have."

"Probably not, but here I am."

His stare is unnerving. Not for the usual reasons, the ones that send my heart into a gallop and make everything female in me unfurl with anticipation. No, right now his gaze knocks me off kilter because it's full of compassion and concern. I swallow, feeling my outrage fizzle under the unexpected warmth of his caring regard.

"How are you holding up, Melanie?"

It's the tenderness in his voice that unravels me the most. "I'm okay."

"And your mom?"

"Better now, thank God. She collapsed after we came home from a day in the park yesterday. The surgeon put in two stents, one of them to clear an eighty-six percent blockage in the left anterior artery. He said that one's the worst kind of blockage to have."

Jared nods grimly. "The widow-maker."

"That's what Mom's doctor called it. How do you know so much about heart issues?"

"My mother had similar problems. She wasn't as lucky as yours. If the heart disease hadn't killed her, the alcoholism and smoking eventually would have."

He's mentioned his family had hardships when he was young, including the financial mistakes of his father that cost the family their horse farm in Kentucky, but this is the first he's shared any of the details of his past. Having come so close to losing my mother now, I can understand some of the pain he must have felt in losing his. "I'm sorry, Jared. I truly am."

He grunts. "Ancient history."

And yet the way he says it, the way the tenderness in his gaze seems to harden, tells me his history isn't as ancient as he'd like me to believe.

"What's the plan with your mom?" he asks, deftly attempting to shift my focus away from him. "How long are they keeping her here?"

"Another day or two for tests and follow-ups. I'm going to have my work cut out for me after she comes home. I swear, sometimes I feel like I'm raising two six-year-olds."

"Your father's not in the picture?"

"No. Just me."

He nods, studying me in that way he has of cleaving through all of my defenses and protective walls. My simple answer gives away nothing of the trauma of my past, yet I sense him waiting for me to tell him more. I glance away, reminding myself that this is Jared Rush, the artist who thrives on dissecting people, peeling them apart to expose every vulnerability. I don't want him to see mine, not now. Not here, in the middle of the hospital corridor.

"I should've seen this coming with her," I admit under my breath. "I knew she looked tired yesterday. I knew her color wasn't good. She had a heart attack last year. I should've known a blood clot was more than a possibility. I should've taken her to the emergency room myself as soon as I noticed how fatigued she looked--"

"Hey," he says gently, as the words tumble out of me in rapid fire. His hand comes up between us but instead of touching me, he lets it slowly fall back down to his side.

"What about you?" he asks, his brows furrowed. "Have you gotten any sleep since yesterday? Gabe said you've been here the whole time."

"I'm fine. I'm tired, but I'm fine. I shouldn't have brought Katie with me, but I had no other choice."

"What about Hathaway? He isn't willing to help out?"

"I didn't ask him to," I murmur, unwilling to tell Jared that we broke up. I've got enough to deal with at the moment without seeing him gloat over my bad choices or the fact that he warned me not to put my trust--or my heart--in Daniel. "I should go look in on my niece."

Jared nods solemnly. "Come on, I'll walk you back to the waiting room."

I know I should refuse. I don't want his comforting any more than I want his charity. But my body is too exhausted to resist when he moves his hand to my back and lets it hover just above my spine, not touching me, yet offering a warm support--a soothing strength--I can't deny.

We walk to the waiting room in silence, and while it should feel awkward, even uncomfortable, after the way we left things between us at his studio a few days ago, all I feel is gratitude for his presence. No, that's not all. I feel a strange sense of calm, too.

God, I must be a fool.

Jared Rush should not be my safe harbor, yet right now, in this moment, that's exactly what he feels like.

We arrive in the family waiting area and I sigh when I see Katie curled up and sleeping like a kitten in the vinyl chair. Her half-empty bottle of grape juice sits on the end table beside her, the magazine she'd been reading still clutched in her small hands.

"She needs to be at home in her bed," I whisper, reluctant to wake her.

Jared glances me. "My car's in the visitor lot downstairs. I can have you back at your house in ten minutes."

I start to shake my head. "I'm sure you have plenty of other more important things to do."

"I don't," he says, his deep voice solemn. "Let me take you home, Melanie."

21

MELANIE

Asleep and belted into in the backseat of Jared's black sports car, Katie hardly stirs during the short ride from the hospital.

Although the gorgeous Aston Martin could probably hold its own and then some on a Formula One racetrack, Jared drives it with reserved control through the busy morning traffic in Queens and zigzagging one-way streets of my neighborhood.

"Thanks for the ride," I tell him as he parks in the short driveway of my little house. "You really didn't have to go to the trouble."

"It's no trouble at all."

I don't expect him to get out of the car, but when I unbuckle my seatbelt, Jared turns off the engine and comes around to my side as I reach into the back to retrieve Katie. She's dead to the world, slumped in the seat, a sprawl of long legs and loose arms, her head flopped down on her narrow chest.

"I can carry her inside for you," Jared offers, moving in to help.

"That's all right, I'm used to this."

He frowns and shakes his head. "You're as exhausted as she is. Let me take her."

As much as I may want to argue against accepting his help, he's right. I am tired. I give him a vague nod, then step aside and watch as he carefully extricates her from the seat and gathers her boneless weight against his strong shoulder.

"Lead the way." The sound of his deep voice pitched to a lower timbre to avoid waking the child sleeping in his arms makes my heart squeeze up like a fist in my breast.

I didn't imagine a man like Jared Rush had any degree of tenderness in him. Seeing him like this makes me wonder what else I've yet to learn about him.

As much as I try to cling to the fear, confusion, and anger I left with the other day at his beach house studio, this calm, steady side of Jared isn't playing along with that plan.

Despite my firsthand knowledge from childhood of how quickly a man can veer from the straight and narrow path of kindness, even charm, to a monster with the ability to destroy everything in his path, I can't reconcile that image with Jared.

Unlike my father, Jared hasn't been violent with me. His explosive reaction when he knocked the bottle of whisky off the counter had been vitriol directed at himself, not me. And while I'd been afraid of the alcohol, and remain disturbed by how readily Jared reaches for it, I haven't ever been afraid of him.

If I were, our conversation today--and whatever it is

that lingers between us now--would have ended back in the hospital corridor.

"We'll go in through the back," I tell him, trying to pretend I don't notice the current of energy that still lives between us, no weaker for the days that have passed since I saw him at the beach house studio.

If anything, I'm even more aware of him now that I know how his mouth feels on mine.

I lead him to the side door of my house, Katie still asleep on his shoulder as I unlock the deadbolt. The house has always seemed small, but the space inside shrinks around the presence of Jared Rush.

"Katie's bedroom is upstairs," I murmur quietly in the stillness surrounding us as I lead him deeper into the house.

It's neither an invitation for him to take her there nor a request for him to surrender her to me so he can leave. To be honest, I'm not sure which I'd prefer. Part of me is grateful for his company today, and for his smooth ability to take control of every situation. That arrogant confidence I found so maddening when I met him is the thing I'm simply grateful to lean on now.

The empty picnic cooler is on the kitchen floor where I left it when I ran to help my mom after she collapsed. In the living room, the overturned end table is still on its side, Mom's reading glasses and book lying haphazardly where they fell. It's difficult to walk past the reminders of how close I came to losing her.

Jared seems to clue in to the weight of my unspoken thoughts. "Are you okay?"

"Yeah. This just brings the reality of it crashing back to me, you know?"

His nod is solemn, something haunted in his grim

expression. It was only days ago that I considered him the last person I'd want to see me vulnerable or hurting. Now, I look at him and find an unexpected reassurance in his perceptive gaze.

When we reach Katie's room, Jared carefully deposits her on the mattress, then steps back to let me take off her shoes and cover her with the blanket folded at the end of her bed.

Once we're back downstairs, Jared moves ahead of me to right the small table. I pick up Mom's things and set them where she'll want them when she gets home.

"Have you been taking care of your niece for long?"

"Since she was an infant. Mom was already living with me here at the house."

"And your sister?"

"Jen had a lot of problems," I admit, frowning at the memories. "She struggled with drugs and alcohol, which didn't make it easy for her to hold a job. She used to leave Katie here with Mom and me when things got rough. She died before Katie really knew her. The medical examiner called it an accidental overdose."

"But you don't believe that?"

"Life wasn't easy for my sister."

"Doesn't sound like it was easy for you, either."

"No, it wasn't." He has no idea how hard things were, and as much as I'd prefer to keep my ugly childhood locked up inside me where I don't have to examine it, I can't stop the words from coming. "My father didn't make things easy for anyone near him. He wasn't always bad, not in the early years, at least. No one realized he had psychological issues. It would've mattered if we did. He was too proud for therapy, not that we could've afforded it. He drank instead. Mom thought she could save him. She tried to be his rock, but he spiraled to a dark place. One day he could be charming, seemingly normal. The next, he was a monster."

"I'm sorry," Jared says, his voice as grim as his expression. "That's no way for anyone to grow up."

"Jen got the brunt of his rage because she was so similar to him. She had his lightning temper, the same habit of lashing out when she felt attacked. She was rebellious, too. That only escalated the conflicts between them, which meant all of us suffered for it."

"How did you manage to turn out so normal? Hell, better than normal."

I shrug, brushing off his assessment with a downward glance and a shake of my head. "I don't know about that. All I ever wanted was to hold the pieces of my family together, whatever it took. If that meant tutoring my middle school classmates for a few dollars each week in order to help put food on our table when Mom's small paychecks didn't stretch far enough, that's what I did. If I had to put myself at the striking end of my father's fists so he didn't end up killing Jen during their fights, I weathered the blows before my mother had the chance to step in and get hurt, too."

"Jesus Christ." Jared reaches out to me, gently stroking my cheek as if he can see the bruises that used to ride there after my father's manic rages. His thumb traces my jawline, his dark eyes smoldering with a combination of outrage and tender concern. "I've never met anyone as courageous and strong as you are. No one, Melanie."

I haven't told him the worst of it. No one knows that ugly truth except my mom, the only person alive who endured it along with me.

His compassion right now is almost too much for me to bear. I turn my face away from the comfort of his caress. I don't want to crumble against him, no matter how tempting it might be to take the couple of steps that would move me into his arms.

"Where is your father now?" he asks, a dangerous edge to his low voice. "How did you finally get away from him?"

"He was killed in a car accident when I was thirteen."

"Driving drunk, I assume."

"No. Ironically, I don't think he'd had anything to drink that night. He was having one of his manic episodes. He started driving erratically, shouting and swearing over nothing. Speeding like a man possessed as we approached the bridge on the freeway."

Jared's brows furrow. "You were in the vehicle with him?"

"We all were. Mom, Jen, and me."

"What happened?"

"We had been at one of my school events, driving home from a regional science fair on Long Island. It was dark and raining that night. Dad was in a mood after hearing he'd been laid off again. He started railing about everything--the gas it took to take me to the event, the storm outside, the injustice of life in general. Mom asked him to slow down, to stop shouting because he was scaring all of us, but he couldn't be reasoned with. There was a wildness in his eyes I'd never seen before, a cold resignation. I saw it when he glanced at me in the rearview mirror in those last few seconds before the crash."

I see it now, too. I close my eyes, but I can't erase

the sight of his bleak stare in that narrow piece of glass. I shudder with the chill of it, even now.

Jared's fingers brush lightly under my chin, coaxing me to look at him. "Tell me what he did."

"He didn't slow down. His eyes were still glued on mine in the mirror when he jerked the steering wheel to the right and hit the gas even harder on the bridge. Another car in the lane beside us clipped our rear bumper and sent us into a spin. It slowed our car down enough so that we only smashed into the guardrail instead of going over it as I'm sure my father intended."

Jared grinds out a curse, his handsome face tight with fury. "That son of a bitch. He couldn't handle his own problems, so he was going to kill you all?"

I nod, because as stark and horrific as the statement is, it's the truth.

"He wasn't wearing a seatbelt," I explain, my voice quiet. "The impact threw him from the car. He died on the scene. Mom and Jen and I all spent time in the hospital with varying injuries, but we survived."

Jared nods soberly. "That scar under your arm. This is the accident you told me was no big deal."

I can't pretend the crash--and my father's cold actions--were anything less than life-altering. Not with this man. His gaze has had the power to look inside me from the very beginning. Even if I tried to hide this pain from him now, I couldn't.

And I don't want to.

I realize it with a clarity that shocks me.

"There are times, even now, when I wake up in the dark bathed in a cold sweat and dreaming that I'm still in that car. I'm twenty-five years old, yet I go to bed sometimes afraid to shut my eyes because I know I'm going to see my father's dead stare looking back at me."

On a groan, Jared gathers me close. "I've been an asshole with you this whole time, Melanie. I'm sorry for that. I'm sorry for what happened a few days ago, too."

"It's okay."

"No, it's not." He draws me away, scowling. "I had no idea what you've been through, or I never would've-
-"

He breaks off on a low curse and shoves his hands into the front pockets of his jeans.

"You never would have what?"

He gives a tight shake of his head. "If I'd known, I never would've started any of this with you. Not the painting, not the contract I made you sign. I sure as hell never would've allowed myself to get half-drunk and then force myself on you the way I did out at the studio."

I can see the torment in his face, the remorse. "I don't like the fact that you drink as much as you do," I admit to him. "If you have problems, Jared, you need to find a better way to deal with them."

"I know," he answers tightly. "Fuck, I know that."

"As for the rest of it, you don't have to apologize."

"Yes, I do--"

I silence him by going up on my toes and brushing my lips against his. His beard-shadowed jaw feels like rigid granite under my palm as I draw back from him. His eyes burn into me, hot with desire. The tender comfort he showed me a moment ago has shifted into a desire I can feel in the heavy throb of his heartbeat, and in the hard length of his erection pressing into my abdomen.

"You don't have to apologize, because you didn't force anything on me, Jared. Not that day out at the studio. Not anytime we've been together. I entered into this with my eyes open. I wanted you, too."

"You shouldn't." His scowl darkens. "I'm not the kind of man you should admit that to, either. Especially not when the only thing preventing me from acting on it is the fact that there's a little girl sleeping just above our heads."

Katie's the only thing that would keep me out of Jared's arms right now, too.

It's a slim tether to cling to, one he seems to be grappling with as much as I am. "I should go, before I prove I'm any more of a bastard."

An electric silence simmers between us for a long moment, only to be broken by my phone's chime sounding from in the kitchen. "I have to answer that. It could be the hospital."

He nods, but doesn't follow me into the kitchen while I run to take the call. It's not the hospital's number on the screen. It's Eve.

"Hey," I answer, a bit breathlessly. "What's going on? Aren't you supposed to be in your client meeting?"

"I'm just heading into it," she says. "Don't hate Gabe, but he literally just told me that he ran into Jared Rush at the Baine offices today. Apparently, Jared's really concerned about you and was going to look for you at the hospital. Gabe told him where you were, Mel. I hope you're not mad."

"I'm not. And he did--find me at the hospital, that is."

"Oh, my God. Is he there now?"

"No. We're at my house. He brought Katie and me home a while ago. She's taking a nap, so now we're . . . talking."

195

"Uh, huh," Eve says, and I can practically hear the wheels of her mind turning. "You and Jared. At your house. Talking."

"Yes." I glance over my shoulder to peer toward the living room, but I don't see him. "Can I call you back later?"

She laughs. "Girl, you'd better call me. I want to know everything."

I murmur a quick goodbye, then drop the phone into my purse. When I walk back into the living room, I find it empty.

The front door has been unlocked, then closed silently behind him while I was talking to my friend. I look out the curtain of the front window just in time to hear his car rumble to life in the driveway.

He backs out onto the street, then he's gone.

22

MELANIE

"Katie, time for breakfast," I tell my niece, popping my head into her bedroom while I wind my hair into a bun and fasten it with an elastic band I pull out of the skirt pocket of my diner uniform. "Brush your teeth and come down to eat before I have to leave for work, please."

"Okay, Aunt Mellie."

I can hear my mom rummaging in the kitchen downstairs while a commercial plays on the TV in the living room. She came home from the hospital two mornings ago, feeling healthier than she had in months. Of course, her renewed energy only makes her harder to manage. She's always had an independent streak, and I suppose I don't have to look far to guess where I get my stubbornness.

I find her in her peach bathrobe and pajamas, bent over in front of the open refrigerator door and reaching in to retrieve an unopened gallon of milk from the back of the shelf.

"Mom, what do you think you're doing?"

Her voice is muffled from halfway inside the appliance. "I'm getting Katie's cereal ready for her."

"Your doctor said no lifting or straining for at least a week." I move around her and take the carton out of her hands. "What did you do with the packet of instructions he sent home with you?"

She gives me a mildly exasperated look. "It's on the end table with my reading glasses in the living room."

I frown, but it's hard to be upset with her when she's staring at me with clear, bright eyes and a healthy pink glow in her cheeks. I consider it my personal responsibility to ensure she stays as healthy as she looks now. "If you're uncertain about what you can or can't do while I'm gone today, promise me you'll follow your doctor's orders."

She sighs. "I've already promised you I would, honey."

Yes, she did, but that doesn't mean I'm not going to worry. "Maybe it's not a good idea for me to leave you and Katie alone so soon."

"Melanie, I'm sixty-two years old. I'll be fine. Besides, Katie and I have our day all planned out. We're going to color and play some board games, then we're going to make sugar cookies this afternoon."

I arch my brows at her. "I must have missed the page that listed sugar cookies as part of your new heart healthy diet plan from the hospital."

"Don't worry, they're not for me. Katie wanted to bake today, and I thought it would be fun if we did something we could decorate together."

"All right," I relent, feeling a bit better about the

situation.

I'd much rather stay home with them, but at least the diner is closeby. Ordinarily, I'd be heading into the city to my part-time accounting job, but after Mom came home I quit the dentist's office in order to pick up extra shifts at the diner.

God knows, we're going to need the money. I don't even want to imagine the size of the medical bill that will be coming soon. My stomach bottoms out just thinking about it.

I can't deny how much I could use the money Jared was going to pay me for posing for him, but that's obviously off the table now. Even though I had decided not to go through with the arrangement after that first day at his studio, Jared's disappearing act two days ago here at my house and the radio silence that's followed has made it clear to me that he has no desire to continue with the painting, either.

When it comes to me, evidently, he has no desire for anything.

I felt foolish enough in the minutes after he left. Two days later, I feel like an epic idiot for letting myself believe there was something more than just the attraction that had been burning between us. I shared a piece of my soul with him that day. I told him things only my closest friends know because I thought he might be the one man who could understand.

I thought he might have cared about me, even a little.

Instead, what he apparently felt for me was pity.

And regret.

I can still see the uncomfortable look on his face, the way he retreated from me physically and emotionally after I told him how my own father had such little regard for me and the rest of his family he attempted to kill us all.

Jared's words come back to me, replaying on the same endless loop that's been running since I watched his car vanish up the street.

"If I'd known, I never would've started any of this with you."

Now he knows, he's gone.

And I'm left feeling like a ridiculous joke.

I thought Jared had been struggling against his desire for me after I kissed him and nearly threw myself at him in my living room. Instead, he was no doubt just waiting for his chance to break away and make his escape.

Since rehashing any of what happened between us is a colossal waste of time, I pour myself a cup of coffee and rally my thoughts back to reality and things I can control.

Or try to control, that is.

I frown when my gaze catches on the piece of paper tucked inside the mystery novel Mom's been reading. Slipped between the pages as a makeshift bookmark is the medicine log I printed for her.

I take it out and unfold it. "Mom, did you take your aspirin and other morning meds yet?"

"Yes, honey. I took them with my oatmeal and tea about a half hour ago."

I wave the blank page at her. "You didn't mark it off on the chart. You do know that's the whole point of keeping a log, right?"

"Rules, rules, rules," she says, as I set the paper down in front of her at the table.

As if I don't have enough to deal with in the handful of minutes before I have to leave for the diner, the front doorbell rings. Setting my coffee on the kitchen counter,

I walk through the living room to see who it is. I open the door and find a middle-aged woman dressed in pink hospital scrubs standing on the stoop.

She glances down to check the clipboard she holds in her hand before greeting me with warm brown eyes and a pleasant smile. "Good morning. I'm Rosa Cortez. I'm here to see Elaine Laurent."

"Elaine's my mother. I'm Melanie. Can I help you?"

"Oh, yes." Her kind eyes flick down to the clipboard again and she nods. "I haven't arrived too early?"

"Too early for what?"

She gives me a confused look. "I'm your mother's home healthcare provider. I'll be coming here to take care of her for the next four weeks."

"I don't understand. No one at the hospital mentioned this to me."

"We're a private service," she says, cheerfully unfastening the work order from her clipboard and handing it to me along with her ID and credentials from what I recognize as the premier in-home nursing firm in the area. According to the document, Rosa has been contracted to provide hands-on care for my mom in our home from nine-to-five every weekday for a full month. Medicines. Meals. Bloodwork. Errands.

The list is extensive. And, I'm sure, very expensive.

"I didn't order this." I shake my head and try to push the paper back at her before I'm tempted to dream I could even begin to afford it. I'll be working for the next twenty years just to pay off Mom's hospital stay, never mind something like this. "I'm sorry, Rosa. You seem very nice, but there must be some kind of mistake. I can't pay for this kind of service."

"Oh, no, miss. It's all been taken care of already. The

contract's prepaid."

I frown. "Prepaid? By who?"

She gestures for me to flip the page over. I scan down to the bottom of it and my gaze settles on the bold, aggressive scrawl of Jared's signature.

Rosa begins explaining more about the services she provides, but I'm only half-listening. As appreciative as I am for the idea of some much-needed help, I don't want his charity. I sure as hell don't want Jared's pity. Especially when it's coming on the heels of two days of nothing but silence and avoidance after I told him about my pathetic past.

Suddenly, the idea that I confided in him about that makes me feel even more foolish and humiliated than the fact that I blurted out how much I wanted him.

I'm mortified. I'm angry, too.

More than angry, I'm pissed as hell.

As much as I'd like to turn Jared's gift away, the sad fact is I do need the help. My mom needs the help, no matter what she'd like me to believe.

I force a smile for the kind healthcare worker and hold open the door for her. "Please come in, Rosa."

I'm still fuming as I make quick introductions and provide the nurse with my phone number in case she needs to reach me while I'm gone. A few minutes later, I'm out the door.

I'm not going in to the diner, though.

After calling in to make my excuses, I head for the subway that will take me into the city.

23

JARED

“Here’s the paperwork you requested, Jared.”

Nate sets the file folder down on the desk in my study, placing it on top of a small stack of other documents that have been awaiting my attention for the past hour.

“We’ve already got a protective order in place for Alyssa, and I’m pulling a few strings to get the restraining order pushed through as quickly as possible,” he says. “At least she’ll have some legal remedies if her ex-boyfriend attempts to harm her or sic any of his thugs on her in retaliation for her helping the police arrest him for the break-in at the rec center.”

“Thanks, Nate.”

I flip through the pages of court documents and attached evidence Alyssa has provided. Printed photos of bruises, abrasions, and blackened eyes she’s suffered over time at Traynor’s hands. Text messages full of vitriol and demeaning insults. Demands for her to get rid of the child she's carrying or face the consequences of Traynor's wrath.

It sickens me.

It also makes me think about another woman and the years of abuse she endured as a girl, not from a boyfriend who claimed to love her, but from a father who should have been the one to keep her safe. A sick, cowardly man who would have killed her and the rest of his family if fate hadn't intervened to keep their car from plunging off a highway bridge in the dark.

My blood seethes at the thought. I'm also filled with a bone-deep relief that Melanie survived the crash and the hell of her childhood. I don't want to imagine the world existing without her--even if I'm determined there can be no place for her in my own.

I suddenly realize Nate hasn't moved from where he stands in front of my desk. When I drag myself out of the grim reminders of Melanie's past pain, I find my friend's piercing stare locked on me.

"You didn't hear a word I just said, did you?"

I grunt. "Sorry. I've got some things on my mind today."

He eyes me skeptically. "You've been prowling around in here grumbling and scowling since the weekend."

I level a dark look on him now, which only serves to prove his point. "What were you saying?" I ask, ignoring his on-point observation.

He points to the file folder. "We're going to need Alyssa to sign those documents so I can file them with the judge. The shelter she's staying at is on the way to the courthouse. I could take the file over to her for signature on my way."

"No. I'd rather bring her here to review the process with us and answer any questions she might have. She'll be more comfortable doing that somewhere other than where she's staying. I want to talk to her about the art program in Chelsea, anyway."

Nate nods. "Let me know if you need anything else on my end."

"Actually, there is something. We need to discuss the Gramercy Park project."

"Sure. What about it?"

"I'm suspending the project, effective immediately."

"Suspending it?" Nate's brows rise. "Meaning you're scrapping it entirely, or putting it on hold for a while?"

"I haven't decided. But as of today, I want Crowne and Merritt cut loose."

Nate lets go of an exhaled curse. "That's not going to go over well. Victor Crowne is notoriously litigious. I'll guarantee you we can expect a lawsuit from him in response."

"Do I look like I give a fuck about that?"

My barked reply comes out hotter than intended. It's rare that I lose control of my temper when it comes to my business dealings. Rarer still that I lose it in front of Nate.

Unlike my art, my clubs and real estate ventures have never meant much to me. They're nothing but diversions, albeit lucrative ones. They've also become a needed distraction from the reality I'm loathe to accept: that my ability to paint is slipping away from me day by day.

And now I have another loss I need to accept.

The dubious look on my friend and counselor's face

intensifies in the wake of my anger. "What's really going on here, Jared? Why am I getting the sense this grudge you have with Daniel Hathaway goes a lot deeper than the seventy-five grand poker debt he owes you?"

I scoff sharply, despite the fact that he's got that much right. But everything's changed now, because of *her.*

"I'm not interested in Hathaway anymore. I took this thing too far. I need to let it go."

Nate studies me. "I think you mean let her go. We're talking about Hathaway's woman, aren't we?"

Hathaway's woman. Melanie doesn't belong to him, not that she ever did. She couldn't have, not if she was able to kiss me the way she did. The way she melted under my touch scorched the truth of it into all my senses. Melanie Laurent is mine.

Damn it, she *should be* mine.

Maybe she could be, if only I were a different man. A better man.

"Just kill the fucking project, Nate."

"All right." He gives me a tight nod. "Consider it done."

"While you're at it," I add, when he turns to leave. "I need you to take care of something else for me, too."

I have a business checkbook in the desk. I take it out and hastily scrawl out a payment. I hold it out to Nate, daring him to mention the subtle tremor that make the paper tremble in my fingers.

He frowns as he takes the check from me and glances at Melanie's name and the figure representing the full amount of our agreement.

"You're cutting her loose, too?"

I drop the checkbook back in the drawer without

answering, then I get up from the chair behind the desk. "I need to get out of the city for a while. I'm thinking I'll spend the rest of the summer in Sagaponack, come back here in a few months. Maybe later."

A look of incredulity crosses Nate's expression. "Holy shit. You really must be falling for her."

Fuck, am I? It sounds ridiculous to hear him say it, yet the denial I want to lob back at him refuses to leave my mouth.

Am I attracted to her? No question. Do I want to be inside her so badly it makes me hard just thinking about it? Hell, yes.

Do I wish I had this whole fucked up situation to do all over again? Without a doubt.

But I haven't survived almost thirty-eight years of living by looking out for myself, only to get tangled up in a relationship that can only end one way--in disaster.

I can't let myself get any closer to Melanie so long as she's playing a part in the payback I wanted to wreak on Daniel Hathaway, and once she learns the truth about that, she'll never want anything to do with me again.

"Make sure that check reaches her ASAP," I growl at Nate. "I plan to wrap up the business I have here in the city, then be gone by the end of the week."

He gives me a grave nod. Before he can tell me what an asshole I am, or that I'm making a huge mistake letting Melanie go, a rap sounds on the doorjamb of my open study.

Gibson awkwardly clears his throat. "Excuse the interruption, gentlemen. Mr. Rush, you have an unannounced visitor waiting downstairs."

Just what I don't need right now.

"Not Alyssa Gallo, I hope." I frown, wondering

what kind of fire I'll need to put out for her this time.

"Ah, no, sir." Gibson looks even more uncomfortable, if that's possible. "It's Ms. Laurent. She's insisting that she see you at once."

Nate smirks at me, as if he doesn't give a damn that I'm his employer in addition to being his closest friend. I should fire the son of a bitch on the spot.

"Guess you'll be able to do your own dirty work on this one," he says, placing the folded check on the edge of my desk. "Good luck, sport."

As he strolls toward the door to make his escape, Melanie storms into the room without escort. She's dressed in a pink-and-white gingham waitress uniform with white-cuffed short sleeves and a skirt that ends just above her knees. Her light auburn hair is gathered into a high ponytail and her long, lean legs are wrapped in white tights and crepe-soled shoes.

It's not the sexiest outfit I've ever seen, yet my entire body ignites at the sight of her as though I've got gasoline in my bloodstream and Melanie Laurent is a lit match.

Desire surges through me, giving me an erection that strains the front of my dark jeans.

Just one more reason I need to cut her loose, and do it quick.

Her blue-gray eyes latch onto me the instant she steps inside. They're as dark as thunderclouds now, and I have to wonder how pissed she was when she set out to find me if she's still vibrating with fury now.

"Sorry, Gibson," she says, flicking an apologetic glance at my dutiful house manager. "I know you said to wait, but what I have to say to the arrogant bastard you work for won't take long."

The old man inclines his head as if she just told him she'd arrived for tea. And I would swear I detect the trace of a smile playing at the edge of his mouth in the second before he bobs his head in my direction, then hastily shuffles for the exit where he joins Nate.

The two men leave, closing the tall doors behind them.

At the soft click in their wake, Melanie charges forward. "What the hell do you think you're doing?"

"Until a few seconds ago, I thought I was having a private meeting with my attorney." I lean back against the edge of the desk, my hands braced on either side of me, mainly to combat the urge to go to her.

She advances until she's within arm's length of me. "You know damn well what I'm talking about."

Reaching into the small crossbody bag slung over her shoulder, she pulls out a folded paper and shoves it toward me. I catch the in-home nursing work order and calmly set it down on the desktop beside me.

My non-reaction only seems to anger her more. "You're unbelievable, Jared. What part of 'I don't want your charity' didn't you understand the other day?"

"As I recall, you said that about indulging a child with some sugary drinks. I didn't think the same rule would apply when it comes to providing your mother with a necessary service."

"It's not necessary," she fires back. "It's excessive. And you have no right."

"Maybe not, but I have the means. I'm sure your mother could use the care, and you can't do it all on your own." My voice gentles in the face of her outrage. "The point is, I didn't think you should have to do it all on your own, Melanie."

Some of the steam leaves her at that, but it's clear she's not ready to back down from this fight. "Again, you have no right to decide what I can or can't handle. When I said I didn't want your charity, I meant it." She folds her arms in front of her. "I'm going to pay you back. It may take a while, but I'm going to pay back every cent, Jared."

"It won't be necessary." I stand and turn to pick up the check I made out to her. "I have something else for you, too."

"What's this?" She eyes it warily, as if I'm handing her a lit fuse. When she reads the amount written on it, her gaze snaps back up to mine in question.

"I'm breaking our contract. Keep the full amount, or give your boyfriend his share. I leave that up to you."

"Daniel's not my boyfriend anymore. I broke up with him."

"When?" I don't even try to hide my surprise.

"Last weekend. The day after I was at your studio."

The day after we kissed and I made her come in my hand. "You didn't say anything about breaking up with Hathaway when I saw you at the hospital."

"You didn't ask."

"You didn't tell me later, either." Later, when she confessed she wanted me, too, and nearly invited me to do a lot more than just fondle her like a hormone-crazed schoolboy.

"Would it have mattered if I had told you? I think you would've left either way."

She's right. I would have gone no matter what. To save her from me.

To save myself, too.

"Why did you break it off with him?"

"Because I'd rather be alone than with someone I can't trust. He lied to me about his gambling and the trouble he's in. I think he's lied to me about countless little things since we met. How can I believe him about anything anymore?"

Her gaze pierces me, and I can see that she's also uncertain if she can trust me. I know the answer to that question, and although I would do anything to shelter her from hurt or harm, right now I also understand that I'm the biggest threat to her happiness.

"You made the right decision. Hathaway doesn't deserve you. He never did."

Before I try to rationalize my way into thinking I can do better, I turn away from her and walk around to the other side of the desk. I feel her eyes on me as I move. I feel her confusion, and her hurt.

"That's it? That's all you have to say to me?"

I meet her searching gaze from behind the safety of the barrier I've just placed between us. It's not easy to hold my resolve in the face of her wounded bewilderment.

"What more is there to say, Melanie? Our agreement is no longer in effect. I have no interest in finishing the painting."

"You mean, you're not interested in painting me anymore."

"Semantics," I reply, knowing it's cruel to let her think I'm as callous as I sound. It's for the best, though. Best for her and for me if she leaves now and never looks back. "You told me at the hospital you didn't intend to continue posing for me. I'm in agreement. I never should've proposed the arrangement in the first place."

She scoffs softly. "Oh, that's right. Because if you'd known about my fucked-up past, you would've had zero interest in me. I thought you only want to paint what's real, Jared. Everything else is a waste of your time and your talent. Isn't that what you said the night we first met right here in this room?"

"That is what I said," I admit tonelessly.

"I guess it's no fun for you now, is that it? There's nothing left of me to peel apart on your canvas, so you can't wait to discard me and move on to someone else."

Her brittle stare shreds me.

"You couldn't be more wrong."

"You want to know what I think? I think you're a fraud, Jared Rush. You're an isolated, lonely man. I think you get off on manipulating people, not only through your art but in your life, too. You relish exposing people's weaknesses only so you can convince yourself that you're superior. I think you surround yourself with beautiful women and wealthy friends, but you're always going to be that tragic, broken boy from Kentucky who's not going to heal no matter how rich or powerful he is."

Christ, her aim is accurate. Mercilessly sharp.

"You've seen through me from the beginning, haven't you?" A dry, humorless chuckle escapes me. "I can see through you, too, Ms. Laurent. You surround yourself with people who lack your strength because deep down, you need to feel needed, indispensable. Because you never want to feel like you don't matter again. You never want to feel like you can be thrown away by someone who should care about you. You never want to feel the way you did in the backseat of that speeding car as your father steered toward the guardrail."

She reels back, her lovely face slack with shock. "I

wish I'd never told you that." Her voice is nearly a whisper. Mutely, she shakes her head. "I wish I'd never met you."

The check I gave her is still clutched in her fingers. On a throttled cry, she tears the paper into confetti and casts it at me.

"Keep your fucking money, Jared. Keep your fucking pity, too. I don't want either one of them."

I've managed to hold myself in check since she stepped into the room, but I can't let her remark go. As she pivots around and starts for the door, I round the desk in only a couple of steps, catching her by the wrist.

"This has nothing to do with pity. That's the last thing I feel for you." My words are clipped and harsh, my teeth clenched with the force of my anger. "I'm ending this because everything you said about me is right. And I'm getting too close, too fast. I care about you, Melanie."

She gapes at me, a guarded look in her eyes. It takes everything I have not to reach up and smooth the wariness from the flattened line of her mouth.

"I had no intention of letting it happen, but it did."

She's silent for a long moment, then she shakes her head as if to deny what I'm saying, not only to me but to herself. "You must be drunk, Jared. Again."

She tries to pull out of my grasp, but I can't loosen my hold. "I haven't had a drop of alcohol in two full days. Not since the last time I saw you."

"I don't believe you."

"It's the truth."

Mistrust still darkens her gaze, but there is curiosity there, too. "Why are you telling me this?"

"I don't know. I guess I just . . . wanted you to know.

Maybe I needed to prove to myself I could get through a day without it. Maybe I wanted to prove it to you."

I step closer, when I should be stepping away. "It doesn't matter why, though, because I need to let you go."

She doesn't blink, doesn't take her eyes off me, as if she's facing a wild, lethal animal and isn't sure whether she wants to run or stand and fight. "You still have your hand on me, Jared."

I incline my head. "I do. Tell me to let go and I will."

She draws in a breath. "Is that what you want me to do?"

"It's what I should want." And yet my fingers contract even more, clamped around her delicate wrist like a shackle. I bring my other hand up to her face, helpless to keep from stroking my fingers along the velvety slope of her cheek. I curse, low under my breath. "I had myself convinced it was what I wanted, until you stormed in here all pissed off and looking sexy as hell."

Her gaze is still wary on me, but her lips quirk just a little. "You have a thing for pink gingham polyester and white tights?"

I scowl and pull her closer. "I have a thing for you, Ms. Laurent. In case you haven't noticed."

At the moment, it would be impossible for her not to notice. The hard-on she gave me on sight when she arrived hasn't abated at all. Now that there are scant inches to separate us, the heat of her nearness, the scent of her flushed skin and fragrant hair, sends all my faculties into overdrive.

I let my hand move down from the side of her face to the elegant column of her neck. She shivers, her breath leaving her in a soft, unsteady sigh. "I'm mad at you, Jared."

I smile against her heated skin. "I know, but you're still going to let me kiss you."

If she intends to deny it, the words are swept away by another quivery exhalation as I lower my head so I can taste the tender skin below her ear. She's sweet and warm against my parted lips, her quiet moan vibrating against my tongue. The curse I hiss through my gritted teeth is a dead giveaway for how close to the edge I am already with her.

I draw back and find her gaze heavy-lidded and simmering with the same desire that's streaking through me.

But there is a trace of mistrust in those storm-colored eyes, too. "Why did you leave the way you did the other day?"

"Wasn't it obvious?"

"I need you to tell me."

"You know the answer." My voice rumbles out of me in a growl. "Because after you kissed me, I knew if I didn't go there'd be no stopping what came next. No stopping this," I murmur, as I lower my head and cover her mouth with mine.

There's no resistance in her at all now, not in the way she melts deeper into my embrace, nor in the way she meets my kiss with equal, burning desire. Her arms move around me, one hand fisted in the fabric of my shirt at my back, the other reaching up to tangle in my loose hair.

The arousal that's owned me from the moment I first laid eyes on her weeks ago in my club now erupts in a need I can no longer deny.

I push my tongue past her parted lips on a snarl. She never should have come here--not with Hathaway that first night, not to pose for me in order to save the son of a bitch, and sure as hell not today, after I gave her a fighting chance to keep well enough away.

I still have time to put a stop to this. If I slam on the brakes and push her away now, I know she'll never be back. It's a thought I should reach for like a life line. Instead, I shove it away and fill my hands with more of Melanie's softness.

A tug of the elastic band holding her hair up brings the flame-hued waves tumbling down around my hand. I twist the silken mass around my fist and drag her closer, tipping her head back so my mouth can feast even more feverishly on hers.

She moans my name, her pulse galloping so hard I can feel it pound against my lips and every other place our bodies are melded together.

As hot as she looks in her little pink waitress uniform, I need it gone. I find the zipper behind her neck and draw it down, baring her from her tender nape to the small of her back.

"I want you naked," I mutter, my voice thick with need.

She helps me slide the one-piece dress off her shoulders and down the length of her beautiful body. The tights and shoes come off next, leaving her standing before me in just her modest white lace bra and panties.

As impatient as I am to have her beneath me, I take my time unwrapping the rest of her. A flick of my thumb frees the clasp of her bra, baring the pretty swells of her perfect breasts. I catch the fullness of one of them in my palm and bend my head to suckle the peaked nipple into my mouth. Her answering sigh is ragged, her groan anguished as I pull away.

I skim my hands along her sides, loving the way she trembles for me. I'm careful with the scar that runs along her rib cage, not because I think she's fragile, but because it reminds me of the strength and courage of the extraordinary woman who bears it.

I meet her gaze as I tenderly caress her, savoring the feel of her under my fingertips. "You're so beautiful, Melanie. Even here," I tell her, carefully tracing my thumb over the raised and ragged skin of the injury that might have killed her.

I feel her tense under my touch. She tries to flinch away from my tender exploration of her scars. "Jared, don't . . . not there."

"Look at me, sweetheart." I still until she finds the courage to obey my quiet command. "You're beautiful, Melanie. You're beautiful especially here, because you survived." With my free hand, I reach up and rest my palm along her cheek. "I've already got every gorgeous inch of you branded into my mind. I could paint you just from memory. Right now, though, I want to taste you."

"Jared . . ." A lost look fills her gaze, but her voice is filled with surrender.

I lower myself in front of her, until I've sunk to my knees. She makes a whimpering noise as I lean in and press a kiss to the scarred gash.

That whimper dissolves into a strangled cry when I move my mouth to the mound of her pussy and nip her over the top of the thin satin of her panties. The scent of her fills my nostrils, sweet and earthy and delicious.

And she's wet. I slip my fingers inside her panties, into the slick heat of her folds. A groan tears out of me, possessive and untamed. Hunger lashes at me, the scent and feel of her on my fingers making me drunk with the need to have my fill.

Touching her like this isn't enough. I need to feel her on my tongue. I move forward, burying my face in the musky sweetness of her. She gasps as I cleave into her pussy, licking and suckling, lapping at her like a cat in the cream.

Her pleasured, wordless cries mingle with the harsh sounds of our breathing. I want to make her scream. I want my whole damn house and half the city to know she's mine now. As of this moment, I refuse to think she will ever belong to any other man again.

"Jared. Oh, God."

The sound of my name voiced around a shuddery moan spurs me on. My mouth moves relentlessly against her tender flesh, my tongue dominating her clit until she's bucking against my face and the scream I need to hear from her suddenly boils out of her, wild and uncontained.

"I'm sorry," she gasps brokenly, her breathing ragged. "I've never made that sound before. I tried to hold it back, but I couldn't."

I grin up at her, my lips slick with her juices. "Darlin', don't ever apologize to me for that."

My hands are rough as I undress her the rest of the way. My breath saws out of my lungs, driven by the racing tempo of my heart. All the blood in my body seems to be flowing in the same direction, making me harder than I've ever been in my life.

My jeans feel like sandpaper against my engorged length. Sweat dampens my bespoke shirt.

My head is filled with a hundred damn good reasons why I should end this now, before things go any further.

Before I allow myself to need Melanie Laurent--to

want her in my life--any more than I already do.

Instead I rise to my feet. Cupping her nape in my firm grasp, I pull her to me for another kiss. Her nakedness sears me through my clothes. Her dusky, pleasured gaze still smolders with desire, reducing all my logic and good intentions to ashes.

Her lips curve playfully as she looks up at me. "How does it always end up that I'm the one standing naked all by myself with you, Mr. Rush?"

Before I can answer, she reaches up and begins unbuttoning my shirt. I don't realize I'm holding my breath until her hands slide underneath the opened front and onto my bare skin. Her touch is light, but sure. Explorative, but not shy.

If I imagined in the beginning that she was innocent because of her prim dresses and fresh-faced beauty, her hands on me now obliterate all those misgivings.

Her palms skim down my abdomen, fingertips tracing the ridges in a way that makes my cock jump in envious anticipation. She lifts on her toes to kiss me while her hands work my belt loose and unfasten the button of my jeans.

I groan in warning as the rasp of the loosening zipper vibrates through my every awakened nerve ending. Her hand slips inside, wrapping around my shaft. If lust were truly combustible I'd be nothing but cinders as she strokes my length, her eyes locked on mine.

"My friend Paige says you're a deviant," she murmurs as she moves her hand up and down on me. "She says she's heard you have orgies right here in your house. Is she right?"

The questions are unexpected, and too much to contend with so long as she's touching me. I scowl, gritting my teeth against the delicious friction of her hand all over my cock. "Is this your idea of torturing a confession out of me?"

She arches her brows. "Would it work?"

"Oh, yeah."

She smiles in response, but then her hand slowly stills. Her touch leaves me, her eyes turning serious. "So, is it true?"

I can't lie to her. I can't pretend I've been a saint when my reputation and my art both speak volumes to the contrary. "Not for a long time."

"How long, Jared?"

"About a year or so." Not coincidentally, around the same time the tremors in my hand became too frequent to ignore. I've been pulling back from everything I used to be, retreating into a self-imposed isolation. I'd almost had myself convinced I was comfortable there. Then I saw her. "What are you really asking me, Melanie?"

She swallows. "I know you've been with a lot of women. I know you probably still are--"

"I'm not. If you're asking how long it's been since I've been with anyone else, it was well before I first laid eyes on you. And there's been no one after."

"Not even Alyssa?"

I chuckle, not only because I hear a note of jealousy in the question, but also because the very idea is so far beyond the realm of possibility I can't help but laugh.

"Why is that so funny?"

"Alyssa Gallo is seventeen years old. She's a student in an art program I sponsor at one of Dominic Baine's rec centers in Chelsea."

"Oh." She frowns, shaking her head. "But that first morning I came here, you let me believe--"

"I only let you believe what you wanted to about me. I thought it would've been easier if you despised me."

I'm lost staring down into her desire-drenched, questioning eyes. All those reasons and rationales I had for inflicting harm on Daniel Hathaway by taking what he cherished most fell away after the first day she showed up to pose for me. The game I was so certain I could master had slipped out of my control before I'd even realized it.

"I thought if you despised me it would be easier for me not to feel anything for you." My hand moves up to caress her exquisite face. "I was wrong about that, Melanie. I've been wrong about everything when it comes to you."

Pulling her closer, I take her mouth in a slow, passionate kiss. Despite the wild gallop of my heart, and the lust that's spurring into me with every hard beat of my pulse, I don't hurry. I want her dizzy with pleasure before I'm finished with her.

I want her to understand all the things I can't summon the courage to say.

That I'm sorry for how we started out.

That I wish I were a better, more deserving man.

If I can't tell her with words, I can tell her with pleasure.

And in that way, I intend to leave no shred of doubt.

24

"Come with me," he says, threading his fingers through mine after his deep, infinitely thorough kiss leaves me out of breath and boneless with need.

I'm too eager to feel his mouth on me again to question what he has in mind. With my hand in his, he starts walking further into the immense study, toward the ornate mahogany millwork of the rear wall. It's not until I see the discreet crystal doorknob that I realize there's a doorway cut into the dark, polished wood.

Jared opens it, revealing another large space. Inside this room is a huge king-size bed with four thick posters at the corners. Luxurious silk fabric in rich, masculine shades of bronze, burgundy, and cream cover both the bed and the walls. The room is decadent, yet classic, a fitting backdrop for the ruggedly gorgeous man standing in it now.

I give him an arch look. "A bedroom connected to

your study? How convenient. I don't suppose I want to know how often your conversations start in the other room and end up in here."

He smirks. "This house has twenty bedrooms. I've never seen the benefit of this one until right now."

Reaching past me, he closes the door behind us. His fingers light gently under my chin, tilting my face up for another of his soul-melting kisses.

"Where'd we leave off?" he murmurs, his teeth gently nipping my lower lip as he draws back to look at me. Desire smolders in his whisky-dark eyes. "Oh, yeah. I remember. I was just about to make you scream again."

He takes my face in both his hands, then claims my mouth in a consuming kiss that's even more possessive than the ones that have come before. I can taste his wild need, his unspoken demand. I taste myself in his kiss, too. The sweetness that lingers on his lips only heightens my arousal. My core pulses with every commanding thrust of his tongue, my nerve endings alive with electricity.

Still kissing me, Jared uses his body to guide me backward, inching us toward the massive bed. I sink into his strength, his masterful domination of my body and my will. Dimly, I remind myself this is the same dangerous, enigmatic man I met a week ago. The same arrogant, merciless artist whose reputation is as debauched as his paintings.

I can't pretend Jared is none of those things, but I've glimpsed another side of him, too. A raw, tormented side of him that I feel instinctively he shares with no one. We're alike in that way. We're alike in more ways than I ever could have imagined.

And then, there is this side of him.

Passionate. Commanding.

Devastatingly seductive.

With our kiss unbroken, his strong hands tremble a bit as they leave my face to roam down the front of me. I'm dizzy with desire, hot all over, my skin aching and overheated as he caresses my naked breasts.

I cling to him, moaning as he lightly pinches my sensitive nipples while greedily devouring my mouth.

His name is a harsh whisper that gusts out of me as another orgasm begins to boil inside me. I'm drenched between my thighs, both from the climax he gave me in the other room and from the unbearable need to have him inside me.

I need him there now. I want him inside me so desperately, I can hardly stand the waiting.

"Jared." I gasp his name as his mouth breaks from mine and descends my throat.

He dips his tongue into the sensitive notch at the base of my neck while his hands caress me with increasing urgency. His palms curve around my backside. He squeezes my ass, parting me, kneading me as his mouth trails fire onto my breasts.

He drags me closer, mashing our hips together. The ridge of his erection feels enormous against my abdomen, the grinding of his pelvis stoking delicious pressure that speeds my pulse and leaves me quivering in his arms.

His low growl vibrates through me as he slides his fingers between my thighs, giving me just a taste of what I really crave. Penetrating me with one digit, he rolls his thumb over my clit until I'm writhing against his palm and nearly out of my mind with sensation.

I need to touch him, too. I reach between us and feel

him as firm as granite, bulging in the unzipped vee of his jeans. I squeeze and stroke his shaft over his straining boxer briefs, reveling in the power that surges against my palm and fingers.

His answering groan only inflames me more. I slide my hand inside to feel the immensity of his arousal. He is a thick column of satin-wrapped heat and power in my hand, hard and pulsing. A bead of slick fluid drips from the crown of his shaft. It coats my fingers as I caress him, creating a wet friction that makes him thrust and surge even harder in my grasp.

"Fuck," he rasps lifting his head to the side of my neck while I run my hand up and down his length. A shudder racks him, his hips bucking in response to my touch. "I need to find a condom. Now."

He takes my mouth in a hard, fast kiss, then breaks away from me on a curse. My legs are practically useless at this point, so I sit on the edge of the bed and watch, breath heaving and heart racing, as he pivots to the nightstand and pulls open the top drawer to rummage inside.

"I thought you never use this room." I sound like I'm sulking, and maybe I am a little.

Jared doesn't look up from his search of the drawer. "I don't use it, but Gibson's in charge of the household staff and inventory, and the man runs a tight ship." He pauses, swiveling back to face me with several foil packets in his fingers and a wolfish grin on his handsome face. "Remind me to give the old guy a raise."

His eyes scorch me as he stands there for a moment and drinks me in.

"Don't move," he orders, his deep voice husky with arousal.

225

He tosses the condoms on the nightstand then paces back to where I wait for him. My thighs are slightly parted and my hands are braced behind me on the mattress to hold my balance. Jared stands between my knees, heat and desire pouring off him. He reaches down and spreads me wider, until I am open completely to his fevered gaze.

"Christ, you're beautiful."

He strokes my inner thighs, his fingers rasping over my tender skin, leaving a trail of goosebumps in their wake. There is a slight shake in his right hand as he caresses me, but his touch is there and gone almost before I even notice it. With my sex entirely exposed to him, he lowers himself in front of me.

"I'm going to make you scream again when I fuck you," he utters as he leans in to nip at my inner thigh. "But first I need another taste of this gorgeous pussy."

"Oh, God." My moan stretches out as his mouth presses into my wet cleft. His beard-shadowed face is a delicious abrasion, contrasted by the slick, soft strokes of his tongue and lips.

I feel unhinged, adrift in a pleasure I've never known before.

I've never known the need to surrender completely to a man, yet that's all I can do as Jared feasts on me with toe-curling passion and a ferocity that sends my pulse into a breakneck pace. His mouth is greedy, possessive, an overwhelming force that sets off a shockwave of sensation rocketing through my body.

I whimper, thrashing under the skill of his talented mouth. It's too much, and I'm too near the edge already. I arch back, my spine bowing as Jared sucks my clit between his teeth and teases it with his tongue.

"Jared, oh God, it feels too good. If you don't stop, I'm going to break . . ."

His wicked mouth shows me no mercy whatsoever. Thank God.

I can't halt the orgasm that roars up on me. I can't slow it down for a second. Pleasure ripples from my clit to my core. I am molten, every fiber of my being splintering in bright shards that erupt in a sea of dizzying stars behind my closed eyelids.

Jared makes a low, animal sound while I come against his mouth. It's the sexiest thing I've ever heard. He rains more kisses on my quivering sex, giving my cleft a long, slow lick of his tongue before he rises up between my sagging legs.

I open my eyes, feeling drugged and unraveled. "That was . . ."

"Just the beginning," he snarls, staring at me hungrily from under the slashes of his brows.

His hooded gaze is primal and ravenous, his face taut with barely contained control as his hands move roughly to remove the shirt I've already unbuttoned. He tosses it aside, revealing bronzed broad shoulders and a muscular chest that tapers to an equally mouth-watering abdomen.

It's all I can do not to drool as I watch him undress for me.

His jeans and shoes go next, followed by the dark boxer briefs that barely contain his impressive cock. When he's naked, I simply stare at the perfection of him. Not a flaw or a blemish on his sculpted body, no hideous scars like the one that mars the side of me.

Subconscious now, I glance away from him, knowing he can have his pick of any woman in this entire city. Probably any woman in the world. Why he chose me--not only for his painting, but here and now--I can't begin to imagine.

"Hey." His low voice cuts into the doubts spiraling through my mind. He lifts my face on the edge of his hand, staring down at me with solemn, smoldering eyes. "Wherever you went just now, don't. There's only you and me in this room. I want your full attention, Ms. Laurent."

"You have it." I let go of a breathless laugh. "After what you just did to my body, I'm not going to be thinking about anything else for days."

"Days." He smirks. "That's all? Darlin', you're not leaving this bed until I'm sure you'll be thinking about me seventy years from now."

Pushing me down onto my back on the bed, he prowls on top of me, taking my mouth in a blazing hot kiss as he covers me with the delicious weight of his body. He feels so good, and I'm so filled with yearning to have him inside me, I can't resist moving beneath him.

"Now, Jared," I pant against his mouth. "Please."

He chuckles, deep in his throat, breaking away only long enough to reach for one of the condoms and tear it open with his teeth. He shifts to the side and rolls the protection on with one hand while I delight myself in stroking the hard contours of his back and firm ass.

After suiting up, he reaches between my legs and torments me some more, teasing my clit and sinking two fingers inside me while he scorches my mouth with another deep, soul-melting kiss.

I moan in complaint when he releases me, but my protest only lasts for a moment. He moves his hips, aligning the broad head of his erection with the opening of my body. Then he pushes inside, inch by glorious inch, a measured thrust that seems to cleave me in two, stretching my tender walls to their limits.

"Ah, fuck," he rasps, his voice strangled against my ear. "You're so tight, sweetheart. You feel so fucking good. Tell me I'm not hurting you."

I shake my head, incapable of words. The fullness of him inside me twines with the soaring sensation in my chest as he begins to move, invading then drawing back, his strokes building with each motion.

I writhe beneath him shamelessly, arching to take the full measure of every thrust of his body within mine. I'm molten for him, and unable to contain the pleasure ratcheting through me.

"Jared." His name boils out of me on a low moan as I bring my legs up around his hips to take him even deeper. "Jared, please . . . fuck me harder."

He growls a wordless sound of agreement and the careful control he showed me a moment ago burns away. I hold on to his shoulders as he drives home, impaling me with long, urgent strokes. Our tempo is fierce, frenzied.

I close my eyes as I start to splinter around him. My breath is galloping, my panting moans building into another wild scream I can hardly bite back.

"Look at me," he commands me hoarsely.

I lift my lids and find him watching me, his breathing ragged as he crashes into me, pushing me toward the crest of an impossibly steep wave.

"Look at me," he says again, more forcefully now. "I want you to see me when you come. I want to hear you say my name."

"Jared," I gasp, consumed by the feel of him. My climax twists ever tighter, driven by the fierce look in his dark eyes as he watches pleasure break over me.

The scream I can no longer contain claws its way out of my throat, and yes, it's his name I call out.

He is all I see, all I feel, everything I never dared to want.

"Jared." I shudder beneath him as the pleasure rocks me. "Oh God, Jared."

His gaze is wild now, matched by the ferocity of his desire. I can feel it pounding through him. His heartbeat is like thunder. His cock surging, battering me, as if he can't get close enough, can't bury himself deep enough.

On a taut snarl, he shifts his position, caging my head between his bent forearms, his fists tangling in my hair. I am riveted to his heated eyes, and to the intensity of his expression as he fucks me.

We are joined intimately, but the connection of our gazes is profoundly deeper. It sears me, branding into me the truth of what I sensed the moment I stepped into Jared Rush's study and everything else crumbled away. He's owned me from the instant our eyes met that night.

He knows it, and in a stunned corner of my own consciousness, I know that I've owned him since that moment, too.

"Melanie." He says my name through gritted teeth like a curse, all his focus locked on me. His strokes grow more untamed, his tempo relentless. I reach down between us to feel the power of him as he thrusts into me. He groans my name again, and this time it sounds like a prayer.

He lowers his mouth to mine and plunders my lips, his tongue echoing the rhythm of his driving hips. It's too much for me to withstand when I'm still lit up like a live wire. I move against him, greedily chasing another climax.

"That's it," he rasps into my mouth. "Give it all to me, baby."

I have no choice but to surrender to the pleasure erupting within me. And Jared gives me no mercy. Holding onto him is like holding onto a storm. He is powerful and overwhelming, electric and unstoppable.

And all the while, he's looking at me as if I'm the one pulling him under, consuming him.

Maybe we're both falling too much, too fast. God knows, I've felt the terror of losing myself to him every time we've been together. Being with Jared like this, feeling him buried so deep inside me I can no longer tell where he leaves off and I begin, there is no room for fear.

If that makes me a naive fool, I can't even summon the will to regret it.

Jared growls my name and I come on a jagged cry, tumbling helplessly into oblivion. He follows me an instant later, his harsh shout gusting hot against the curve of my neck and shoulder as his big body convulses with the force of his release.

25

MELANIE

For a long while afterward, neither of us moves. Jared kisses me again and again, his hands rough in my hair, infinitely gentle when he caresses the side of my face. I encircle my arms around his shoulders, not yet ready for our connection to end. Maybe he feels the same way, because instead of pulling out of me, he rolls onto his back, taking me with him until I'm settled over the top of him.

His heart thuds heavily beneath my cheek as he strokes my bare shoulder. We lie in contented silence, suspended in a moment neither one of us seems eager to break. His erection is still firm inside me, still pulsing with aftershocks. I don't want him to withdraw, but eventually Jared kisses the top of my head and moves to get rid of the spent condom in the adjacent bathroom.

I hear the water run in the sink for a moment, followed by the soft hiss of the shower turning on. He strides back out to the bedroom like a big cat on the prowl, all gorgeous muscles and athletic motion. His mussed, golden-brown hair completes the effect, grazing his broad shoulders like a wind-tossed mane.

He meets my appreciative gaze and gives me a slow, lopsided smirk. "That looks says you'll be thinking about me for more than a few days."

He's right, and I don't even try to contain my satisfied smile. "So arrogant, Mr. Rush."

"Confident," he counters, grinning now. "Big difference."

"Mm, so I see." My eyes travel to the jutting, bare length of him as he approaches me on the edge of the bed. His erection grows even harder in the few steps it takes for him to reach me. I want to lick him so badly, I practically groan. "Jared, I should go."

"Go?" Frowning down at me, he palms the back of my skull, his strong fingers playing in my loose hair. "Darlin', I'm not even close to finished with you yet. Besides, if you were on your way to work, you're already late."

God, I'm tempted. I look up at his devilish gaze and shake my head. "A coworker picked up my shift. It's my mom I'm worried about. I should be with her."

"She's got someone with her," he reminds me. "I reviewed the nurse's credentials myself before the agency sent her over. They assure me Rosa's the best they have on staff."

"Jared, about that . . ." I slide off the mattress to stand with him. "I appreciate the gesture, but what just happened between us doesn't change my mind. I can't accept your help with my mom's care. I'm going to pay you back."

"I won't take your money. Not before I was inside

you, and sure as fuck not after." He kisses me as if the matter is settled. "Come on. You can argue with me some more in the shower."

I follow him into the bathroom, then into the glass-walled shower that's already filled with billowing steam. We don't continue our argument under the warm spray overhead, but instead take our time soaping each other. We kiss and stroke every inch of each other's bodies until the water runs cold and we've both come multiple times.

It wouldn't have taken much convincing at all for him to get inside me again, but the fact that he didn't even try without the benefit of protection only makes me want him more now that we're out of the shower.

With a towel fastened around his trim hips, Jared wraps me in another one, then draws me against him. I am blissfully caged within the circle of his strong arms as he brushes his lips over mine in a tender, yet hungry kiss. He groans as he pulls back, both of us breathing heavily. I feel boneless and loose, but he's a coil of tension against me, the ridge of his cock nudging into my hip.

"I knew you were going to be a problem for me," he murmurs as he stares down into my heavy-lidded eyes. "I just didn't realize how much. I can't get enough of you, Ms. Laurent."

My smile is slow, seeming to curl up from the very center of my being. "That's only going to be a problem if you think I'll be able to get enough of you."

He arches a brow. "You will, eventually. I'm still the same insufferable prick I was when we met. The only difference is, now I know how to make you come."

"Yes, you do." I want to keep the moment playful

and light, but I've never been more serious in my life. "You've ruined me for anyone else, Jared. I knew it that first night I came here with Daniel. I wanted to despise you, but instead I just . . . *wanted you.*"

He makes a low, approving sound in the back of his throat, his gaze burning with desire and a fierce tenderness that astonishes me. "You are unlike any woman I've ever met. So genuine and honest. Tenacious and loyal. Stubborn as hell, too."

"So I've heard, once or twice," I admit, smiling.

"And you're beautiful," he adds, reaching up to caress the side of my cheek in his palm. "You're more than beautiful, Melanie. Your goodness glows from inside. You take my fucking breath away."

A soaring kind of warmth opens up in my chest at his words, and at the earnest way he says them. His name is a sigh, my breast too full with emotion to form any true sound. I turn my face into his gentle hand, pressing my lips to the center of his palm. I can feel the throb of his pulse there, beating strong and heavy.

But I feel something else, too.

His fingers tremble against my cheek. More than tremble, they're shaking.

He draws his hand away from me, letting it fall slowly down at his side.

"Jared." I look at him in alarm, realizing the tremors I noticed in his hand when we were making love and that I dismissed in the heat of the moment were something more than I thought as well.

I reach for his hand, but he moves it behind him.

"Don't, Melanie." His deep voice is clipped, toneless. "It's nothing."

"No, it isn't," I reply, cautiously because I can see

how ready he is to deny it. To shut me out completely.

I can't let him do that. Not now, when I've let him into my body, into my heart.

"What's wrong with your hand, Jared? Please, let me see."

His eyes hold me in an inscrutable stare, bleak and unblinking. I can see him wrestling with the decision to let me in, debating whether he can trust me. Like a wild animal caught in a snare, he watches me, coiled and ready to lash out.

"It's okay," I assure him. "Let me see."

He stands so still I don't even hear him breathing as I reach down and take his strong hand in my grasp. The spasm has worsened, affecting not only his fingers and hand but vibrating up the muscled length of his forearm.

"It'll pass in a few minutes," he murmurs, his eyes still trained on me. Searching for cracks in my reaction, I have no doubt. The way he stares at me, it's as if he's waiting for me to shrink back and turn away. Or daring me to. "Early onset Parkinson's disease, in case you're curious. A little DNA parting gift from my old man."

The explanation hits me like a physical blow. Not because I consider it a death sentence, but because it's immediately, painfully, obvious to me what that kind of diagnosis means to someone like Jared.

"My father's tremors came on around the same age as mine, so I guess I shouldn't have been surprised." He shrugs. "I had my first noticeable symptom a couple of years ago. Blew the shaking off as a consequence of too many bad habits and a few too many long nights in places I shouldn't have been. But it wasn't just one time. It kept coming back. Kept getting worse and more frequent, until I couldn't ignore reality anymore."

I'm amazed he's still allowing me to hold his hand while it shakes in my light grasp. That edge of wariness hasn't left his sober gaze, though, and I wonder what it must cost a strong, larger than life man like Jared Rush to be forced to confront this kind of mortal vulnerability.

I want to apologize for what he's going through, but I know he doesn't want my sympathy. I'm not even sure he'd accept it.

What's more, every time I've looked into his haunted brown eyes I could tell that he's been through far worse than any physical challenge could ever pose. I bear my scars on the outside of my body. Jared's are buried deep.

And now, this.

"Two years ago," I whisper, glancing away from his gaze to look at the elegant fingers that are normally so in control, so brilliantly gifted. The tremors are small, but bad enough to make holding a pencil difficult, never mind a paintbrush. "That's why you stopped painting. I accused you of letting alcohol interfere with your art, but that wasn't the problem, was it?"

"No," he says. "I had myself convinced the drinking helped smooth out the shaking. Sometimes, it did. But drinking's only given me an excuse to ignore the truth."

"Can you paint at all?"

"On good days I can. Those are becoming fewer and fewer all the time."

"But you were willing to pay me to pose for you."

He nods, and I'm not sure if the regret I see in his eyes is because of his declining ability to pursue his art or something else.

"I thought I could give it up." He reaches up with his other hand, the one that's steady and infinitely gentle as he sweeps his thumb across my lips. "I likely would have walked away from my art for good, but then I saw you."

I can't pretend it doesn't move me to hear him say that. Yet it confuses me, too. "Today you said you weren't interested in painting me anymore."

"That's right."

"Why not?"

"Because it was a mistake to drag you into my problems."

I shake my head. "You don't hear me complaining, do you? After all, it brought us here."

A growl rumbles in the back of his throat as I lift his afflicted hand up to my lips and kiss his clenched fingers. He doesn't pull away, but I can see him retreating emotionally. He wants to say more, but something holds him back. His gaze is shadowing over like a door being slowly closed.

As much as I want to coax all his secrets out of him, I know him enough to understand that if I push too hard, he'll only close that door even tighter.

"Maybe you were right," he says gruffly. "You should go home now."

"Don't do that. Don't shut me out." I let go of his hand and reach for his handsome face instead, framing his whiskered jaw in my hands. My gaze implores him to see me, to let me in. "Please don't act like you want me gone. Don't act like you want to be alone when it seems to me you've been alone for most of your life."

"Alone?" He chuckles humorlessly as he lowers my hands. "Look around you, darlin'. I'm surrounded by people."

"How many of them know about your tremors? Does your lawyer know? Seems like you and Nathan

Whitmore are good friends, but I'll bet he's got no idea. What about Gibson?"

Jared nods now, a wry twist to his mouth. "He's the only one. I used to send the old man out for my prescriptions, back when I was still taking them. But I think he knew even before then. He notices too much, rather like someone else I know."

"He cares about you," I tell him gently. "Like someone else you know."

His gaze searches mine for a long moment. He wets his lips, then leans forward and gives me a heartbreakingly tender kiss. "Finish drying off and get dressed. I'm going to take you home."

He turns away from me and grabs another towel from the rack. I watch as he runs it roughly over his damp hair. His movements are tight and aggressive, not only due to the tremors that still have a hold on him. He's retreating from something more than just me. I can practically see the talons of his past sinking into him.

"You said your father came down with early onset Parkinson's, too. Was that how he--"

"Died?" Jared finishes for me when I break off. There's something cold in his eyes when he swivels a glance at me. "No, it wasn't the Parkinson's that killed him. It was the shotgun he put under his chin the day the bank sent their foreclosure letter on our horse farm."

"Oh, my God. Jared . . . I'm so sorry."

"Shit happens, right?" On a heavy exhalation, he tosses down the towel he used to dry his hair. "I only wish I'd been able to keep my mother from running in behind me after we heard the blast from inside the house."

I close my eyes, trying not to imagine the horror of

that moment. "Why would he do something like that to both of you? He had to know the pain it would cause."

"He had his own pain. First the disease that was slowly devouring him, then the shame of losing everything he and my mother had worked for."

"But that wasn't his fault," I point out, recalling that Jared relayed some of the story to me at his studio. "He was cheated in a Ponzi scheme."

"Yes, he was. Although I imagine that was cold comfort to him during the months when the creditors were clawing at the door and all my parents' rich society friends turned their backs to avoid being tainted by the scandal." Jared shakes his head. "My dad ran the farm his whole adult life. His investments were supposed to carry us once he became too weak to work. The really fucked up thing about a Ponzi scheme is that it takes years to perfect. Years of deliberate, calculated deception. It starts with a lie to build trust, and then the one running the game keeps those lies coming, building on one another. The bastard who got to Dad knew he was sick, so he preyed on my father's fears of leaving his family behind to fend without him."

My heart aches to consider it. It aches for Jared, too, because he's lived with this pain and loss for so long.

"I was twelve," he says, "old enough to recall the day my father brought Denton Sweeney to our house. He wore a nice suit and polished shoes, and his brand-new Bentley had New York license plates. Mom didn't appear to like him much, but my dad seemed to hang on every slick word that came out of his mouth. After Sweeney left, he called the house at least once a month. Seemed like Dad was always going to the bank for one thing or another. In the beginning, he was cashing in proceeds from Sweeney's investments every other week. They were big checks, so Dad kept investing more and more. Apparently, he trusted Sweeney so much, he finally staked the farm, too. The scheme went on for more than two years before some other men in nice suits and cars with New York license plates showed up at the farm to talk to my father. These men also had FBI badges."

"Sweeney was found out?"

Jared scoffs under his breath. "Not until after he was dead. He had a stroke on the toilet in his 5th Avenue apartment. It took a couple of weeks before the overdrafts started piling up and his clients started to wonder what was going on. By the time the authorities started sniffing around, Sweeney's wife had fled the country with their young son and all the money Denton had stolen from more than two dozen investors. The pair were never located, not for lack of trying."

I close my eyes, appalled by the brazenness--the sheer cruelty--of the crime. "And all the people Denton Sweeney cheated, people like your father, who just wanted to take care of their families--they had no way to get their money back?"

Jared shakes his head. "It was all gone. Unfortunately, for us, that also included the farm and all our horses."

"Jared, I'm so sorry." I go to him. Whether or not he wants my comfort, I need to be near him. I need to touch him and let him know that I'm here, that I care about him--so profoundly, it's an ache filling my chest. He doesn't flinch away from the hand I lay tenderly on his shoulder. "How did you and your mom get through all of that?"

"Not easily," he admits, his deep voice low and raspy. "Mom sank into an immediate tailspin. The awful way he died, the financial worries, our eviction from the farm . . . it all weighed on her, more than she could bear."

"At the hospital, you told me she drank and smoked."

He nods. "That didn't start until after we lost everything. It was a blood clot that stopped her heart, but I think she went downhill so fast because her heart was broken. She just . . . gave up."

"What about you? You were so young. It couldn't have been easy for you, either."

He shrugs, as if his pain was inconsequential. "I couldn't give up. I had my mom to look after."

"Didn't she or your father have any family who could help you?"

"Mom had a sister, but my aunt wanted nothing to do with her after the farm was lost. Dad was an only child from the other side of the tracks. All they had was each other."

"And you."

"I wasn't enough reason to make my mother live," he states flatly. "She used to draw and paint from time to time, but she had no interest in art after Dad was gone. The only work she knew was on the farm. I tried to earn money around town, but there's only so much a fourteen-year-old kid can do."

I reach up and smooth some of the damp tendrils of hair away from his furrowed brow. "I can't imagine how hard it was for you." I had my struggles growing up, but at least I had my mom and Jen. Jared had no one. "When we were at your studio, you said you left Lexington and came to New York when you were sixteen."

"The day after I buried my mom, I spent my last few dollars on a bus ticket and never went back."

"Did you know anyone in the city?"

"No."

"How did you get by all by yourself? This isn't an easy place to navigate as an adult, let alone a boy on his own at sixteen."

"I did what I had to. Some of it was even legal."

"And the rest?"

Those shadows that so often lurk in his eyes are there again as he meets my questioning gaze. I don't want to guess at the things he might've had to do in order to survive, but the only thing worse than guessing is hearing Jared confirm my dread.

"The only things of value I had were my wits and my body. I used both."

"Is that how you met Kathryn Tremont?" I'm aware of his affection for the wealthy socialite who'd been both his lover and his friend over the years, but part of me will never forgive her if she preyed upon Jared when he was at his most vulnerable. "Did she pay you for sex?"

"No. She pulled me out of that world. Nate actually made it happen. He knew her before I did, and he persuaded Kathryn to let me live at the mansion and earn my keep in other ways. Art turned out to be one of them. She was a collector, also a patron for new talent. She helped me get my start, introduced me to the right people and made sure my work was shown in the right galleries."

My hackles smooth a bit, concern replaced by a feeling of gratitude for the woman I'll never know. "I'm glad she was there for you. God knows, you needed someone to lean on after everything you'd gone through,

Jared."

The words come out a little choked, and he frowns at me.

"Christ, don't look at me like that. Do not feel sorry for me. Pity's the last thing I want to see on your beautiful face."

"I don't pity you or feel sorry for you. I care for you, Jared."

God help me, it's more than that. This feeling that's been growing inside me goes deeper than simple affection. Deeper than the desire that consumes me every time I'm near this man, or the longing I feel when we're apart.

It's so engulfing, it terrifies me.

And as I hold his searching gaze, I glimpse a trace of that same stark alarm in Jared's eyes, too.

"You deserve more than I can ever give you," he says softly. He raises his hand and I feel the tremors as he lightly caresses my face. The shaking has lessened since we've been talking, reduced to a small tremble in his fingertips. He exhales, his sensual mouth twisted with regret. "Nothing's going to cure it. There won't be some miracle to fix me. Not even you."

"I'm not looking to fix you, Jared. I'm just trying to be your friend. And I don't turn my back on the people I care about."

"No, you don't," he says, his gaze moving from my eyes to my parted lips. "You make me wish I were a better man, Melanie."

Lifting up on my toes, I cup the back of his strong neck and bring his head down to meet my kiss. I take my time, savoring the feel of his mouth on mine, tasting the hunger in him that erupts on a low growl as I sweep my tongue inside to tease his. He encircles me in his arms, pulling me against the firmness of his muscled body and the very clear evidence of his arousal.

When I draw back to catch my breath, he groans, his gaze hot with desire.

I run my fingers through his thick hair, on fire with need for him all over again. "If you were any better, Jared, I'd never want to leave your bed."

His mouth curves. "That can be arranged." Reaching down, he grabs my ass in both hands and grinds his erection into my abdomen. "In fact, let's start that plan immediately. As I mentioned, there are twenty bedrooms in this house. I think you should see all of them."

I laugh, despite the heaviness of everything he's just shared with me. Neither one of us can change our pasts or the people who hurt us, but we're here. We've both survived.

And, at least for now, we have each other.

He kisses me again, melting away what little resistance I have when it comes to him.

"I'm serious," he murmurs against my lips. "I don't want to let you go."

"Rosa only works until five," I remind him.

"I'll pay her overtime. I'll move her into your house."

I smile and shake my head. "I have a class in the morning."

"I have internet. You can take it online."

Laughter bursts out of me as he holds me in the circle of his arms and the overwhelming intensity of his hungered gaze. Dipping his head to the side of my neck, he kisses a trail of fire from my ear to my shoulder.

A shivery sigh slips past my lips. "You're very

persuasive, Mr. Rush."

"You have no idea." A nip on the tender curve of my neck sends need spiraling through my veins. "I need you in my bed now, Ms. Laurent."

I moan. "Persuasive and extremely bossy, too."

He draws back, grinning as he shakes his head. "Confident."

"Oh, that's right." I reach down, taking his erection in my hand. "Big difference."

"Yes, it is." One of his brows wings up over his blistering gaze.

It's all the warning I get. In the next instant, my feet leave the ground and I'm suddenly tossed over his shoulder in a caveman hold and he carries back out to the waiting bed.

26

JARED

Eventually, I did have to let Melanie escape from my bed and take her home for the evening.

My hunger for her has hardly abated by the next day as I wait in the lobby of the university building to pick her up after her morning class. I'm earlier than I'd planned, having spent the first part of the morning at the house, meeting with Alyssa about her court documents and all the other things the teenage mother-to-be will need to consider when it comes to mapping out a future for her and her child.

Not that I'm anyone who should be offering advice on life. My own has been fucked up for so long, I'm not even sure I know what a normal, happy future would look like. All I know is, right now, I want my days and nights filled with a certain fiery-haired, stubborn beauty who makes me feel more alive than I have at any other time in my whole existence.

My chest constricts at the sight of Melanie walking

into the lobby from her class. She's dressed in white jeans and sandals and an off-the-shoulder top, her hair tumbling loose in a coppery cascade down her back. She looks fresh and innocent, but everything male in me flares hot when I think about all the deliciously dirty ways we enjoyed each other less than twenty-four hours ago.

A small group of classmates surround her as they approach the lobby exit, all of them chatting and laughing over something one of them said. While the other young women are attractive enough, I only have eyes for the beauty at the center of the small gaggle. As her friends break off to go their separate ways, Melanie spots me and her entire face lights up with a bright smile.

Christ, she's gorgeous.

The power of all that joy aimed at me is almost too much to bear. Still, I greedily soak it up, reveling in the way this woman can make me feel like a fucking god just by looking at me.

The bigger miracle is that she can make me feel that way in spite of the reality that I'm nothing if not physically, pathetically, human. She's seen the weakness I've hidden from nearly everyone close to me, yet it hasn't seemed to dim how she views me.

The affection in her eyes wraps around me like silk bonds, a connection I haven't truly earned. Guilt over that fact still claws at me after everything we shared yesterday. It was selfish and cowardly to keep the truth from her in the beginning. All the worse to keep it from her yesterday, too. But no matter how I tried to frame the explanation she needs to hear, the words stayed jammed in my throat.

Even though I know delaying the inevitable will only

make things worse, there is a part of me that would like nothing more than to put the entire matter of Daniel Hathaway behind me and forget I ever heard his name.

Melanie's smile only grows as she nears me. "You're early."

"You're beautiful." I cup her nape and drag her to me for a kiss I've been waiting hours to claim. "Ready to go?"

She gazes up at me with her lip caught between her teeth. "More than ready."

I take the book-laden tote off her shoulder and lead her out to my waiting car. When I open the Aston Martin's passenger door for her, she peers into the backseat at the bags of fresh produce and meats I picked up on the way, then shoots me a quizzical look. "What's all this?"

"Lunch."

I drive us to a private airport nearby, where the small plane I've chartered is already fueled up with the pilot waiting for us. She doesn't hide her surprise, nor her relief that we'll be making the flight to my Hamptons house in something other than a helicopter.

"You didn't do this for me, did you?"

"I did." I kiss her again, groaning at the way my body throbs to be inside her. "Traveling by plane also shaves ten minutes off the flight, and that's ten extra minutes I'd rather have to spend naked with you today."

She laughs. "I can get on board with that plan."

"Good." I pass her a bag containing a couple loaves of warm French bread and vegetables for salads. "You take this one. I'll grab the rest."

An hour later, I'm flipping burgers on the big deck of the house in Sagaponack while Melanie's got a feast set up for us on the table overlooking the beach and ocean. She carries out a big bowl of salad from the kitchen, then pours a couple of sparkling waters over ice and brings one to me at the grill.

Her kiss lands light and tender on my jaw. "This is amazing. Thank you for bringing me here again today."

"Consider it a do-over." Trading the bubbly water for the sexy woman standing beside me, I encircle Melanie in my arms. "I wanted to make this right."

"It already is." She sets her glass on the edge of the deck railing and gazes up at me, her eyes reaching inside me the way no one has ever done before. "I mean, come on. Sand, salty summer breeze off the water, a private lunch being served up by the hot, handsome man who made me come so many times yesterday I lost count? What more could I possibly want?"

I grunt, unable to curb my grin. "Just wait until you see what I've got in mind for dessert."

She tips her head back and laughs, giving me a welcome excuse to run my mouth along the pretty curve of her throat. She sighs as I skim my lips and tongue down to the small hollow, a small shiver coursing through her.

My cock surges, desire already sinking its hooks into me. I groan and lift my head from the silky sweetness of her skin, giving her firm little ass a playful smack of my palm.

"Lunch," I growl. "Before I decide to make an appetizer out of you."

We work together to put the rest of the food on the table. It strikes me how natural it feels to have her here with me. How easy and relaxed it all feels. The way it just feels . . . *right.*

As we eat, I watch, amused and more than a little turned on, as she bites into her burger with complete abandon.

"Mmm," she moans, closing her eyes for a moment. "This is so good."

No dainty nibbles or false declarations that a few morsels are all she needs to sustain her. While Melanie is naturally elegant no matter what she's doing, there's something viscerally primal about the way she eats. I could study her doing the most mundane things and never get bored.

She must feel the weight of my stare because she abruptly glances over at me and pauses. "What is it?" She sets the half-eaten burger on her plate and picks up her napkin. "Do I have ketchup on my face?"

I chuckle, mutely shaking my head. "You're perfect. Tell me about the classes you're taking."

She waves her hand in front of her face as she chews, then takes a drink from her glass. "I'm a semester away from finishing my MBA. That's why I'm taking summer courses. The sooner I finish up, the sooner I can start looking for a full-time position in the city. Waiting tables at the diner pays the bills, but I'm not going to get ahead like that. Besides, I really want a career, something more challenging."

"Like what?"

"Numbers come easily to me, so most likely I'll start out interviewing with some of the big accounting firms." When I purse my lips and take a drink of sparkling water, she tilts her head at me. "You don't think it's a good plan?"

I set the glass down and lean toward her. "I think you can do anything you set your mind to. You're intelligent, creative, tenacious--"

"But what?"

"I think you should aim higher. Anyone can work at an accounting firm. You need to think bigger. What would make you happiest?"

"I like helping people. I like to think I'm making a difference in someone's life." She shrugs, suddenly reticent. She looks down at the napkin in her lap. "You were right, you know? When you said I need to feel indispensable. That I need to feel I matter, and that I won't be . . . thrown away."

My chest constricts at the reminder of that insensitive comment I made yesterday. Her quiet reminder of it now makes me feel as if I've just been kicked in the solar plexus. I fucking should be. "I was a prick to say that to you. I'm sorry. I didn't mean it."

She glances up at me, her gaze tender, apologetic. "I didn't mean any of the awful things I said about you, either. But you were right about me, Jared. I've been taking care of my mom and Katie because I like knowing they need me."

"No." I reach over and wrap my fingers around hers. "You've been taking care of them because you're a good person. You're strong and loyal, the kind of person everyone wishes they had in their life. You're the most incredible woman I've ever met."

She smiles, turning her hand so our fingers are laced together. "I think you're pretty special, too. I thought I had you figured out the moment I met you, but I was wrong. You're so much more than you want people to believe."

"I'm not." I pull my hand away, uncomfortable with her praise. Especially when there are too many things she doesn't yet know about me. Things that would bring this moment crashing down around me. "Just because I've given you a few spectacular orgasms, don't make the mistake of thinking I'm not the same self-absorbed, overbearing asshole you first met."

She slowly shakes her head. "I don't know many self-absorbed, overbearing assholes who sponsor art programs for underprivileged kids."

I'm shocked she remembers I told her that. Then again, nothing should shock me when it comes to her.

"Tell me about the rec center program you mentioned." She lifts the burger and takes another bite, patiently waiting for me to speak.

"Dominic Baine's fiancée, Avery, persuaded me to get involved in that. She and I met at Dominion gallery the same year she hooked up with Nick."

"I know her work," Melanie says. "She's an incredibly talented artist."

"Yes, she is. She's also got a kind heart, like you. The rec center in Chelsea means everything to Nick and her. It's the first center he built, and the one where they test out new programs and events for the kids. She'd been wanting to install an art program for a while. Not the typical paint-by-numbers bullshit kids might expect, but something to truly inspire as well as instruct."

"It sounds amazing. What's your role in the program?"

"I help fund it, primarily. I also call in favors and twist arms within the art world to bring in creators to talk to the kids and teach an occasional class. I have to admit, I'm proud of the people I've been able to introduce the kids to. These are artists the public would generally only recognize by their works on display in important galleries and museums."

She grins. "Wow. What a self-absorbed, overbearing asshole you are, Jared."

I chuckle, marveling at the ease with which she can draw me into her light. "If you want to know the truth, I'm doing it for Kathryn. Helping the kids at the rec center--especially good kids who just need a break, like Alyssa--makes me feel I'm doing something worthwhile. Alyssa's got a real gift for painting. With the right guidance and opportunity, I think she could turn that natural ability into something truly extraordinary."

"And that's what you're providing for her and the rest of those kids in the program. Guidance and opportunity. Even more than that, I think."

"I want to give them a chance to lift themselves up, not let a few bad choices or a shitty home life destroy them for good."

"Because that's what Kathryn Tremont did for you."

I nod. "It's the only way I know how to pay her kindness forward."

Melanie's gaze is soft and thoughtful. "I'm sure she'd like that. Have you ever considered starting a school of your own?"

"Christ, no. Even if I had the interest, I don't have room in my life for the kind of commitment that would require. I've never been a long-term kind of guy. And now . . ."

I don't have to say the words out loud for Melanie to pick up on them. She studies me with a compassionate, yet practical gaze.

"You can't stop living or doing the things you enjoy, Jared. That includes painting. I think you should keep creating as long as you can. I think you need to paint, almost as much as you need to breathe."

I feel myself nodding in agreement, even though there's a gnashing fear inside me that's screaming at me to let my art go. To give up.

Melanie's tender affection is the only thing that's ever been powerful enough to silence it, even for a minute.

I push my empty plate away and hold my hand out for her, an invitation for her to come sit with me on my chair. She steps over and settles on my lap. I hold her there, both of us looking out at the calm tide for a long while.

Her fingers play idly in my hair. "You seem so much more relaxed out here than in the city."

"I love the ocean," I admit. "Especially when the waves are green like they are today. They make me think of Kentucky pastures, all the rolling hills on the farm. There's nothing in the city that evens me out like being here does."

"Have you been back to your family's farm since you left?"

"Only once, seven years ago. I wanted to see the bulldozers roll in and knock every building down. I stayed until they had plowed the whole damn place under."

She goes utterly still in my arms. Then she carefully lifts my chin, coaxing me to look at her. "Who did that to your home, Jared?"

"I did." I think back on that day, all my anger. All the pain I wanted to bury along with the barns and the beautiful, rambling house I once loved. "After my first multi-million dollar auction for one of my paintings, I used most of the proceeds to buy back the farm from its new owners. The ink wasn't even dry before I arranged for the wrecking crew to come in and raze the whole property. I didn't want the reminders. I didn't want to think about someone else living in a place that should have been ours. I left as soon as it was done and haven't been back."

"Jared." Melanie's gaze has never looked so sad, so bleak. She's shocked at what I've done. Appalled, even. But there's an anguish that goes deeper than that. Anguish for me. "I hate Denton Sweeney for everything he did to your family, and the others he bilked. I hope he's rotting in the worst kind of hell."

Her voice is filled with quiet fury. There is a fierce protectiveness in her words and in her beautiful, sad eyes, as if she would defend me to her last breath--or burn down the world before she'd let anyone do me harm.

I've never seen anyone look at me like she is now. Her caring rocks me to my core. So does her strength. She's a lioness, a warrior queen.

And she's mine.

At least, I want to pretend she is. I want to pretend I'm worthy of the devotion I see in Melanie's lovely face. That I might one day be deserving of her.

A low rumble of thunder in the distance warns of a coming storm. The clouds are darkening overhead, the winds kicking up from the water.

"We can't stay like this," I murmur, wishing I could hold her in my arms forever. I reach up and smooth some of the bright copper tendrils of her hair away from her cheek. "We should go inside."

She nods silently, her gaze still holding mine with a tenderness that nearly breaks me. "I'll get the plates and glasses."

We clear the table and take everything into the house just as the rains begin to sweep in from the horizon. She puts the condiments away while I load the dishwasher and turn it on. Without speaking, she briefly caresses my back, then places a warm kiss between my shoulder blades.

The air stirs as she moves away, but it takes me a minute to realize she's no longer in the kitchen with me.

"Melanie?"

I step through the empty living area, hearing nothing but the sound of rain pattering on the roof and against the windows. My bare feet carry me to the studio at the back of the sprawling beach house, and there I find her.

Standing in the center of my workspace, she's just taken off her white jeans. My mouth waters at the sight of her long, bare legs. She pulls her top over her head and lets it fall from her fingertips to the floor.

I step inside, drawn as surely as a moth to a flame. "What are you doing?"

"Making the most of a rainy day." Smiling, she removes her bra and panties, then closes the distance between us. "You're overdressed."

She unbuttons my shirt, then peels it off me. I can't resist the urge to kiss her. Wrapping my hand around the back of her neck, I pull her against me and cover her mouth with mine. Our kiss is unhurried and tender, despite the rising demand of our mutual need for each other.

When we part to catch our breath, there is a gleam of mischief in her eyes. She reaches down to the work table next to my easel and picks up a paintbrush.

"I'm feeling creative," she says, unscrewing the cap

from one of the jars of paint.

I arch a brow, but watch without resistance as she dips the brush into the black acrylic then brings the soft bristles up to my bare chest. Her little hum as she paints a large circle around my pectoral makes my cock go hard. When she leans in and traces a tighter circle around my nipple with her tongue, the low, carnal growl that rumbles in my chest is as deep as the thunder rolling outside.

I take the brush out of her loose grasp and paint a small heart around one of her perfect nipples. "Exactly how creative are you feeling, Ms. Laurent?"

"Extremely."

I grunt, hunger in the sound. "That's a dangerous thing to say. I might just decide to test your limits."

She gives me a saucy smile. "I'm not sure I have any limits with you."

With nimble fingers, she unfastens my jeans and sweeps them over my hips along with my boxer briefs. My cock springs loose, jutting upward like a spear. Aching for her attention.

She doesn't disappoint.

Pushing me down onto the stool behind my easel, she removes my pants then sinks to her knees in front of me. She teases my erection with a flick of her tongue, wrenching a desperate moan out of me. Then her hands cup my shaft like an offering before she takes the head of me into her hot, wet mouth.

Ah, Christ. I'm on the razor's edge of exploding as she runs her tongue and fingers all over it. My blood races, need lashing me at the mere idea of taking Melanie any way I can imagine.

I refuse to picture introducing her to any of the

private kink clubs I used to frequent around the city, because fuck if I would even consider sharing her with anyone. I was done with that life even before I met her; now, she's the only thing I crave. Still, my mind runs wild with endless erotic possibilities for us to explore together, all the countless ways I want to make her come.

I let my head fall back on a groan as she takes me deep into her mouth, then draws back on a slow, torturous slide up my length. The wet slurping sound as my engorged head slips out of her mouth wrenches a hard hiss through my gritted teeth.

"Feeling inspired, Mr. Rush?"

I drop my chin and open my eyes to find her gazing at me in wicked delight. "Fuck yes, I'm feeling inspired. And about a hundred other things."

"Good." She licks her lips, but instead of taking my cock for another spin inside the heat of her gorgeous mouth, she moves away from me. She stands up between my parted thighs while I gape at her in bewilderment, every fiber of my being coiled with the need for more of her.

She hands me the paintbrush we used on each other a moment ago.

I frown. "What's this?"

"You can have me any way you like," she says, leaning close, her pretty breasts not even an inch away from my face. "After you fill that empty canvas in front of you."

I reach for her and she dances backward. I scowl, my balls in a knot and my erection setting off a blaze of raw need in my veins.

Grabbing a clean paintbrush from the collection on the table, she walks across the studio to the overstuffed chair facing me. Challenge glitters in her stormy eyes as she brings one foot up onto the cushion, her other leg spread at just the right angle to give me a perfect view of her pussy. The pink folds are slick and swollen, ripe for my taking.

But it's clear she's not going to let me.

Not until I put some paint on my damned canvas.

At first, all I can do is stare, dumbfounded and frustrated. My cock stands as tall as a flagpole, my chest heaving with every raw beat. I've never painted with a hard-on before. No matter how erotic or sexual my art is, I've always approached it with pure objectivity, saving my emotion for the result on the canvas.

With Melanie, it's impossible to separate how I feel for her--how intensely I want her.

To say she inspires me is more than understatement. I'm obsessed. She consumes me, and has from the start.

Now, she owns me in ways I never dreamed were possible.

Tapping the bristles of the paintbrush against her parted lips, she smiles at me while I drink in every nuance of her beauty and light.

"You can begin anytime, Mr. Rush." Her eyes locked on mine, she slides the paintbrush over her chin and down between her breasts on a slow path toward her parted thighs. When the long bristles reach the seam of her sex and begin to play in her wetness, I feel it like a spur to my sides.

"Holy Christ," I utter, my vision hazing over with lust.

I stab my brush into the open paint pot, then bring it to the empty canvas. There's no need to sketch anything first. My hand moves as if it's possessed.

The image comes to life in what seems like seconds, and while it's only black strokes and far from finished, I'll be damned if it isn't one of the best things I've produced in years.

Possibly ever.

"Are you going to show me?" Melanie asks, starting to get up from the chair.

"Later." I toss down the paintbrush and stalk toward her. "First, I mean to claim my reward."

27

MELANIE

It's mid-afternoon, the rains long cleared, when Jared and I touch ground again at the small airport in Queens.

Our day at the beach house was so incredible it feels like a dream, one I never want to wake up from. Seeing Jared at work in his studio, being part of it with him, was a gift all of its own. The rest of it--the hours of phenomenal sex and sensual games that pushed us both to the limits of how much pleasure we could bear--are moments I'll carry with me for the rest of my days.

And then there was the painting. Although I'd been familiar with his inimitable style, the arresting sexuality of Jared's art, I hadn't been prepared for seeing myself through his artist's eye.

Raw, intimate, real. He captured me physically, erotically, but he also seemed to peer into the depths of my soul, into the place where I can't conceal my feelings for him. Somehow the man I didn't want to like in the beginning has become the one I don't want to imagine living without.

If he could see all that when he painted me, I wonder if he can see it now, too, as he glances at me while the private plane taxis in from the short runway. Smiling, his eyes are tender on me as he lifts our joined hands to his lips and kisses the backs of my fingers.

"Next time, we should plan to stay overnight," he says, his deep voice full of sensual promise.

He looks calm and relaxed in his seat beside me, his muscled thighs spread and his thick mane of hair still damp, like mine, from the shower we took together before leaving the beach house. He's so irresistibly masculine and sexy, it's all I can do not to unbuckle my seatbelt and climb on top of him.

And, yes, I believe he can see through to my heart even now. The look he gives me is pure fire, banked but still smoldering in his whisky-dark eyes. "How soon do you think you could get away for a weekend?"

The thought of filling three days--and the nights-- with more of what we did today speeds my pulse and makes me squirm in the leather seat. "If Mom continues doing well these next few days, I could probably sneak away at the end of this week."

"Good. If you'd feel better having twenty-four-hour care for her, I can make the arrangements and have the staff in place as soon as tomorrow."

I arch my brows at him. "Haven't we discussed this? You've already done enough."

He grins. "Ah, but my motives are purely selfish now. It's going to be hell waiting for the next time I can get you naked."

I can't hold back my smile. I can't hold back the

soaring elation that's battering inside my ribs like a caged bird, either. Dear Lord, I'm falling fast.

No, it's worse than that.

I'm already there. My heart belongs to this man.

And in some hopeful corner of my soul, I think he might be at least a little bit in love with me, too.

His phone chimes with an incoming text. He scans it, his expression contemplative. "It's from Dominic Baine. He must've sent it just as we were taking off."

"Is everything all right?"

"Yeah. He and Avery are at the Chelsea rec center. A shipment of new equipment for the art classroom arrived today. They're asking if I'd like to weigh in on the installation."

"Right now?"

He nods. "It's okay, I don't need to be there. By the time I drop you at home, it'll be too late to get to Chelsea before they're gone."

"No. You should go, Jared." I squeeze his hand. "It's your project, too. They wouldn't have asked you if they didn't think it was important for you to be there. I can catch the subway home from here."

He balks, scowling. "Out of the question."

"Then I'll call an Uber or take a taxi. It's really not a big deal."

He shakes his head in refusal. Then he hesitates, searching my gaze. "Would you like to come with me?"

"I'd love to."

The youth recreation center is an impressive community campus situated on a residential block in the heart of Chelsea.

Although it's clear the beautifully designed complex is relatively new construction, the grounds are bursting with mature shade trees, lush green spaces, and plantings abloom with a rainbow of summery flowers. A group of boys are playing basketball on one of the outdoor courts. In another area of the sun-filled yard, a Tai Chi instructor leads a class of young people through a series of fluid, meditative moves.

"What an amazing place," I remark as Jared parks the Aston Martin in the side lot of the large, inviting brick-and-glass building at the heart of the property.

He nods. "Wait until you see the inside."

With his hand resting warmly at the small of my back, he walks me to the building's entrance. Beneath our feet in the spacious lobby, gleaming tilework is inlaid with an inspiring quote about overcoming adversity. Above our heads in the soaring rafters, colorful kites give the impression of open sails carrying us somewhere exciting and full of promise. A cheerful, welcoming children's mural knits the entire room together with hand-painted, random vignettes of nature, friendship, and community, obviously created by an army of small hands.

I glance at Jared and find him watching me. "Is this something that came out of your art project?"

"No. That's all Nick. He had a vision for what he wanted this center to be. True to form, he exceeded it."

I nod in agreement. "It's magical."

The sound of an opening door to our right draws our attention. A stunning blond in slim-fitting beige jeans, flats, and a crisp white blouse steps into the lobby, her smile as bright as a ray of sunshine.

"Jared, there you are!" Her megawatt smile grows

even warmer as she approaches us. "I wasn't sure you were going to come."

"I didn't get your text until we'd touched down after a day out at Sagg."

"You were out at the studio?" At his nod, her curious gaze flicks toward me for an instant. "Well, I'm glad you came. Both of you."

Emerging right behind her is an arrestingly handsome man in dark suit pants and rolled-up shirtsleeves. He's tall and broad-shouldered, a dark-haired force of nature with eyes the color of tropical blue water. Although I've never met Avery Ross or Dominic Baine, their energy alone leaves no doubt who this power couple is.

"This is Melanie Laurent," Jared says, making introductions as he and Nick shake hands and Avery greets me with a hug as if we're already friends.

"It's nice to meet you," I tell them.

Avery smiles. "You, too, Melanie. I understand you're friends with Evelyn Beckham."

I'm not sure how she knows that, but I suspect the brief look exchanged between Jared and Nick helps explain it. "Eve's my best friend. We've known each other for years."

"Then you probably know she's designing the lingerie for my upcoming wedding and honeymoon in a few months."

I nod. "I've seen some of the pieces. They're absolutely gorgeous."

"They are. Eve's designs have blown me away." She gives me a conspiratorial smile. "I have photos from our last fitting on my phone, if you'd like to see them."

"Hold on," Nick interrupts, one black brow winging

up. "Why have I not seen these photos?"

Avery pivots toward him, placing her palm on his chest. The huge diamond on her engagement ring catches the light, sparkling like a star on her finger. "If you see them before our wedding night, it'll ruin the surprise."

He makes a low, appreciative sound in the back of his throat. "Seeing them early won't ruin a thing for me. I'll still be the lucky bastard who gets them off you."

Their heat is almost palpable. So is the depth of their love. It radiates between them as they look at each other, a thousand silent promises in that brief moment their eyes hold.

At my side, I feel Jared's hand brush mine. That subtle stroke of his fingers is our own private communication. That's all it takes for my senses to quicken, every fiber of me tuned solely to him. When I glance over and meet his gaze, the connection sends a spiral of longing through me.

"Have you been to the rec center before, Melanie?" Avery asks, her attention returned to me.

"Um, no. This is my first time."

"Then, follow me. Nick and I will give you a tour on our way to the art center."

The four of us set off together, Avery leading the way and pointing out all of the fascinating details and thoughtfulness that went into the facility's design.

"Nick wanted to create a true gathering place for the kids of the community," she tells us as we progress from one end of the modern, beautifully laid out building to the other. "The goal was to offer not only a place for them to come and relax or exercise their bodies, minds, and imagination, but also provide a safe shelter for the ones with nowhere else to go."

I nod, awestruck by the care that went into every aspect of the center, from the motivational words of encouragement and strength that decorates each room and common area, to the spare-no-expense equipment and supplies.

"I grew up dirt-poor," Nick adds, a surprising statement coming from a man who built one of the most formidable business empires in the country, if not the world. "For kids like me, having somewhere to go, somewhere safe, could've meant the difference between having a reason to live or just praying to make it out of a bad situation alive."

I remember that Jared explained his feelings regarding the center's role in similar terms. I could tell then that he was reflecting on his own past, too. He's gone still beside me while his friend speaks, and I wonder how much these two powerful, wealthy men had to overcome to get where they are now.

I sense it took some courage for Dominic Baine to reveal this much of his personal life and struggles, particularly to me, someone he doesn't know. I don't have to wonder where he gets his strength.

Avery gives him a gentle, yet proud look. "And now you've given that chance to hundreds of kids, Nick. You're making a big difference, not just here with this first center, but with all the others you've built since."

Jared nods. "I think it's a great idea to expand the concept nationally. Hell, take it worldwide."

Avery's blond brows lift. "Does that mean you're ready to sign on to help bring art programs to all our centers?"

He chuckles. "Like I've told you, I'm on board for

whatever funding or advice you need. You want additional artists to commit to lectures and instruction? I'll make it happen for you."

"There's one artist in particular who's proving to be quite the challenge," Avery replies, slanting him a wry look. Then she glances at me. "I've been working on him for months, trying to persuade him to come in and teach sometime. We have some really gifted students in the classes, and I think they could learn a lot from Jared. Besides, the kids adore him."

"I'm not surprised." I glance at him, unable to curb the warmth I feel toward him.

I'm not about to comment on the idea of Jared instructing a class. As wonderful as I think he'd be, I won't add to the tension I feel coming off him right now. He's obviously close to Nick and Avery, but I know they're unaware of the neurological disease he's been grappling with the past couple of years.

It's a secret he entrusted to me, and I'll keep it for him as long as he wants me to.

I'll protect it, and him.

I know he hears that promise, even though I don't speak it aloud. Our hands brush again, and this time he threads his fingers through mine.

"Let's have a look at the new classroom equipment," he says, his deep voice casual and nonchalant, as if it's the most natural thing in the world for him to be holding my hand in front of his friends.

We follow Nick and Avery to a large art classroom that's currently in use by a dozen teenage kids. Bright and spacious, it's set up with easels and workstations for twice as many students, with skylights overhead and lots of windows providing beautiful natural light.

The kids aren't painting today, but are instead raptly listening and watching a tattooed female artist who's demonstrating how she works with metal sculpture.

Avery signals to the instructor with a friendly wave. "Sorry to interrupt, Lita."

"No problem," she says, setting down the piece of hammered metal she was displaying for the class. "We were just about to break for a few minutes, anyway."

Some of the kids file out as we step inside, offering smiles and chatty greetings to Avery, Nick, and Jared. I'm a bit taken aback when one of the girls in the class, a petite, curvy brunette with big doe eyes and a sweet, crooked smile walks straight up to Jared and wraps her arms around him.

Immediately, I recognize the affectionate embrace is simply that. Jared chuckles, releasing my hand to return the girl's brief hug.

"Hey, Alyssa. What'd I do to deserve this?"

When she draws away from him, tears shimmer in her eyes. "The restraining order was approved. I just found out around an hour ago. Chad isn't allowed to come anywhere near me again or I can have him arrested."

"That's great news."

She sniffles, giving him a jerky nod. "Thank you for doing it for me. If you hadn't helped me through all the legal stuff, Chad and his stupid friends might've never left me alone."

"No." Jared rests his hands on her shoulders, looking at her intently. "You understand it wasn't me who made this happen, right? It was you. It took real guts, Alyssa. I'm proud of you."

She hugs him again as if she just can't help herself.

Belatedly, she notices me standing beside Jared and gives me a shy smile.

"This is Melanie," he says. "Melanie, this is Alyssa."

I smile back at her. "Hi, Alyssa. Jared tells me you're a wonderful artist."

"He said that?"

"Yes, he did. He also said he thinks you have a great future ahead of you."

She glances at him, then smiles down at her weathered sneakers for a moment. "Okay. Well, I gotta go get some water before the class starts again. Nice to meet you."

"You too."

"Good kid," Nick says after she's gone.

"They all are," Avery adds. "All they need is a chance, and someone to show they truly care, that they can be trusted."

"Isn't that what we all need?" I ask, my gaze returning to Jared.

He nods, but doesn't speak, his expression pensive and somehow distant.

In silence, he takes my hand again as Avery and Nick bring us into the art room to review the newly arrived equipment and supplies.

28

After an amazing day spent with Jared, and a restless night alone in my bed at home, I'm practically giddy when he calls me at work the next day to invite me out for dinner.

Rather than going somewhere trendy or exclusive on a busy Friday night in the city, he surprises me with an intimate rooftop table at a quiet little French restaurant in the Meatpacking District. We spend three unhurried hours talking and laughing over five delicious courses and a dessert of chocolate soufflé that's so heavenly it makes me moan almost as blissfully as I do for the impossibly sexy man seated across from me.

As far as perfect evenings go, I'm hard-pressed to think of anywhere I'd rather be than caught in the smoldering, fathomless heat of Jared's eyes. If I've tried to stop myself from falling for him, I realize now that there's no use in denying it.

I'm already halfway in love with him.

More, my reckless heart corrects.

And if being together feels so right, so effortlessly natural, this soon, I can only guess at how good things between us have yet to be.

Jared pays for dinner, then leads me out to his car waiting with the curbside valet. A nod and a large tip pressed into the attendant's palm sends the young man away. Jared opens the passenger door for me, but I'm not ready to get in yet.

Wrapping my arms around his neck, I kiss him right where we stand, a soft summer breeze stirring the skirt of my red dress and the sounds of the city buzzing all around us.

"Thank you," I murmur against his lips. "Not just for dinner tonight, but for yesterday at the beach and at the community center . . . for all of it, Jared."

His mouth curves, his dark eyes so tender on me it sends a pang of yearning straight to my soul. It's not only his body I crave right now, but this--the connection I feel toward him when he looks at me, as if I'm the only woman in the world.

The only one for him.

There is a part of me that's desperate to believe that.

If I'm only imagining our bond--or worse, if it's only me who's feeling it so profoundly--I don't want to consider how much it will break me if I'm the only one falling.

"You belong to me," he says, his deep voice vibrating with solemnity as well as demand. "You're mine now, Melanie."

Maybe he senses the fear bubbling up inside me, the uncertainty that I can trust everything I'm feeling. Maybe he reads it in my eyes. God knows he's been able to tune in to my feelings, good and bad, ever since we met.

His gaze burns into mine. "Let me hear you say it."

"I am," I whisper, barely staving off the emotion that swells inside me. "There's nowhere else I'd rather be, and with no one else, Jared. I'm yours."

Pulling me into his arms, he kisses me with a sweetness that rocks me even more than the explosive passion I know he's capable of. I sway against him on the sidewalk as he holds me, our bodies moving in a slow rhythm all our own.

A low, rolling sound builds in his chest, somewhat like a purr. "I love the way you feel like this in my arms. I should take you dancing sometime."

"I'd like that." I lift my head and smile at him. "How about now?"

"Tonight?" He chuckles. "I had a different kind of dancing in mind, Ms. Laurent."

He kisses the tip of my nose, and even that sweet gesture stirs a growing heat inside me.

"I do like how you think, Mr. Rush, and I intend to take you up on that very enticing offer. But first, I want you to take me dancing." I look at him from under my lashes. "As I recall, there's a hot new nightclub not far from here."

He frowns. "Muse?" He shakes his head. "There are plenty of other places I'd rather bring you. Muse is for a different crowd, not you."

Grinning at his sudden uncomfortableness, I give him an arch look. "Are you afraid I'll ask you to take me into one of your VIP rooms?"

He stills. "Is that what you want?" His voice is gravel, dark interest flaring in his serious gaze.

"I want you, Jared." I trace my finger along his

beard-shadowed jawline. "I want all of you tonight, even your wildest side."

His answering growl is pure animal. I love it. I also love the heat I see in his gaze, so blistering it practically melts my panties off my body.

"I'll give you anything you need, Melanie. All you ever have to do is ask." He kisses me again, his mouth carnal and possessive. It's a wonder my knees don't crumble beneath me. His big hand palms a handful of my ass. "You want to go dancing? Get in the car, baby."

He speeds us to the packed club, parking in a reserved space near the door. Music throbs from inside, strobe lights flashing behind the top-floor windows of the multi-story building.

Jared links his fingers through mine as he smoothly leads me past the beefy bouncers checking IDs at the entrance. The men greet their boss with friendly deference, giving me respectful nods of acknowledgment as we pass.

Once we're inside, Jared pulls one of his staff aside and tells the muscular man in the dark suit to prepare the owner's suite for us. I probably should feel embarrassed by the request, but all I feel is excited. And so in love with Jared Rush it makes my heart feel as though it wants to leap out of my chest.

"Come with me," he says, bringing me out to the crowded dance floor.

The song pouring out of the sound system is a slow, sexy one. Jared pulls me against him and cages me there with his arm around my back. The feel of his hard body pressed to my curves ignites every nerve ending, all of that hot energy pulsing in time with the music.

"This was a great idea," he murmurs, his mouth

brushing the shell of my ear. "You feel so good in my arms, and you're fucking scorching in that dress. I'm the envy of every man in here."

"You say the most charming things, Mr. Rush. If I didn't know better, I'd think you were just trying to get under my skirt."

He chuckles, the dark, rich sound of it vibrating deliciously everywhere we touch. "Oh, I have every intention of doing that. But I'm serious, too. I've been wanting to feel you dancing against me since the night I saw you on this dance floor."

Confusion scrapes through my rising desire. "I was only here one time, a few weeks ago with my friends." Although he continues to hold me, his body still swaying against mine, I sense an edge of tension in the muscles that surround me. I draw back. "Were you here that night, too?"

He's silent for a moment. Something in his eyes makes my pulse race. He shrugs, but the movement seems anything but nonchalant. "Muse had only been open for a week. I was here every night making sure operations went smoothly."

"Jared," I say, expelling a confused laugh. "Why didn't you ever mention to me that you saw me?"

I've never seen this utterly confident man look uncertain until now. "I'm sorry." He smiles, but it doesn't quite reach his eyes. "I guess it just never came up."

And just like that, I am jolted back to a different moment, with a different man.

Daniel said something similar when I questioned him about his gambling, the secret he'd been keeping from me for the entirety of our months-long relationship.

A sense of déjà vu grips me, both alarming and disturbing. *But Jared's not Daniel,* my heart hurries to remind me. Forgetting to mention he'd seen me in a nightclub is a far cry from withholding the truth about a habit that would eventually embroil me in its problems, too.

Isn't it?

Jared stares at my conflicted expression, his own face taut with an emotion I can't name. Or maybe I'm afraid to, because what I see in his eyes looks remarkably like guilt.

He lets go of a low, vivid curse as he stares at me with bleak resignation. "There's a lot I should've told you before now, Melanie."

Despite the driving rhythm of the music and the noisy crowd packed into the club, I can hear every word quiet Jared's saying. All my senses are locked on him, searching for some truth that's either going to allay my mounting dread or crack me wide open where I stand.

"We should leave," he says, his face so grave and filled with anguish I can hardly draw my breath. "There are things you need to know, but not here."

"No." My voice shakes, but I don't care. "Whatever you want to say, Jared, I think I need to hear it right now. What's wrong? You're scaring me. Tell me what's going on."

He swears again, frowning as he rakes a hand over his head in a violent motion. The noise around us seems to expand, punctuated by a sudden, sharp ruckus taking place near the club's entrance.

A drunken male voice raised in fury reaches my dazed consciousness. The voice is familiar, if totally unexpected. "Where is he? Goddamn it, let go of me! I saw him bring her in here!"

Daniel.

Jared recognizes the angry shouts, too. Gone is the torment I saw in his face a moment ago, replaced by an all-business coldness I've only witnessed in him one time before--the night Daniel and I first stood before him in his study.

He signals to one of the suited bouncers nearby. "Get him out of here. Now."

"What are you doing?" I gape at Jared as the man runs off to carry out the order. "Jared, don't let them hurt Daniel."

He slices a dangerous look at me. "Still ready to defend him, are you? Don't worry, my men are only going to take out the trash, not harm the son of a bitch."

The music is still playing, but the din of conversation and other noise has now dried up as Daniel's disruption captures the attention of everyone in the club. The bouncers close in on him, but he keeps yelling, his wild gaze searching for us among the throngs.

"Rush, you bastard! You sick, conniving fuck! I know what you're trying to do! I know why!"

I look at Jared, afraid to guess at what Daniel's accusing him of. "What's he talking about? What does he think you've done?"

Two of Muse's staff latch on to Daniel and begin wrestling him toward the door. I know they could easily overpower him. I know any one of them could silence him with a blow, but as Jared assured me they would, his men refrain from violence.

Daniel takes advantage of the small mercy and manages to break loose. His drunken gaze homes in on me where I stand beside Jared and he charges forward like a mad bull, the bouncers right on his heels.

"Mel, get away from him! He's using you!"

Jared swiftly moves me around to his back, shielding me with his body.

Daniel is undeterred. "You don't mean anything to him! All Rush's wanted to do is destroy me! He's been playing us both this whole time!"

The guards make a grab for him, yanking him off his feet. They restrain him without any hope of his getting loose now, but he keeps screaming in crazed fury, acting as if he wants to protect me.

I'm bewildered and unsure I can trust either of the men in front of me now. Daniel's unhinged rage is shocking enough, but Jared's chilling silence scares me even more.

"It was all a setup, Mel!" Daniel shouts. "The construction project. The poker game. Pretending he wanted to paint you. It's all been some twisted game of revenge for this sick son of a bitch!"

His accusations sink into me like sharp-edged blades. The pain of it makes a cry build in the back of my throat. When I step around Jared and see the bleakness of his expression, those knife points cut even deeper.

"What's he talking about, Jared? Is he right?"

My voice is so quiet, I'm amazed Jared can hear me. But he does.

And there's no need for him to answer, because I see the truth written all over his rigid face.

29

JARED

The pain in her beautiful face wrecks me.

Her cheeks are bloodless and pale, the lips that only earlier tonight had been so loving and warm on mine are slack with shock . . . and dawning horror.

"Is Daniel right?" Her voice is soft, hardly more than a whisper, but it cleaves into me sharper than any blade could wound me. "Are you playing some kind of game, Jared?"

I slowly shake my head, casting inside myself for the words--any words--that could help her understand that no matter why I started this regrettable plan, none of it means anything to me now.

Only she does.

And she's looking at me warily, as if suddenly realizing I'm every bit the ruthless beast she judged me to be that first night when this whole fucked-up situation began.

"I never believed it was just about the money Daniel owed you," she says. "So, tell me now, Jared. Why?"

"Because he figured out who I am," Hathaway puts in bitterly, his gaze crackling with contempt. His breath reeks of alcohol I can smell from three feet away. "It took me until a couple days ago to piece together how he could know that, or why it mattered to him."

He's still struggling uselessly against the security detail holding him. One of my men looks at me in question. "You want this piece of shit kicked to the curb now, Jared?"

"No. Let him go."

As much as I'd like to erase Daniel Hathaway from this conversation, the damage is already done. Hell, it's all self-inflicted. He's not telling Melanie anything I haven't owed her from the start.

I dismiss my men with a curt nod. They release him, stepping back, but hanging close just the same. He staggers forward a pace, his eyes glazed but seething.

"What do you mean, he figured out who you are?" Melanie asks Daniel. Then her head swivels back to me, understanding putting an even starker expression on her lovely face. "Oh, my God . . . Denton Sweeney. That's what this is about, isn't it?"

"He was my father," Hathaway announces. "I didn't have any part in what he did. I was a kid for fuck's sake. My mother didn't tell me what he'd done until much later. It's not as if I even knew the names of the people who invested with him."

"Invested with him?" I exhale a sharp, humorless laugh. "He cheated dozens of victims out of millions of dollars. He would've kept on bilking even more if he hadn't died at the height of his scheme."

"You don't know that," Hathaway shoots back hotly. "You don't know anything."

"I know enough. I know that you and your mother used the money he'd stolen to flee to Montenegro, where you changed your names and disappeared for years afterward. I know that after she died, you returned to the States with what was left and you squandered it on gambling and expensive toys."

He shrugs while I recount the details my investigator gave me a few months ago, and it's all I can do to contain the contempt rising in me. He may not have committed his father's crimes, but he's hardly the better man.

"Those were people's lives your father stole. The money you lived off and then threw away was stained with blood off your father's hands, and you knew it. None of that meant anything to you."

He sneers. "You're no fucking saint, Rush. Reeling me in, dangling a multi-million dollar construction project in front of me like a goddamn lure, knowing I'd take your bait. You had no intention of building that project with me. Just like when you invited me to your poker game knowing I was desperate for a windfall. You only wanted to watch me lose."

I stare at him, feeling no remorse for those deceptions. I needed a means of getting close to him, of earning his trust--just like he'd done with my father. The difference is, I didn't put the rope around Hathaway's neck; I simply handed it to him and waited to see if he would do the work himself. As I expected, he didn't disappoint.

"Rush set me up from day one, Mel. Everything he did was to destroy me."

Melanie listens in utter silence. After becoming so

close to her that she almost feels a part of me, now I can't tell what she's thinking at all.

"I should've told you." I swallow past the knot of bile that's forming in the back of my throat. "As soon as I realized you had no idea about Hathaway's past or who he was, I should have told you, Melanie. *Fuck*. I'm sorry-_"

"Don't believe him, Mel. Come with me instead." Hathaway takes a step forward under the spinning lights of the strobes. My men situated behind him are coiled vipers ready to strike on my command. If I turn them loose on him now, I'll lose Melanie for good. I see that cold truth in her uncertain eyes.

"I should've told you everything," I murmur, self-loathing making my voice scrape like ashes on my tongue. "I should have told you how much you mean to me, too. Because you do, Melanie. Christ, you mean everything to me."

Gently, I reach out to her, trying to show her I mean no harm. I never could where she's concerned.

"He's playing you just like he played me," Hathaway urges, his voice rising in hysteria. "He killed my project, Mel. I lost my fucking job because of him. How long do you think his interest in you will last now that he's got what he wanted out of ruining me?"

"Shut the fuck up," I warn him as Melanie draws out of my reach, my gaze never leaving hers for a second. "He's wrong. What we have together has nothing to do with him. You have to believe that. Please, let me prove it to you."

Hathaway cackles now. "This son of a bitch is still playing you, don't you see that? He's using you. For fuck's sake, Mel, be smart and think about it. When he could have any other woman he wants, why the hell would he choose you? "

I see her flinch at that cutting remark and rage explodes inside me. "You fucking bastard."

When I lunge toward Hathaway, Melanie's voice stops me the way nothing else could.

"Jared, don't."

I wheel back to face her, my breath heaving out of my chest. "He's wrong. What he said isn't true at all."

She stares at me. "Which part? The fact that you used me to get back at Daniel? Or that you're still using me, even now?"

My sternum feels as though a jackhammer is blasting into it. She's slipping away from me. I can see it in her anguished eyes. She doesn't believe anything I've said. "Melanie, please forgive me--"

"I'm taking her out of here," Hathaway interrupts. He makes his move, jolting forward and snagging her by the wrist. She tries to jerk loose and he clamps down so hard she cries out.

My fist flies at him like a reflex. It connects with his jaw, snapping his head back on his shoulders. He goes down to the floor like dead weight, half-dazed and losing his grasp on Melanie.

I nod to my staff and they swoop in. "Call the police and tell them we've got an intoxicated patron for them to pick up."

"Glad to," one the men snarls, before the security detail drags him away.

"Show's over," I bark to the spectators who've gathered to watch my life fall apart before my eyes. "We're closed for the night, effective immediately."

The crowd moves off. In the next moment, the

music stops and the lights come on. My staff starts corralling people off the dance floor and away from the bar.

Without a word, Melanie starts walking away from me.

"Wait." My stride carries me in front of her. "Please . . . wait. Hear me out."

Her stormy blue-gray eyes seem huge, brimming with hurt and unspilled tears. "What more do I need to hear, Jared? Are you going to try to tell me that getting revenge on Daniel for his father's sins isn't the entire reason we're together?"

"It's not."

She scoffs, scathing me with her doubt. "You wanted to hurt him. You wanted to take something away from him as payback for what his father took from you."

"Yes, I did." I shake my head, unable to justify any of those motivations when she's looking at me with such raw despair. "I wanted him to feel what it was like to lose everything that mattered to him. Including you. Especially you."

"So, you used me. Just like he said." Her mouth twists with pain. "Why else would you have ever wanted to paint me?"

"No. Jesus, no." I want to touch her, but I know there's no soothing I can offer her now. Only the truth. "You're all I thought about after I saw you here with your friends that night. Not because of Hathaway. Because I'd never seen a woman I craved more than you."

"Did you know Daniel and I were in a relationship?"

I nod soberly. "I also knew he wasn't who he pretended to be. The private investigator I hired had already given me his full report. The night of the poker game, I realized you didn't know what Hathaway was keeping from you. Not the gambling problem or the debts he'd racked up in Vegas, and certainly not the truth about who he really was."

"You could've told me."

"I should have. I should've explained everything to you that first day you came to my house without him, because by then I no longer wanted you to be part of this. I would have released you from our agreement. There was a part of me that hoped you'd tell me to go to hell and never come back, but you were stronger than that. You weren't going to break. That only made me want to know you more. It only made me crave you more."

Instead of softening some of the woundedness I see in her, my confession seems to build a wall inside her. "You had so many chances to tell me everything, but you didn't, Jared."

"I didn't want to hurt you."

Her answering laugh is a choked, bitter sound. "What do you think you're doing now? You lied to me. You used me. You're breaking my heart."

"Nothing between us is a lie. Nothing. Daniel Hathaway may have been the start of this fucked-up situation, but he's got nothing to do with us, Melanie. He's got nothing to do with how I feel about you. I care about you, more than anyone I've ever known in my life. Melanie . . . I love you."

"Don't say that." She closes her eyes for a moment, exhaling a shaky breath. "Don't you dare say that now."

"It's the truth."

"How do you expect me to believe that when

everything we've shared has been built on your lies? How do you expect me to ever trust you again?"

"You can start by giving me a chance," I suggest solemnly. "I know I don't deserve it--"

"No, you don't." She takes a step away from me, folding her arms in front of her like a shield. "I can't give you another chance to break my heart, Jared. I don't want to hear any more. I don't want to be here. I'm going home."

"I'll take you."

"No." The word is crisp and final, as sharp as a slap. I feel it inside me, the sting of her disappointment in me flaying me alive. "You made me think you cared about me. You let me tell you things I never told anyone but my most trusted friends. Just like with your paintings, you peeled me open to my soul, Jared. And now there's nothing left."

"Melanie." I hold my hand out to her.

There's a tremor shaking my fingers, but I don't give a damn. I thought she'd already seen me at my weakest the day she learned about my disease. I was wrong.

I've never felt more useless or broken.

"Please, come home with me. Let me try to make this right between us."

She glances down, mutely shaking her head. When she looks up at me again, I know I've lost the battle. Even worse, I've lost her.

"I'm leaving," she says softly. "Don't come near me again, Jared. I don't ever want to see you."

She pivots away from me and starts walking into the departing crowd, a red dress in a sea of black. I drift after her, hanging back several paces only to avoid the urge I have to physically keep her with me.

As soon as she's out of the club, I see her hand go up to hail an idling taxi at the curb.

She gets in, then the car speeds away.

30

MELANIE

It's been a month since I walked out of Muse in pieces.

One month, but to my broken heart it feels like a century. I've carried on with my life and school, with my family and friends. Thank God for my friends.

I'm only half-listening to Evelyn seated across from me for lunch at a table in Vendange, one of our favorite places in the city. Despite my inattention, I'm grateful for her company and conversation. Her excitement for her lingerie shop's soaring success helps distract my mind from all the things I can't avoid thinking about when I'm alone.

Especially at night, when my longing for Jared and my pain for what I've lost--for what I possibly never had with him to begin with--is at its worst.

My friends have held me together when it feels like I'm comprised of a million fractured shards, kept in place by sheer will alone.

I'm surviving without Jared these past weeks because I have no other choice. I told him to stay away from me, and he has. Evidently, he's handling our breakup with a lot less anguish than I am.

Eve takes a sip of her iced tea and waves her hand in front of her. "Blah, blah, blah. Enough about me. Congratulations on getting that job offer from the firm in Midtown. I'm so happy for you!"

"Thanks."

"When do you start?"

"I go in for a day of introductions and training next week, but I won't officially start until my classes are over and I graduate with my degree at the end of the semester."

Eve raises her glass to me. "Here's to getting your MBA. You did it, girlfriend."

I smile as we clink our iced teas in a toast. Although the full-time accounting job will help pay the bills the way none of my other work could, I'm not as excited about it as I should be.

At one time, landing a safe, long-term position with a stable company was all I wanted. Now, I can't think about it without hearing Jared's advice to aim higher, do something more challenging, more rewarding to me personally.

Someday, maybe I will. And someday, maybe I'll make it through an entire day without looking back in regret or yearning on our brief time together, too.

I hope that day comes soon, because so far it feels like a hurt that will never fade.

Eve swallows a bite of her sandwich, looking at me as if she can tell I've drifted back into difficult waters. "How's your mom doing, Mel?"

I smile with genuine joy. "She's doing great. She's keeping active, walking every day. I haven't told you yet, but she and Katie talked me into getting a dog a couple of days ago."

"What?" Eve gapes. "Oh, let me guess. Something adorable, right? A cute little lap warmer that you can carry in your purse?"

I laugh and shake my head. "Actually, that's what they both wanted, but when we got to the shelter we all fell in love with a sweet pit bull mix named Sadie who'd been surrendered when her owner passed away. She's a bit big and rambunctious for our small house, but we're making it work. Between the daily walks to the park and the tail-wagging affection, Sadie's already doing wonders for Mom's heart."

"How's your heart holding up?"

I sigh. "Not so good. I'm trying to keep myself busy so I don't think about him. I miss Jared something terrible, Eve."

"You're still in love with him," she gently points out.

"Will this awful ache ever go away?"

My friend's smile is tender with sympathy. "I'm the wrong person to ask. I'd never been in love until Gabe. Since we met, my feelings for him have only gotten stronger. I don't think I could turn it off even if we weren't together."

I groan, miserable to consider this may be my new normal. I've wanted to call Jared so many times. I've yearned to see him, but I'm afraid of getting hurt again. I'm terrified to think this pain could go any deeper.

"I can't excuse what he did," I murmur. "But there's a part of me that can't hate him for it, because if he hadn't exposed Daniel, how long would it have taken me to unravel Daniel's lies and secrets on my own?"

Eve nods, her expression grim. "I'm not sure it even occurred to Daniel that his gambling problems and the debts he racked up in Las Vegas could've put you in jeopardy, too."

"I'm not sure he cared about that," I admit. "Daniel's top priority is himself."

"Any sign of that loser since his drunken spectacle at Muse?"

I shake my head and glance up at my friend. "I went by his apartment in Midtown the day I interviewed for the accounting job. His landlady was on her way out of the building as I arrived. She asked me if I'd heard from him recently, said his rent was overdue and she had no way of reaching him since he'd left for Europe a few weeks ago to look after his sick mother."

Eve snorts. "His mother who's been dead for more than a decade?"

I nod. "He's long gone and never coming back."

"Good riddance," Eve says, her tone effectively closing the chapter on Daniel Hathaway. She stares at me for a long moment, a look of question in her pale green eyes. "Aren't you going to ask me about Jared? Gabe and I have invitations to his exhibit later tonight at Dominion. It's the talk of the town."

I'm well aware of Jared's heralded return to the art world stage. I'm genuinely happy for him, too. The city has been buzzing all week with excitement for his new show, anticipation at a stratospheric level for him to reveal his first paintings in two years.

His career reboot is guaranteed to be even more successful than he'd been originally. It's been in the headlines everywhere that Jared Rush is painting with a renewed passion for his work, creating in his Hamptons studio like there's no tomorrow.

There's been no public mention of the disease that's got its hooks in him. Evidently, it's a secret he intends to keep. I've honored the faith he showed me in telling me what he was going through. No matter what else has happened between us, I'll never be the one to betray his trust.

After all this time, I'm not certain he feels likewise when it comes to me. I can't help thinking about the erotic painting he made of me that day in his studio. While our agreement forbade him from revealing my identity in his finished work, that contract was no longer in play when I gave him all of me, both on his canvas and in his arms.

He's under no obligation to honor any of our terms now, not even the compensation, so I have no choice but to wait like the rest of the public for word on what the master reveals at his exhibit tonight.

As much as I dread he might take out some measure of revenge on me by putting my body on full display at Dominic Baine's gallery, I'm even more loath to imagine Jared in his studio with any other woman.

"You should join us, Mel." Eve smiles up at the server as he leaves our bill on the edge of the table. "Gabe's got extra tickets. I think you should come."

"No." I push my empty plate away, panic beating in my breast. "No way. I can't see him again."

As much as I might hope to see him again someday, I'm not ready yet. I don't want to be swayed when I'm still picking up the pieces of my broken heart.

"Gabe and Nick both say he's miserable without you." She stares at me as if considering how much to divulge. "Did you know he sold Muse?"

I shake my head. "When?"

"The day after you and he broke up. He sold all of his clubs, Melanie. The Lenox Hill mansion is up for sale, too. He's moving to the Hamptons permanently next week."

I draw in a breath. Why does hearing he'll be moving out of the city make me feel as if my heart is being ripped out all over again?

Because I know if he leaves, the chances of bumping into each other one day when it might not hurt so bad will be next to nil.

I should be relieved by this news. Instead I feel as if I'm mourning the imminent loss of a friend. More than a friend, a part of myself.

"I think you should talk to him, Mel."

I wince, wishing I didn't want to take my friend's advice. "What would I say?"

"That you forgive him. That you miss being with him and you don't want to live without him anymore." She smiles softly. "Just tell him how you feel. Tell him the truth."

"The truth is the one thing he couldn't give me. Not until his hand was forced."

Her gaze holds mine with tender understanding. "You have the truth from him now. It's up to you to decide what to do with it."

31

MELANIE

I'm in the kitchen that evening with Mom cleaning up after dinner when the front doorbell rings.

My heart stutters at the sound, and at the unusually late interruption at eight o'clock on a Sunday night. Sadie lets out a string of barks from the living room where the dog had been cuddling with Katie in front of the TV after we ate.

Mom sets her dish towel down on the counter. "Whoever could that be at this hour?"

I don't know, but for some reason a wild hope gallops through me as I turn off the water and dry my hands. "Stay here. I'll go answer it."

I haven't stopped thinking about my conversation with Eve this afternoon. Jared's gallery showing should be in full swing by now. His paintings will have been unveiled. He's no doubt basking in the adoration of the city and the press.

So why I'm walking to the door with my heart in my

throat, I have no idea.

Katie calms her furry best friend, but the protective dog remains at attention as I reach the door and peek out through the small windows. The fluttering in my breast dies out in an instant when I see it's only a delivery person standing on the stoop.

The man is wearing a private courier's uniform. "Package for Ms. Melanie Laurent?"

"That's me."

"Great. Sign here, please." He thrusts an electronic pen and sleeved tablet at me. "I'll go get your package."

I add my signature to the line he indicated, then watch as he gingerly retrieves a large rectangular object out of the back of his van. It's wrapped in thick brown paper and twine, not the kind of packaging I'd expect if the item had been shipped from somewhere far away.

No, this package hasn't traveled far at all.

And as he cautiously carries it to me where I wait inside the door, I don't have to guess what's beneath the unmarked paper.

"Here you go," he says. "It's fragile, so take care with it."

I nod and trade him the pen and tablet for the large, framed painting. Feeling it in my hands, my heart starts pounding again, though not with the same anticipation as before. I'm all but certain I don't want to see what's inside. And most certainly not with my mother and young niece underfoot.

"Oh!" he adds. "Almost forgot. There's a note with it."

He pulls a black square envelope out of the sleeve holding the tablet. The envelope is familiar to me, and so is the antique gold wax seal on the back of it, stamped with the initials *J* and *R*.

"Have a good night," he says, jogging back to his vehicle.

I set the envelope down on the console table and carefully lean the painting against the wall while I close and lock the door.

Katie bounds over to inspect the mysterious delivery. "It's big. What is it, Aunt Mellie?"

Mom's gaze meets mine from where she stands in the kitchen doorway. "It looks like a painting to me, honey."

I've told her about Jared--including the details of how I arrived at posing for him. She knows how foolishly I fell for him, and that I'm still miserably, hopelessly, in love with him.

Katie glances up at me in excited curiosity. "Aren't ya gonna open it?"

"Not right now," I tell her, steering her away from the artwork she's at least ten years too young to see.

Make that twenty years, I mentally amend, flooded with memories of the day I posed for Jared in his studio . . . in between marathon sessions of incredible, bone-melting sex.

I'm not even sure I'm ready to see that painting again.

Especially not now, when every reminder of my time with Jared carves away another piece of my heart.

I need to get back to normal again, back to my real life. Jared has his own life, one that's going to be filled with even more wealth and fame and beautiful women than before. He'll move out to his beach house in the Hamptons and I'll go to work at the accounting firm in the city.

He'll forget me before long, I'm sure.

And me? I'll survive. I'll survive for Mom and for Katie, because that's what I've always done.

Somehow, it will have to be enough.

Pasting a smile on my face, I crouch down in front of Katie. "Who's up for some ice cream?"

"Me!" With a happy squeal, she skips off to the kitchen with Sadie trotting along behind her.

Mom's still looking at me with soft, caring eyes. "You don't even want to read his note?"

I shake my head, glancing mutely at the elegant black envelope. "Let's go have some dessert, okay?"

Nearly two hours pass before I step back into the living room again.

The house is quiet. Katie is dozing on the sofa with Mom, Sadie resting contentedly on the floor beneath them. The dog looks up as I pad through, but she doesn't stir from her new favorite spot.

I'm tempted to sit and enjoy the tranquility with them, but I can't stop my feet from carrying me to Jared's note and the painting I've been trying to ignore since it arrived.

I still don't feel ready to revisit my humiliation with him. I'm not sure I'll ever be ready, but I also realize that if I mean to move on, I'm not going to start by running away from the pain or sheltering myself from hard truths.

Silently, I pick up the envelope and the painting and bring them both upstairs to my bedroom.

Once I'm closed inside, I take a fortifying breath and break the golden seal on Jared's handwritten note.

As soon as I start to read his words, a knot of emotion tightens in my throat.

Melanie,

I am so sorry for the hurt I've caused you.

For too many years, I have been consumed by anger and pain. It showed in my work, and in the selfish ways I lived my life. I thought revenge was the answer, the thing I needed in order to finally move on. I was wrong.

I had no right to pull you into my world, into my troubles. Least of all, into my cowardly, pointless game of retribution. You are good and kind and courageous, the most beautiful woman I've ever seen, both inside and out. The light you've brought to my life has changed me. You've made me better. You showed me all the things I was missing because I hadn't let go of my past.

And now, I've lost you because of it, too.

Maybe this is the best thing for you. I've stayed away because that's what you've asked of me. But please know my love for you was, and always will be, real.

Yours, Jared

Tears blur my vision as I glance down at the wrapped painting on the bed. I cut away the twine, then begin to remove the paper.

I realize at once that this isn't the portrait I was expecting.

I am the subject of the painting, but I've never seen this one before. I never posed for it, yet he's captured me in arresting detail.

I gasp in astonishment as, bit by bit, a portrait of me standing on the deck at his beach house emerges. Jared's painted me as if I'm gazing directly at him, the wind catching my loose hair, green waves rolling in the distance behind me like the Kentucky pastures he clearly loves and misses.

He's remembered every detail of my face. The precise shade of my eyes. The soft expression on my face instantly calls back all the feelings I had for him on that perfect day we spent together. The love I felt for him then . . . and still do.

Vaguely, I hear the soft knock on my door. I don't realize I'm sobbing until my mom pokes her head in to make sure I'm all right.

"Oh, honey," she says, stepping inside to wrap me in her comforting embrace.

I sag against her shoulder and weep. I can't help myself. I can't harness the tumult of emotion and confusion that engulfs me.

She lets me cry only for a moment before drawing me away from her. Sweeping my tears away with her thumbs, she cradles my face in her hands. "My sweet girl. Look at how he sees you. The man who painted this portrait knows my daughter better than anyone ever will. And he loves you, Melanie. He loves you very much."

I glance back at Jared's painting, unable to deny what my mother is saying. I can hear his deep voice echoing in my head as the words from his note play back to me now. The hurt I've been carrying around for the past few weeks starts to crumble away, replaced with a burgeoning hope.

"I love him, too. I love him more than anything, Mom."

Her mouth curves. "Sweetheart, why are you telling me? Jared's the one who needs to hear it."

"You're right." I swallow, wiping my cheeks as I get up off the bed. "I have to see him. I have to go to him right now. Oh, God. I have to hurry!"

32

JARED

She's not coming.

I don't know why I thought she might.

A pathetic, desperate part of me wanted to believe she might be feeling as miserable and empty as I've been this past month without her.

That's some of the reason why I sent the portrait to her house tonight. I thought she might see it as the peace offering I intended it to be. I had hoped the note I enclosed would be the declaration of love she refused to accept when I feebly blurted out those inadequate words that awful night at Muse.

But she's not coming.

The courier should have arrived at her house more than a couple of hours ago. Ample time for her to decide if she can forgive me.

Evidently, she can't.

Somehow, I need to find a way to be okay with that decision, despite that it feels like a crushing weight seated on my chest.

"Jared," a female voice calls to me through the clusters of patrons gathered around my unveiled new works. Dominion's manager, Margot Chan-Levine, glides toward me with a dour-looking gentleman in a stuffy suit and bow-tie. "I have someone I'd love for you to meet."

I spend the next ten minutes answering questions from the French art critic and pretending to be interested in his attempts to impress me with his credentials.

I've long grown accustomed to the fuss my art usually stirs up at its debuts, but even I have to admit this level of excitement is astonishing. Not even the drizzling rain that started in the past hour has slowed the traffic of invited VIPs and patrons packing the gallery. If I was uncertain how the change in my artistic style and subject matter might impact my return after a two-year absence, this exhibit erases any doubts.

And I couldn't be more bored.

For the past three hours since my newest paintings were unveiled at the reception, I've been glad-handed by reporters and patrons, and toasted with a seeming endless flow of champagne--none of which I've imbibed.

All around me, I hear effusive praise for the trio of paintings dominating the focal wall of the gallery . . . and whispered speculation about who is the mystery muse depicted in my new work.

Unlike the portrait I gave to Melanie, none of these show her lovely face. That's a privilege I don't intend to share with anyone.

In the first painting on display, she's standing alone

on a beach illuminated in soft sunlight as she looks out at the tranquil water. In the next, she's seated on the edge of a bed, as serene and protective as an angel while she watches over a sleeping little girl.

The third is a painting I almost didn't allow the gallery to have tonight. In it, Melanie is bared from the waist up, her face tilted away from the viewer with her long red hair flowing down the elegant length of her back in a fiery cascade.

Each of them means something different to me, three different facets of an infinitely intriguing, extraordinary woman. A woman I was fortunate to have in my life for a brief moment, and too unworthy to keep.

"Quite the turnout, my friend." Dominic Baine steps up to me with Avery on his arm. He's wearing a dark suit, holding a glass of champagne. Avery glows in a black cocktail dress that sets off her green eyes and golden blond hair.

"I think half the New York art world is here," she adds, lifting up to kiss my cheek. "Congratulations, Jared. Your paintings are absolutely gorgeous. Everyone's raving over this new direction your art has taken."

"Thanks." I smile at my friends, genuinely warmed by their praise. "I was glad you agreed to host me here at Dominion tonight."

"Are you kidding?" Nick grins. "I'd have been insulted if you'd gone anywhere else."

Avery nods. "Margot says she's already received half a dozen eight-figure offers on the collection. You sure you're not interested in selling any of them?"

"I'm sure." I glance over the throng of admirers gathered around the three images of Melanie. "I could no more part with them than I could my right arm."

As we talk, Gabe and Evelyn step in to join us. Melanie's best friend apparently overheard my comment. "Have you called her yet, Jared?"

"No." They all know how I've felt since my epic fuck-up with her. They know my planned relocation to the Hamptons and the sell-off of all my clubs and entertainment venues in the city is all in an effort to put some much-needed distance between myself and the anguish of losing Melanie. "She doesn't want to see me, and I have to respect that."

Eve gives me a sympathetic look. "Mel's stubborn sometimes. She guards her heart because as tough as she's had to be all her life, that's the one place she's vulnerable. She let you in, Jared. That's not easy for her. You really hurt her."

"I know. Damn it, I know that." The words grate out of me, my self-loathing hardly lessened since that night at Muse. "I fucked up with her, big time."

"Yes, you did," Eve says. "But I don't think you've lost her completely. Not yet."

I shake my head. "I think you're wrong. I sent her an apology tonight. It didn't make any difference. She's shut me out, and I don't have anyone to blame but myself."

Gabe frowns. "You really love her, don't you?"

"Christ, yes. I didn't realize how much I could need another person, but I need her. Melanie's my light. She's everything to me. I don't know how I'm going to live another day without her in my life."

My heart pounds as I let the words spill out of me. I don't care if my friends think I'm a pathetic, lovesick idiot. Hell, that's exactly what I am. I've been in a tailspin of misery for the past month. I don't want to imagine how much worse I'll be hurting in another month, another year. Or longer, for the rest of my days.

What's more, I refuse to imagine that kind of pointless existence.

I can't.

She may hate me. She may not want to see me, or hear anything I have to say, but if she thinks I'm going down without a fight, she has no clue how much she means to me.

Melanie is mine. She has been, right from the beginning. Now, I just need to convince her of that.

"I've gotta go."

Eve and Avery both nod at me, their gazes soft with understanding and approval.

Nick cuffs me on the shoulder. "About time you figured that out, brother."

Gabe nods and grins, then he glances past my shoulder and arches a brow. "Looks like you don't have to go far."

I wheel around and all the breath gusts out of my lungs.

It's Melanie. She's just arrived inside the gallery. Her hair, navy-blue T-shirt, and jeans are drenched from the rain. Her cheeks are flushed as though she just ran for a solid block. Her gorgeous blue-gray eyes are red-rimmed and puffy, as if she's been crying.

I cut through the gathering with singular purpose, stopping just a few feet away from her. All I want to do is pull her into my embrace and never let her go.

She holds up a soggy letter, black ink dripping down her hand. "I got your note. I got your painting, too."

Her gaze moves over the packed crowd inside the gallery, then to the wall where my paintings hang. Her eyes are already soft with emotion, but their color changes to something even more tender as she sees herself in my art.

"They're amazing, Jared. I'm really happy for your new success."

I take a step forward. "I'm only painting again because of you. I've found my true muse. The only one I need."

She swallows. I can feel people starting to look at us. They're looking at her, realizing she's the mystery woman gracing these new portraits.

She stares at me, uncertainty in her gaze. "I should've changed into something more appropriate."

"You look perfect." She's never looked more beautiful to me than she does now, soaked and breathless, just out of my reach. I take another step, removing the distance.

"I left in a hurry," she says. "I was afraid you'd be gone soon, and I didn't want to miss you. I wanted to thank you for my gift."

Hope ignites inside me. My heart is banging in my chest, about to burst out of my rib cage. "I didn't think you were coming. I thought maybe you didn't like the painting, or what I had to say."

"I love the painting." Her eyes glisten, not with raindrops but with raw, tender emotion. "I loved your note. And I love you, too, Jared."

"Thank God."

I pull her into my arms, cupping her nape as I take her mouth in a kiss I've been dying to taste for four long weeks. She's wet against my suit and open-collared shirt, her face and skin still dripping with rain. I hold her to me as if I've been starving for water. I truly have been starving for her, for the feeling of her in my arms.

I draw back from her lips on a groan. "I should've told you I loved you, even before that night. Melanie, I'm sorry. I should've told you everything right from the start. That I love you. That I need you in my life. It's been fucking agony without you."

"I know," she whispers, bringing my face back to hers and kissing me again. Her salty tears blend with the raindrops on her lips. "It's been awful for me, too. I've missed you so much. I love you, Jared."

"You're mine." I say it fiercely, needing her to understand. "I love you, Melanie Laurent. For the rest of my life, I'm going to love you."

"You'd better," she replies, happiness radiating in her smile as the sounds of cameras snapping photos and shocked murmurs travel the gaping crowd.

I hardly notice the hubbub we're creating. I have all I need in the circle of my arms.

I kiss Melanie again, whispering tender promises against her lips, which taste like heaven to me.

No, she tastes so much better than that.

She tastes like forever.

Like coming home at last.

Epilogue

One month later . . .

MELANIE

I stand next to Jared under a clear blue Kentucky sky. Green rolling hills and acres of lush pasture edged with miles of pristine white fences spread out before us. Under a copse of shade trees near the recently erected barn, a dozen brown horses graze on clover, their black tails swishing, silky manes riffling in the breeze.

He's been quiet for a while, looking out at the property he knew as a boy. The home that was taken from him and his parents, then won back by Jared years later if only so he could try to erase all his hurt by tearing everything down.

We've rebuilt most of it now, together.

The main house and new horse barns. The sprawling guest house crafted to accommodate twenty people at any given time. Alyssa Gallo is our first, arriving with her nine-month-old daughter just last week. She waves to us from the patio behind the main house, her baby in one arm, a basket of fresh-baked cornbread in the other.

"Chef says it's almost time to bring the ribs out," she calls out to us.

Chef being Gibson, who's practically become a permanent fixture in the months since Jared and I have moved up to the farm with my mom, Katie, and our dog, Sadie. Gibson and Mom have tried to pretend their friendship is purely platonic, but I can't remember when I've ever seen her smile and laugh as much as I do when he's around.

Today, the pair insisted on cooking for us and our friends.

Nick and Avery, Gabe and Eve, along with Nathan Whitmore and my friend Paige are gathered and conversing on the big patio and deck at the main house, all of them having come for the weekend ground-breaking of the new art studio on the property. Jared still paints when we're living in the Hamptons beach house, but here is where he and other visiting artists will teach the kids and young adults in need who come up from the city to stay with us and to learn.

As for me, I turned down the position with the accounting firm in the city. Instead, I'll be putting my MBA to work at the foundation Jared and I have started to benefit gifted young artists and promising students in need of scholarships and grants. The work we do together is challenging, exciting, and, yes, deeply rewarding.

"I don't know about you," Jared says, reaching over to hold my hand. "But I'm not quite ready to join the others yet. I'm enjoying having you all to myself."

I snuggle closer to him. "I like the sound of that."

"Good, because I don't plan on ever letting you go."

We kiss, wrapping our arms around each other and staring into each other's eyes. His face grows solemn as the moments pass. "I didn't think it could be possible that I could fall any deeper in love with you than I already was. But I was wrong. You're as vital to me as air, Melanie. You're my heart."

"And you're mine, too. I think I'm alive just so I could eventually find you."

He makes a tender sound as he bends his head down and kisses me again, slow and deep, as if nothing else exists in the world except the two of us and our love.

I want to hold him like this forever, but he slowly draws away from me.

I frown, feeling lost without his warmth around me. "What's wrong?"

"Absolutely nothing." His smile is warm and full of devotion as he reaches into the pocket of his barn jacket. He pulls out a small ring box.

I exhale a shaky sigh. "Oh, my God."

He chuckles, his grin making my legs go a little weak beneath me as I watch him sink down onto one knee in the grass before me. "Melanie Erin Laurent," he says, holding me in his steady, intense gaze. "My beauty, my light, my love . . . I have never known the kind of happiness you've given me this past year. I've never known this feeling of completeness, this whole-hearted faith in another person in all my life. I don't know how I lived before I had you in my life, but I do know I never want to be without you in it ever again."

"Jared," I whisper, a sob building in my throat.

He takes out the stunning diamond ring and reaches for my left hand. His fingers tremble, not with the tremors that come and go, but with the force of his emotion. The depth of his devotion for me, which I see shining in his eyes.

"I'm down on my knees," he says, holding my hand in his big palm. "Please, say you'll marry me, Melanie. Be mine forever."

"Yes." I nod my head once, then again and again. "Yes, Jared. Oh, my God, yes!"

He slips the ring onto my finger and a round of cheers and applause goes up from our friends and family gathered at the house.

I hardly hear any of it. I don't hear the birds singing in the trees, or the sound of the sweet, country breeze rolling over the hills and pastures. All I hear is the strong beat of Jared's heart drumming in perfect tempo with mine.

I look into his eyes and I see the promise of our future together.

This man, his heart, his love.

It's everything I'll ever need.

~ * ~

Never miss a new book from Lara Adrian!

Sign up for Lara's VIP Reader List at
www.LaraAdrian.com

Be the first to get notified of new releases,
plus be eligible for special VIPs-only exclusive content
and giveaways that you won't find
anywhere else.

Sign up today!

ABOUT THE AUTHOR

LARA ADRIAN is a *New York Times* and #1 international best-selling author, with nearly 4 million books in print and digital worldwide and translations licensed to more than 20 countries. Her books regularly appear in the top spots of all the major bestseller lists including the *New York Times*, USA Today, Publishers Weekly, Amazon.com, Barnes & Noble, etc. Reviewers have called Lara's books "addictively readable" (Chicago Tribune), "extraordinary" (Fresh Fiction), and "one of the consistently best" (Romance Novel News).

Writing as **TINA ST. JOHN**, her historical romances have won numerous awards including the National Readers Choice; Romantic Times Magazine Reviewer's Choice; Booksellers Best; and many others. She was twice named a Finalist in Romance Writers of America's RITA Awards, for Best Historical Romance (White Lion's Lady) and Best Paranormal Romance (Heart of the Hunter).

With an ancestry stretching back to the Mayflower and the court of King Henry VIII, the author lives with her husband in Florida.

Visit the author's website at **www.LaraAdrian.com**.

Find Lara on Facebook at
www.facebook.com/LaraAdrianBooks

Have you read the 100 Series? Don't miss this sexy trilogy featuring alpha billionaire Dominic Baine and struggling artist Avery Ross!

For 100 Days

Available Now

eBook * Paperback * Unabridged audiobook

"Adrian simply does billionaires better."
—*Under the Covers*

Nick and Avery's story continues in the suspenseful, scorchingly sensual second novel!

For 100 Nights

Available Now

eBook * Paperback * Unabridged audiobook

"PHENOMENAL."
—The Sub Club Books

Nick and Avery's story concludes in the
emotional, romantic third novel in the series!

For 100 Reasons

Available Now

eBook * Paperback * Unabridged audiobook

**"An emotional and powerful conclusion that
validated every word in this sensational series."
—*Smut Book Junkie Reviews***

Get all three books now in a digital box set!

The 100 Series Complete Collection

Available Now

Save on the eBook editions when you buy
the complete series in this digital-only bundle.

www.LaraAdrian.com

Wounded combat vet Gabe is supposed to protect beautiful lingerie designer Eve, but duty's no match for desire in this 100 Series standalone!

Run To You

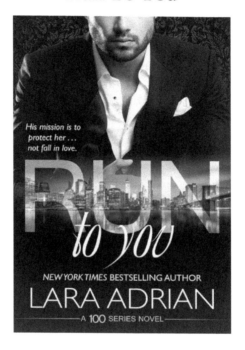

His mission is to protect her . . . not fall in love.

RUN

to you

NEW YORK TIMES BESTSELLING AUTHOR

LARA ADRIAN

—A **100** SERIES NOVEL—

Available Now

eBook * Paperback * Unabridged audiobook

"A home run! Run To You is a wonderful story of self-discovery, second chances, and love."
—*Reading Divas*

Love paranormal romance?

Read the Midnight Breed vampire series

A Touch of Midnight (prequel novella)
Kiss of Midnight
Kiss of Crimson
Midnight Awakening
Midnight Rising
Veil of Midnight
Ashes of Midnight
Shades of Midnight
Taken by Midnight
Deeper Than Midnight
A Taste of Midnight (ebook novella)
Darker After Midnight
The Midnight Breed Series Companion
Edge of Dawn
Marked by Midnight (novella)
Crave the Night
Tempted by Midnight (novella)
Bound to Darkness
Stroke of Midnight (novella)
Defy the Dawn
Midnight Untamed (novella)
Midnight Unbound (novella)
Claimed in Shadows
Midnight Unleashed (novella)
Break the Day

. . . and more to come!

Discover the Midnight Breed
with a FREE eBook

Get the series prequel novella
A Touch of Midnight
FREE in eBook at most major retailers

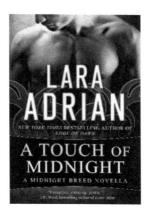

After you enjoy your free read, look for Book 1 at a
special price: $2.99 USD eBook or $7.99 USD print!

Look for the next book in the bestselling
Midnight Breed Series from Lara Adrian!

Break the Day

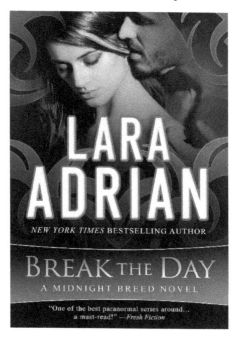

Available Now

eBook * Paperback * Unabridged audiobook

**For more information on the series and upcoming
releases, visit:**

www.LaraAdrian.com

The Hunters are here!

Thrilling standalone vampire romances from Lara Adrian set in the Midnight Breed story universe.

AVAILABLE NOW

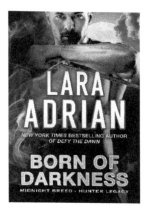

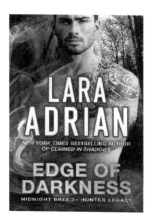

Award-winning medieval romances from Lara Adrian!

Dragon Chalice Series
(Paranormal Medieval Romance)

"Brilliant . . . bewitching medieval paranormal series." —Booklist

Warrior Trilogy
(Medieval Romance)

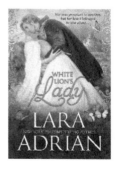 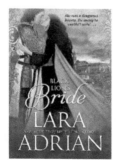 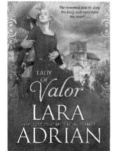

"The romance is pure gold." —All About Romance

Connect with Lara online at:

www.LaraAdrian.com

www.facebook.com/LaraAdrianBooks

www.goodreads.com/lara_adrian

www.instagram.com/laraadrianbooks

www.pinterest.com/LaraAdrian

CPSIA information can be obtained
at www.ICGtesting.com
Printed in the USA
LVHW011951300820
664591LV00008B/1180